Tailor-Made Candy

Tailor-Made Candy

A novel written by

Erskine Harden

Rev. date: 06/27/2014

To order additional copies of this book, contact:
Xlibris LLC
1-888-795-4274
www.Xlibris.com
Orders@Xlibris.com
616327

To Ebony Gibson—thank you for showing me my gift, and teaching me how to use it. Thank you for seeing the best in me when I was down and out. I'm indebted to you for life!

On behalf of Lavish Life 88 Entertainment, we would like to dedicate this page to Dr. Maya Angelou who passed away on May 28, 2014.

Dr. Maya Angelou, who has been hailed as the Global Renaissance Woman, inspired me to develop this company as a means to publish the work of talented writers. Her work as an educator, novelist, poet, civil rights activist, and historian (just to name a few) has changed the literary world and will be never be forgotten.

Lavish Life 88 Entertainment would like to extend our condolences to the family of Dr. Maya Angelou. She was truly a remarkable woman who touched the lives of many.

Darnell Jacobs
Lavish Life 88 Entertainment

Acknowledgments

I'd like to thank God for giving me the intellect to create this project. Sending positive energy to my family. (Harden, Peterson and Carter, Ferrell, Tisdale, Dillard, Harris, I love you all.)

To my mother for giving me my literary foundation, among other skills. I love you. Thanks to my sister Mychel for always being there in spite of my foolishness. A blessing to have all my cousins, aunts, and uncles—what a great family.

I know things looked hopeless for me to the unfaithful eye. Thank God for making me a resilient, ambitious winner. Shout out to my hometown friends from Newark, New Jersey, a.k.a. Brick City. Also to all the friends I've made along my travels in North Carolina, South Carolina, Atlanta, California, Las Vegas, New York, and definitely Chi-town! Can't forget all the brothers I rocked with on lockdown. Never give up, 'cause the darkest part of night is just before daylight. Your day is coming; until then I'll shine for us both. To the readers who pick up this book and support the Tailor-Made Candy series, thank you. I hope I did my job trying to bring you a solid body of work. To the young lady who bears my last name, Eursla Lamonica Harden, Daddy loves you. I plan on doing whatever it takes to make our relationship the best father-and-daughter relationship ever. Special thanks again to Ms. Ebony Gibson for teaching me that writing with skill is a legitimate form of power.

I leave you all with this food for thought. The only disability in life is a bad attitude. Smile!

Sincerely,
Erskine "E-class" Harden
New Jersey's finest

Shout-outs! To one of the hottest chicks in the game, the diva and fashion icon Tyra Banks. I like your style and respect your business savvy. I hope to meet you one day, keep doing your thing!

To Sean "P. Diddy" Combs—You've been an inspiration to me from a distance. Your hustle and grind is equal to excellence. I'll take your advice. Get money and don't stop!

Erskine "E-class" Harden

From the Author

While much of what I have written about China, Switzerland, California, Atlanta, New York and surrounding areas is true, some is fictional. I'm totally to blame for any errors of fact, geographic locations, or opinions, international or otherwise.

Erskine "E-class" Harden

Prologue

The church was filled with a dry, dark, and gloomy aura flowing from family to the friends assembled. Everyone wore their best and sat in a humble state of disbelief. It would be a Friday they definitely wouldn't forget. Outside was a medium-sized crowd having conversations about rumors. A fleet of exotic cars filled the parking lot. While inside, flowers and old spiritual hymns made the whole ordeal feel so surreal.

It was the home-going service for one Candice Gray, one of California's elite. Family and friends still couldn't believe she was gone at such a young age. No one was more hurt and shocked than her longtime lover and fiancé, Eric "Swave" Hawkins, dressed in a tailor-made navy-blue pinstripe double-breasted suit with banker's cuffs, Gucci loafers, and garnished with a red carnation. Swave sat staring at the coffin trying to make sense of this nightmare. Next to him was Tosha, Candice's younger sister, holding his hand for moral support. At least that was what he thought she was doing. She had loved her sister but secretly lusted after Swave. Two years of love and romance—lavish vacations, shopping sprees, and intimacy—were all over. This was way too much for him to bear, especially all alone. He thought back a few years ago, how they met while he was still in fashion school (Otis College of Art and Design). She was an up-and-coming model building her portfolio. He was an unknown designer trying to get free advertising by offering models to wear his clothing to upscale events that the city of Los Angeles hosted.

He was canvassing the parking lot of a trendy spot (Bar Fly) within Hollywood, handing out his colored flyers showing two current designs with his phone number, website, Facebook, and Twitter. Bar Fly was hosting a contest by Neon Vodka to find a new face for the product. The winner got a one-year advertising and modeling deal and fifty thousand dollars. It was a sixty-city tour and choice of clothing designers they'd like to represent. This would be a golden opportunity to get discovered through advertisement. Even though it was a long shot, Swave took a chance.

After two hours of handing out his flyers, there appeared a beauty of angelic proportions. She was 5'10", almost 6' with her heels. Carmel complexion, light-brown eyes, long brown curly hair, and a small waist. The clincher was a walk that made you say wow! She was a pleasant vision straight out of the pages of a fashion magazine dressed in a cream Michael Kors short-cut top and Sergio Valenta jeans, Jimmy Choo pumps, and Dooney & Bourke arm bag, her accessories and makeup flawless. She was a former contestant for a popular reality modeling show. Candice and Swave's eyes met, and it was an instant attraction, he being an attractive, muscular chocolate brother with boyish smooth skin, always turning women's heads. But he was only concerned about building his brand, so romance took a backseat to his dream of being a world-renowned designer. He handed his flyer to Candice and flashed his pretty white teeth. Before she said a word, he grabbed her hand. "Promise me one thing, sunshine, when you win the contest tonight, you'll wear my clothing line!"

The morning traffic in Los Angeles was hectic as it always was before noon. After being in Cali for two years, Swave still hadn't adjusted to the West Coast style of living. Born in Bronx, New York, and raised in Newark, New Jersey, he was an East Coast guy at heart.

After high school, he had worked various jobs but wasn't pleased with a dead-end future. So he decided to follow his heart and attend fashion school, which was his passion, and he was great at making outfits from mere rags. Raised in a single-parent home with only his mother—no brothers and sisters—made him extremely close to his female first cousins and aunts. Being around women gave him a love and respect for females. Not only did he learn their interests, he was taught how to make clothes, which birthed his incredible fashion sense and an eye for intricate detail. Aunt Barbra Ann and Grandmomma Lucille were master seamstresses who could sew anything and made outfits for the entire family, being lower-class working people. It was cost-efficient, especially with a family full of young girls. Occasionally Swave sat around Auntie or Grandma and picked up tricks for the trade, learning how to measure material, cut patterns, visualize, and sew the linen together on the sewing machine.

Unexpectedly he was a natural and went from an amateur to a decent seamster, taking over projects for his Aunt Barbra Ann making his two first cousins (Tijuana and Bridgette) Easter dresses. While other teenage boys played sports and chased girls, Swave was designing clothes and starting to build a portfolio. Not only did he make women's clothing, he made and wore the sleekest fly men's apparel. In fact, that's how he got his nickname Swave—because he stayed dapper. Surprisingly he wasn't teased by the neighborhood teenage boys for making clothes for women. They admired the fact women always wanted to be in his presence. If not wanting an outfit customized, they just wanted to hang out with the smooth, attractive, sensitive guy.

Secure in his manhood, there was no mistaking the fact Swave was 100 percent heterosexual. If any of his peers wanted to test him, he had an explosive knockout punch. In the streets it was called a one-hitter quitter! However, disrespect was never an issue; he was respected as a good person and a popular guy.

In his last year at Otis College of Art and Design, Swave balanced a full class load with advanced assignments, also putting the finishing touches on his signature line while working as a bartender at an upscale bar called the Polo Lounge in Beverly Hills. The money was good, but between living expenses and funding his clothing line, he often ate oodles of noodles for dinner.

Monday morning after stopping at Starbucks for his daily caramel latte, he entered the campus with his new creation for the wild and sassy outfit challenge given to the senior design students, by head instructor Lex Hamington. Lex was a middle-aged Asian fashion guru. He had thirty years of experience in the world of fashion working for major fashion houses such as Gloria Vanderbilt, Liz Claiborne, and Donna Karan. Circumstances in the corporate world proved to be overwhelming, so he quit, turning to teaching to help the future creative minds achieve success in the industry. He was highly respected and regarded as an influential educator; his students learned all sides of the business. Lex saw great promise in Swave and his eye for colors, how he blended them together. He also respected his tenacity and pride he poured into the designs. Lex was very critical and demanding when it came to Swave's work, wanting to bring the absolute best out of the future household name. So average wasn't acceptable; Lex always demanded mind-blowing creativity. Sometimes Lex got on his nerves, but Swave built a tolerance for high standards.

"What surprise creation do you have today, Swave?" Kym asked.

"You've got to wait like everyone else, short stuff." He gave his friend and classmate a wink and smile. Kym V was Swave's closest friend at the school, a cute country girl from Charlotte, North Carolina. She won his friendship and respect with her loving heart and caring ways. Kym was more of an accessories designer than anything. The two often brainstormed together, making some fierce ensembles. They made a pact—whoever blew up first in the industry would take the other one with them. Having

Swave as an ally insured her of getting passing grades in the class, him being the absolute bright star of the advanced design department. His only competition and obvious hater was Maria Cherry, a self-proclaimed diva and trendsetter who wanted to be famous. The fact that Swave was supremely better than her and wasn't attracted to her like most men made Maria dislike and want him that much more, proving the old wise tale right—you always want what you can't have.

"I can't stand his sexy black ass," she often mumbled under her breath.

He had many desirable qualities a woman wanted in a mate. Very respectful to women, a gentleman, a hard worker, and driven towards success. Swave was spiritual and believed in honoring a relationship. He was truly waiting for Mrs. Right and not Mrs. Right Now. Combining his practiced beliefs and being absolutely handsome made women want him for their lover. He stood 6'4", 240 pounds with a muscular frame, short, clean-cut, pearly white teeth, and a mocha-chocolate complexion.

Maria Cherry thought he was an amazing designer and admired his work from afar. It was hard to accept after being the center of attention in her short career. She had made a name for herself in South Central Los Angeles for selling custom-made T-shirts and jeans. Generating a small amount of money, she felt her calling was designing clothes. After attending the school full-time, Maria realized she was out of her league. Clinging to a small piece of hope, she might get a job in sales or merchandising.

Maria's clique were the twins Melissa and Patricia from Phoenix, Arizona, also Mary Beth Clinton from Seattle, Washington. All were below-average designers who had some years of growth ahead.

There were two other guys in the class, but they lacked Swave's creativity. Besides him being an innovator and visionary, who assembled different styles together to form something hot, he was gifted when it came to using the sewing machine, crushing his competitors with flawless stitching and precision. Speed was also a superior factor, giving him forty-seven wins out of the last fifty challenges.

This day and challenge was different from all the rest. The Wild and Sassy challenge was going to be judged by an industry insider, Kellia Rogers, former student of College of Art and Design who was making a noticeable mark in fashion, currently working in New York. The winner of the challenge would assist Kellia in a project for the Harlem Fashion Row's fashion show and be paid for being an apprentice and have the opportunity to show their talent on a professional level.

Everyone in the design department was putting finishing touches on their work. Mannequins were clothed with dresses, short and long. Skirts, shorts, and sexy tops, headwear and accessories. The students were nervous and filled with emotion, excited for a chance to earn some money. Flying to New York for a week or two was an extra bonus for locals. Lex and Kellia walked around the studio and conversed very intensely. Most of the work was decently average at best, nothing breathtaking. The twins had taken the wrong approach in trying to use leather as a hot summer look (a mistake). The two guys, Billy Owens and Steve Connor, weren't finished on time, disqualifying them. Mary Beth's design lacked the necessary colors that would bring her vision to life.

The last of the competition in the senior class was Maria Cherry. Lex found humor in her attempt to duplicate a Liz Claiborne sundress from the 2009 summer collection. The funny thing was Lex was cocreator of the dress and recognized his work. Nothing worse than a copycat in this industry—a true designer was original. This proved she was sublevel to the devil when it came to creating a fresh new look.

The grand finale was Swave's vision of wild and sassy. Lex and Kellia both stopped in their tracks, looking at each other, circling the mannequin several times, looking up and down, both smiling in agreement of the feature. Everyone in the studio knew Swave had pulled it off once again. The mini pleated spaghetti-strap dress was amazing. The colorful pink, grey, purple, and lavender was indeed wild and sassy, marketably breathtaking! Kym's expertise in accessories was the icing on the cake. A colorful rhinestone and beaded necklace and bracelets set the outfit off magically. Lex was beyond delighted, feeling blessed to have nurtured this great talent.

Kellia made the formal announcement that Swave was the winner. All eyes were on Swave as he hugged Kym and they pumped their fists over the victory. Maria Cherry gave him a long scornful sneer, imagining being in his arms and accepting the honor. Swave shook Mr. Hamington's hand, graciously giving everyone's project a thumbs-up as a manner of respect and professional courtesy. Honestly in his heart, he knew they couldn't compare, but he always remained humble. This is what made him irresistible to women. He was a superstar among designers but never let it go to his head. Secretly Maria Cherry vowed to get him between the sheets one way or another just for the sport of conquering a sexual quest that seemed unattainable.

George and Vanessa Gray were a loving, God-fearing couple from Fresno, California. They met in high school and started dating in their junior and senior years. George was a year older than Vanessa, but they were mentally equal. He was the star quarterback on the varsity football team; Vanessa was the captain of the cheerleading squad, a perfect couple to all that viewed them from the outside.

George was a tall hunk, standing at 6'5", strong as an ox. His athletic ability was superior to most high school quarterbacks in the state. He also ran track, which explained him running a 4.3 in the forty-yard dash. He was a hard worker and the oldest of four, his dad's head helper on their farm. George Gray Sr. was a dairy farmer and a workaholic. If George Jr. wasn't at football practice or study hall, he was working hard on the farm milking cows and doing all sorts of chores, occasionally stealing some time to spend with his high school sweetheart.

She didn't mind him being busy because she knew he was definitely sprung. She was amazingly beautiful; he would be a fool to ruin a good thing. She was tall and slender and with curves in all the right places. Tan complexion and long black hair, which came from her Indian heritage. George had hit the jackpot with his Indian beauty and worshipped the ground she walked on.

His senior year, George led the Fresno Lincoln Ducks to a state championship! He was the talk of Fresno; everyone was proud to be associated with George "the Arm" Gray. USC, Norte Dame, Ohio State, and Fresno State wanted him bad. Before he could answer any college, an unexpected turn of events occurred. Vanessa found out she was three months pregnant. Not only was that a blow to the gut and life-changing, his father suddenly died from a heart attack. *Wow*, talk about Murphy's Law. His life was turned upside down in a matter of days.

He had to man up and take care of the family that Dad had left behind. (Mom had one brother and two sisters.) He had to run the farm as his father had taught him from childhood. Being Christians, George and Vanessa decided to get married and have the baby. The family was happy on both sides, and they started a life together. College and football were in the past. He had too many people depending on him at an early age. Things seemed to have been going fine, but life played yet another cruel trick on the young couple. Vanessa had complications with the pregnancy and lost the baby. They both were devastated but grew closer. George threw himself into his work on the farm; Vanessa suffered from depression. They both couldn't understand why God would take their child.

Fast-forward five years, and things were good on the farm. Hard work made the family business stay afloat and make a profit. His mother was taken care of along with his three siblings. Vanessa was a great wife, but there was something missing in their life. They tried having another child over and over again unsuccessfully. Her gynecologist told Vanessa her chances were slim to none. Her ovaries had been damaged, so the production of eggs was affected. The young couple agreed adoption was an option for starting a family. Six months later, seven-month-old Candice

Gray was the new addition to the Gray family. The precious baby brought lots of joy into the lives of her parents.

Two years later, God blessed the couple again totally unexpectedly. Vanessa miraculously got pregnant and carried the baby full–term, giving birth to a beautiful baby girl. Now Candice had a little sister, Tosha Gray. The girls were instantly close, sharing everything, and had a great childhood. Both were cute little girls and grew into beautiful young women. Even though technically they had no blood relationship, they favored each other very much.

The family all knew about the adoption, but the subject was never a topic of conversation. George and Vanessa never treated one better than the other. Tosha was on the wild side, experimenting with weed and alcohol, while Candice followed in her mother's footsteps, becoming a cheerleader. In fact she was captain of the squad, just like dear old Mom. Candice made good grades, worked around the farm, and was active in the church. Tosha couldn't care less about anything else except partying and boys.

The summer after Candy's senior year in high school, she sent a video profile to the top-rated modeling reality show, *Models on the Rise*. She was handpicked by the executive producer, Diva Dominique Aroacho, the international Puerto Rican fashion icon. Candice never really thought she would make it out of thousands of entries. To her surprise, Candice got a final interview; she aced it and was offered a spot on the show. The whole family was excited that she was on her journey toward success. This would be her first time leaving Fresno, for the city and bright lights. Mom and Dad had some advice: Keep God first and remember to stay grounded. Humility will take you a long way where arrogance won't.

Filming started immediately in Los Angeles. Leaving Fresno behind was a major step. Candice was determined to make it in the modeling industry. Failure wasn't an option, and she was prepared to work long, hard hours. She told herself she would never come back home to live. "Sink or swim" was the mind-set. Thoughts of living on the farm as an alternative weren't appealing. The allure of glamour, fame, and the spotlight had sucked her in. Still a virgin and naive to the game of life, she was a mark for a slick-talking-player spitting game.

The goal for all the girls was to make it to the final ten contestants. Usually with the exposure, they could land a career in the industry. Modeling agencies partnered with the show to recruit fresh new faces. Being around beautiful young women didn't intimidate her at all. Self-assurance made her believe she had the right to be there. Twenty women all shared one extravagant mansion aiming for one ultimate goal: to be the nation's next big model. Every trick known to man would be played; there was no honor amongst thieves. Being the captain of the cheerleaders in high school was one thing. Here she was among women trying to compete on a not-so-even battle field. Some had better bodies, and a few had better looks. The one thing that made a difference was experience. Most of the young women had prior modeling experience and healthy sized portfolios.

Taping the show was nothing like what was aired on TV. From the moment the women got there, they were put to work. Everyone had chores and lots of photo shoots along with various challenges, mini contests, wardrobe fittings, and exercise. Every day was filled with more and more adventure. It was like a fashion boot camp for beautiful women. After sitting in the makeup chair for hours, changing outfits for photo shoots, they had Q and A time to evaluate how much they knew about fashion. If nothing else, Candice was getting an advanced professional inside look at the industry.

Tammy Lynn and Constance were her roommates. Tammy was a blond-haired, blue-eyed girl from Houston, Texas. Constance (Conni) was a black beauty from Memphis, Tennessee. She liked them both; however, they were out to sabotage anyone standing in their way. A naive little country girl like Candy was an easy picking. All the women hated on each other, and competition was fierce. Backbiting, slander, gossiping, and tampering with wardrobes were commonplace. Week after week someone was packing and being sent home. The celebrity judges pulled no punches, and the Diva Dominique expected perfection.

When things got extremely difficult, Candice would call her mom for guidance. Through it all, she knew it was an opportunity of a lifetime. Not only was she getting first-class experience in the field and national and international exposure, and networking and making contacts, she was able to build an awesome portfolio and get paid in the process. Her first experience in the industry couldn't get any sweeter. Working with a fashion heavyweight and legend, the Diva Dominique Aroacho, said it all. The ultimate supermodel!

Fifth week of competition, and things were getting heated between cast members. Conni had been sent home. Tammy Lynn and Candice weren't getting along. Although Candice had been earning great scores for her challenges. The photographer had been capturing her in an awesome light. She was very photogenic; her hair, makeup, and attitude were impeccable.

Fourteen women left and the fight was on, trying to get to the final ten. The next two weeks were double elimination weeks, getting down to the final ten cast members. The contest level was raised up another notch. Only the absolute best would survive another week in the mansion. Candice dug down deep and performed to the highest level of professionalism, advancing the next two weeks to earn a spot in the final ten. She accomplished her goal, and it felt wonderful. Just being among the final ten was good enough for her. However, Mom kept encouraging her to keep the first prize place in her eyes.

Two weeks later, it was down to eight, and a curveball was thrown in the game. This challenge wasn't a glamour one but a difficult horror demand. They wanted to take the models out of their comfort zone and photograph Halloween pictures complete with costumes, wild hairstyles, and bright, robust makeup to see who had the versatility to pull off the look in photographs. No one really kicked butt in this challenge, but Candice failed miserably. She couldn't adjust to the whole horror concept; as a consequence, she was eliminated. No doubt she gave a valiant effort for an amateur in the industry.

Earning several thousand dollars for lasting that long, she didn't leave the show empty-handed. In fact, armed with a BlackBerry full of numbers and contacts in the industry, along with direct access to the show's employment website. The game was just starting for Candice. Dominique liked her attitude so much she hooked her up with a modeling agency in Los Angeles. The Diva Dominique also set up a few photo shoots for small advertisers. The advice given to her was "Stay on the grind, answer casting calls, enter contests, and go to photo shoots. Take whatever work you can get until you're on top. Modeling is a young woman's game, so the rule is to work while you can." So Candice got a permanent address in Los Angeles and started her grind!

To: Candygirl@yahoo.com You've got mail!
From: Spectacularlooks.org

Dearest Candy,

I have a photo shoot lined up for you Tuesday for Pantene hair care products. They're advertising a new conditioner for women of color. The checks came in for your past few print ads. Also Neon Vodka is hosting a modeling contest at Bar Fly in Hollywood. One-year contract with a sixty-city tour, and 50 thousand cash. Sounds like a great opportunity! I advise you to enter the contest, give me a call ASAP!

Lola Hemmingway
Spectacular looks
CEO

"She's a natural!" Vice President Carl Mills whispered to his subordinate Leslie Clark. "Who's that, Mr. Mills?"

"Number 18 with the short-cut cream top."

"Yeah, she's cute."

Leslie knew Carl had already made his choice; it was now just a matter of formalities. Carl, being the vice president in charge of advertising, had an eye for the company's image. *I've seen her before*, went through his mind. Then it hit him like a baseball bat—the modeling reality show, *Models on the Rise*. Yes, she would certainly represent their product well. Out of the many beautiful and voluptuous women, he wanted to make her the new face of Neon, and tasting her sweetness in the process. Candice became an object of his affection.

As Carl Mills made the announcement congratulating Candice for being the winner, handing her a fifty-thousand-dollar check, the lights from the camera flashes blinded her. Overwhelmed by the accomplishment that was major, mesmerizing thoughts played in her head of the sexy chocolate brother who said she'd win the contest. His business flyer was safely tucked away in her purse. "I've got to give him a call—if for nothing else, to thank him for the vote of confidence."

Charlotte, North Carolina, the city that Bank of America moved their home office to, helping to expand the economy. Home of the Carolina Panthers and the Charlotte Bobcats. Michael Jordan and rapper Nelly, being the Bobcats owners, also helped the city's revenue. Charlotte was a nice layover for northerners headed to Atlanta or Miami.

The biggest attraction by far was the NASCAR museum. Between the Charlotte speedway racetrack and the museum, NASCAR fans came from all over to watch races and view the exhibitions. A medium-sized city with a pretty skyline. The largest in the state and the liveliest. With a happening nightlife, young professionals kept the Uptown Epic Center area busy. On the urban side of town, the city birthed official pimps, players, and hustlers. One of the most active parts of town was the west side. In West Boulevard, in the Wilmore section, were the city's elite hustlers.

OGs from other states, while passing through, would stop to pay homage to OG Darryl Moffitt Sr., an old-school player who had the respect of his city and other states. Illness and old age forced him to sit his player's cup down, the one he received from the pimp extraordinaire Bishop Don Juan. A major accomplishment for a North Carolina pimp, to be honored at the Players Ball in Chi Town. Darryl Moffitt Sr. was now out of the limelight. His son Darryl Moffitt Jr. picked up the reins but not traditional pimping. He was known to his street comrades as Young Heat and was a whole new breed of hustler, not conforming to drug dealing and old-school pimp idealism.

Young Heat was a thinker and tactical wizard. White-collar crimes were his forte. Embezzlement, credit card scams, checks, and real estate schemes were how he lived. The secret to his longevity in the game was women. He used women to commit the crimes inconspicuously. His best asset was his mouth, using slick game to manipulate naive women. A combination of poetic lyrics in the ear and being a provider made his pimp game tight. So he never had to do the dirty work, just plan and command his troops from afar. An average-looking guy with a refined edge to him, his style was versatile and very unique at the same time. Sharp dresser, not flashy, just a clean-cut playboy. Young Heat had the love for the finer things in life and stayed on the cutting edge. He lived a lavish lifestyle—not a millionaire but hood-rich. Driving expensive foreign cars was a must.

The only thing he loved more than cars was women. He kept an assortment of different sizes and flavors, all serving one common purpose—to make him a myriad of money. Out of all of them, he kept three as his home team: Jackie, Karen, and Page. All were ride-or-die chicks and knew about each other. There was never beef between the home team. Each knew her role and played their position. He treated them well and provided for every need.

There was no obvious favoritism in public, but Page was the favorite. It was known by all, and the other women accepted her being the bottom bitch. As Holly was in Hue Heffner's trio, so was Page in Young Heat's stable. She was the youngest, finest, and the most loyal of the three. Jackie was the eldest, and longtime homie, lover, and friend to Young Heat. Short, dark, and thick with an ass that would rival Buffie the Body. She was the muscle in the crew. Karen was a redbone with green eyes and sexy bow legs, biracial and used for multicultural marks. She was used as the bait. Page was a baby doll—tall, small waist, light-brown eyes, and long brown hair. She could easily be a model with her stunning looks. She was the closer, the quarterback in an offensive setting, always on point like a sniper.

Out of all three, Page's loyalty ran deepest because Young Heat literally took her off the streets. The switch from living in a homeless shelter to designer clothes, jewelry, and exotic cars made him win her heart with unconditional love for him. Truth be told, it was much more than material things. Young Heat was the only man or person that showed her any love. Raised as an orphan, she never knew the love of a family. Never had a man she could trust in her life. Biological mother was a drug addict and gave her up for adoption. Her adopted mother died when she was five, and she grew up in foster care. Never knew her father but always wanted to know her family's history. One day she planned to contact the adoption agency to find out who were her parents. For now she wanted to enjoy the love she was receiving from YH. It wasn't every day a girl met a baller that offered her a change of lifestyle. Young Heat kept Page hot—hair and nail salon every week with an exclusive wardrobe, dynamite footwear, and access to his fleet of customized cars. To make it even sweeter, she lived with him in his leased Ballantyne mini mansion.

"Hey, baby, everything went as planned." Page handed Young Heat an envelope containing six thousand dollars. "That's why you're my number-one chick." He hugged her after counting the money all in hundred-dollar bills, handing her two thousand for her part in the caper. Playing fair was a way to keep his women honest with the take. Also a major reason why his women stayed and put up with his antics. "Did Jackie and Karen get their cut, baby girl?" Which was a rhetorical question because he knew the answer. "Yes, and they're ready for something else soon." They always spent money so fast the next job was always needed. YH had to constantly stay aware of opportunities so his team could eat, and eat well.

Young Heat had contacts everywhere, inside people he paid for info. People in restaurants, clothing stores, and gas stations anywhere credit cards and checks were used. He also had a girl that worked at DMV and made multiple IDs for identity theft. "I have to get some payroll checks" was one of his more lucrative hustles. They would steal the checks from business mailboxes, erase the stamped signature with a razor blade, then type a new name with a typewriter, neat and precise. Page would cash them with one of her many IDs he provided. She didn't have any record, so her face and fingerprints weren't in the system. He schooled her on the art of disguise, eye contact, and diction. Karen handled the business owners, Jackie did the theft, and Paige cashed the checks. Young Heat planned, instructed, and watched from a safe distance. When credit cards and checks weren't available, he used the women as bait to burglarize wealthy men's homes (usually widowers). They would find the marks in various places, profiling them, of course. They were a well-oiled machine when it came to picking apart a mark. Everything they did was carefully planned to the last detail, YH being the ultimate mastermind.

Sam Walters was a highly respected jeweler in the university area of Charlotte. He was a widower and father of two grown daughters. Walter's Jewelry was famous for custom-made authentic pieces. Prices were costly, but the craftsmanship and quality was undeniable. He made his mark in the city. Businesspeople, ball players, and the wealthy were his clientele. He was like Leonardo da Vinci, an artist in his own right, sculpting fine gold and diamonds together and creating future heirlooms. He was a breast cancer prevention activist and community leader, always helping fund programs for underprivileged children and families, constantly appearing in the *Charlotte Observer* for his contributions and volunteer work for breast cancer. After losing his wife, Margret, to the disease, he vowed to help fund breast cancer research, every year organizing and taking part in an annual walkathon. A full-page ad was in the *Charlotte Observer* featuring Sam Walters, showing his goal to raise one million dollars for the Mary

Margret Walters research fund. The money would go directly to help the fight against breast cancer. The *Observer* also featured a small biography about Sam Walters. The article caught the attention of Young Heat, who found this man interesting. Being a very analytical thinker, he knew Mr. Walters was a sweet target. He immediately started to formulate a plan to strike like a king cobra snake and disappear like a weasel. Operation and surveillance was underway.

Young Heat sat the women down and briefed them on the present mission. Sam Walters would be their next mark and donate to their lifestyle. YH did his homework and found out Sam was an art and antique collector. He owned the city's premier jewelry store and had lots of money. His one weakness that they would capitalize on was alcohol. Sam was an alcoholic and frequented a piano bar in the Epic Center, Howl at the Moon. His late wife was a concert pianist and music teacher at UNC Charlotte. He would sit there for hours listening to the piano, drowning his sorrows in Scotch or Merlot wine. It was apparent he was lonely and still in the grieving process. His daughters were married and living out of state. He was all alone in his huge estate in Myers Park, a very wealthy community.

As always, Karen would be the point guard for the team. Her biracial appearance made it easy to fit in with anybody. She also was very articulate and knowledgeable about world events, which made her able to converse about anything. Her green eyes had the ability to change colors, depending on her mood or clothing. Men would be smitten and caught up in a trance by her beauty and seductive voice. To her it was just a game, and Karen loved to win, and win at any cost.

The plan was for Karen to befriend Sam and make him interested in dating her. Casually start dating and, when the opportunity came, rob him blind. The beautiful thing about this mark was the team would hit him twice. Once at his home for hidden treasures, then again at the jewelry store. Step one put Karen into place as bait, finding out as much info as possible.

Thursday night at the piano bar was very popular with high society. Most of the city's professionals and wealthy socialites were regulars. In her character, "Diana Colby," Karen sat at the end of the bar nursing a cosmopolitan. Hair wrapped in a French twist, very little makeup. Navy-blue Christian Dior pantsuit, cream-colored pumps to match her blouse, and a Fendi handbag. She looked very conservative, and the Dolce & Gabbana frames secured the look. Turning down several offers for free drinks by a few different men, Karen tried to stay in her character and remember why she was there after an hour of being bored. *This isn't my type of crowd*, she thought to herself. Finally her mark, Sam Walters, walked in. He sat directly across her at the bar. It was showtime. She opened her purse looking at a photo YH had given her earlier to make sure it was, in fact, her mark, Sam Walters. Guy after guy would approach her, but she politely waved them off. After making eye contact with Sam, she smoothly took off her glasses and started to massage her temples, appearing to be having a severe headache. This was an old trick of the trade Young Heat taught his women. Men seem to offer a kind word to a woman who appears to be in pain.

Sure enough, it worked. With her eyes closed, working her temples, she heard a soft, gentle voice say, "May I teach you a breathing exercise?" She opened her eyes to find Sam standing next to her smiling.

"What kind of exercise?"

"It's called pranayama, three-part breathing, and I learned it in yoga class."

"Sure," Karen replied.

He taught her a series of breathing techniques to ease the tension. "I hope that makes you feel better, breathing helps the mind soothe the body."

"Thank you, I feel better." It, of course, was a lie.

"I'm Sam Walters, nice to meet you." He held out his hand.

"I'm Diana Colby." She reached to shake his hand.

"I see your drink is empty, may I buy you another?"

She smiled and nodded. "May I have a seat and join you, Diana?"

"I'd be delighted!"

He waved to the bartender for another round as he took a seat next to Karen. They began talking and hit it off instantly. Karen told him she was a young widow, and he felt like they had something in common. Her story was she was a widow of two years and an ex-stockbroker, financial planner, and money coach.

Sam found her even more interesting at the sound of money. Wealthy people always like to make more money. "I've always wanted to play the stock market, do you have any advice?"

She turned to him and smiled while eating the cherry out of her drink. *Man, those lips look so soft,* he thought to himself.

She placed her hand on his and began to give advice. "The trick is finding the best all-weather stocks because there will be lots of volatility in the years it takes our current economy and financial system to recuperate. The best way to find these companies is to look for businesses that raise their dividends year after year. Wal-Mart is a solid investment!"

Wow, he was blown away by her financial knowledge. Even though he was thirty years her senior, he found himself attracted to her mind. They talked about stock a bit more, then he talked about his jewelry store, also the volunteer work for breast cancer he was involved in. The night was going well, and Karen didn't want to overplay her hand. She finished her drink and took a $100 bill out for the drinks. Before he could speak, she put her index finger on his lips. "This one's on me, I can't remember when I've had a better conversation."

"Thank you," he said.

She turned to walk away, and he gently held her arm. "Diana, may I call you sometime?"

"How about I call you, Sam?"

He handed her his business card. "I would love to take you to dinner."

"Maybe we can arrange that, Sam, good night." She turned and walked away, smooth and confident like a female Mack who had just scored. She couldn't believe how much she learned from watching CNN and reading *Wall Street Journal*.

Sam couldn't believe it; the first time since Margret's death, he actually had a hard-on. *Wow, Diana Colby, I must have her for self like wealth!* Karen walked past YH's car (an Audi A8) and hopped in a cab just in case Sam was watching. Her cell phone rang.

"Did everything go as planned, baby?"

"Yes, he's all mine, baby."

"That's why I count on you, Karen. Meet me at the Westin, room 108."

"I'll be there, baby kisses!"

Young Heat had different spots he took each woman; the Westin was Karen's spot. He realized that keeping them happy meant spending time together. Page understood and stayed home watching movies; Jackie was cool as long as she made money. She required the least amount of attention since she was the oldest. They stayed in a suite that included a bar sink with a granite countertop and microwave. The amenities were a heated hot tub, laundry facilities, free Wi-Fi, and flat-screen TVs starting at $141 a night.

YH took the liberty of chilling a few bottles of rosé. He brought several bags of chocolate, which Karen loved. Hershey's Kisses with almonds, Reese's peanut butter cups, Almond Joy, and Kit Kat. Something about chocolate turned Karen on. When she walked in the room and saw the candy and rosé, she felt the moisture between her legs. YH had purchased a cobalt-blue sheer teddy from Victoria's Secret and body spray. YH hit the automatic switch to the hot tub and started to heat the water. Karen took off her clothes, then she started to undress YH. Standing totally naked, they embraced and tasted each other's tongues. He popped a bottle and poured them some champagne. They adjourned to the hot tub, drinking and kissing. Running his fingers through her hair and sucking on her neck turned Karen on. He fed her some Hershey's Kisses then slowly began to suck her round D-cup-sized breast. His manhood stood at full attention; Karen stroked it gently. "I want to feel you inside of me, Heat." "Be patient" was his reply. The flat screen had the Sirius Satellite Radio playing tuned to the R & B station. The smooth sounds of Rick James and Teena Marie, "Fire and Desire," played in the background. They held each other and relaxed in the hot water, enjoying the moment. He carried her to the bed and towel-dried her body sensitively. He put on a condom and entered her body strong and firm, just the way she wanted.

"Slow motion, slow motion for me, slow motion" was what he whispered in her ear. Her legs were spread apart, and YH was deep inside her stroking rhythmically, making her feel like everything she did for him was worth the trouble. She knew only a piece of him was hers, so she wanted to enjoy her portion. With one last thrust with his pelvis, he released inside the condom. She held tight as she felt the warm sensation of an orgasm. Lying on his back, Karen put her head on his chest. "Young Heat, you're the best, baby boy, you're simply the best!" He kissed her on the cheek and they fell asleep.

In the morning, they made love again and, afterward, enjoyed a large breakfast from the restaurant in the Westin. Then YH drove her home to her luxury two-bedroom condo she shared with her cousin. "OK, baby, handle business like we discussed." Heat schooled her on how to play their mark. She would check in daily with a progress report.

After a week, Karen called Sam. He was so happy to hear her voice. They had lunch at the Cheesecake Factory and dinner later on that week at P. F. Chang's. Talking on the phone and meeting for drinks at the piano bar became common. Karen had to admit she was learning a lot hanging out with Sam. He broadened her mind on art and culture; he taught her about the flaws and quality in diamonds. He shared valuable info about his business when he started drinking. Karen found out he had his diamonds imported from Africa—a private gem distributor from Nigeria—usually receiving his stones once a month or according to sales and demand. When she visited his home for dinner, he took her on a tour of his cherished artwork. A valuable Picasso was among his many treasures. When she got the chance to browse around while he took a shower, Karen uncovered a safe in the wall of his study. Not to mention various diamond rings, bracelets, and watches he had in his jewelry box.

Candice was caught off guard by his faith in her abilities. "Do you think I have a chance?"

He responded, "If God made a woman more beautiful than you, he kept her in heaven for himself!"

She was flattered, took the flyer, smiled, and walked in the club. The boost of confidence made Candice hold her head up high. A sea of beautiful women in all shapes and colors were in attendance for the competition. Swave wanted to enjoy the festivities, but he couldn't afford the entry fee on his tight budget. Besides, he had class the next morning and a product assignment that was due. Driving away in his beat-up '89 Honda Accord, thoughts of the beautiful model and her name haunted him. He was upset with himself for not seizing the moment. Well, it was a shot in the dark trying to land an advertising deal. "You've got to be in it to win it" was his motto!

Opening his eyes and seeing Candice in a box snapped his mind back to reality, the here and now. So many plans for the future that would never ever materialize. Dreams of having a family and growing old together was a distant memory. Time to say good-bye to his one true love; it was hard, but he had to be strong. Like a short cool breeze on a spring day. Gone too soon, gone too soon. *I love you, Candice!*

Fond of Sam as she was, Karen had to remember her duty to Young Heat. She had never slept with a white man, but the inevitable was sure to happen. Gathering all the intel she could and noticing he didn't set the security alarm once inside the house, it was time for her team to activate their mission. A month-long courtship made Sam drop his guard and look forward to spending time with Diana (or so he called her). They fooled around, and she let him fondle her a little, but they never had intercourse. The time had come, and she told him she was ready to go all the way!

Jackie, Page, and YH had a complete diagram of the house and Sam's neighborhood. YH put together the plan and instructed the women on their roles. Only thing left to do was wait for Karen to give the go-ahead through her signal. YH made sure the women had black clothing and gloves, also face masks. The plates were changed on the rented van he had secured with a fictitious ID and credit card. The women both had Beretta handguns—not to hurt anyone, mainly as a motivator.

Thursday afternoon and the plan was for Diana (in her character) to meet Sam at the jewelry store. She showed up in a cab, telling him her car was in the shop. Her carrying an overnight bag let Sam know tonight was the magic night. While in the store, she inconspicuously took pictures of the inside with her phone. That would be for part two in the future. When the last customer left, Sam and his employees Sue and Helen locked up the store. Putting Diana's overnight bag in the trunk of his Benz CLS 550, they headed to Ruth's Chris for dinner followed by the piano bar for drinks, then finally to Sam's house for relaxation and more drinks.

Sitting in the den, Sam and Diana (Karen) drank a bottle of Columbian Crest Merlot. Then she insisted on taking a shower. She told him she wanted to be absolutely fresh when she gave herself to him. She carried her overnight bag into the bathroom, turned on the shower, and pulled out her cell phone, speed-dialing YH. He answered immediately. "Hey, baby, are you in position out there?"

"Yes, we're all set waiting for the signal."

"OK. Be ready, I'll signal you in about an hour." The line went dead, and she took a quick shower. While she was in the shower, Sam set the stage. He put Kenny G on the CD player—"Silhouette." Then he sprayed the room and bed with Febreze, peach flavor. He didn't want the smell of Cuban cigars to ruin the mood. He opened another bottle of Merlot, poured a glass, and sat on his Italian Corinthian leather chair, trying to fight the thoughts of Mary Margret in his mind. The time had come for him to move on with his life. When Diana (Karen) appeared from the bathroom, it was like an angel descending from heaven. She wore the sheer Victoria's Secret teddy that YH had brought her. She smelled like vanilla with the VS body spray. Her hair was wet, giving her an exotic look, eyes following with the color pasture green. Thong panties, sexy bow legs, and pretty polished toenails. Her breasts were round and firm, nipples hard and calling to Sam's wet mouth. He couldn't believe how incredible she looked from the wet hair to her pretty toes. His lower half started to circulate blood to his manhood quickly. This was the second erection he'd had while admiring Diana (Karen). *Good thing they invented Viagra for men like me*, he thought to himself.

He stood and greeted her with a kiss, revealing his excitement between his legs. She kissed him back and gently rubbed his manhood.

"Why don't you take a shower, Sam."

The only thing he was able to say was OK. He handed her a glass of wine and stepped into the master bathroom. Karen waited a few minutes until the shower was going, then she made her move. Headed downstairs, she went to the back sliding glass door connected to the kitchen and sunroom. She unlocked the door and flipped the light switch off and on three times. That was the signal to let the team know to move in thirty minutes. She quickly went back upstairs, undressed, and lay on the huge king-sized bed naked. Sam dried off, rubbed on some Calvin Klein Eternity lotion, and sprayed the cologne. He looked at himself in the mirror and said, "Go get 'em, Tiger."

When he walked out of the bathroom, she was on the bed, legs spread, poking her finger in and out of the beautiful, well-manicured kitty kat. "Wow" was all Sam could say; he dropped his clothes and jumped into bed with his seductress. She was surprised that for a sixty-year-old man, he was still in good shape. She guessed yoga was helping him.

"Diana, I want you so much, darling."

She was doing her best not to laugh. "I want you too, Sam, let's not wait any longer." They started to kiss and touch each other's bodies. Despite this being a paid acting part, Karen found herself enjoying his touches. Truth be told, she was slightly attracted to him and his power and prestige. Not to mention he was very compassionate. *Shake it off, shake it off.* She reminded herself of the mission and obligation to the team.

Meanwhile, Jackie and Page were entering the house from the rear. The nearest house was one hundred yards away, perfect for their plan. YH parked fifty yards down the street where he could watch both ends of the street. They were dressed in all-black, with flashlights, ski masks, twin Berettas, and two-way radios. It was radio silence until they secured the house. They knew how the house was built and walked up the stairs quietly, guided by their flashlights. They headed straight to the master bedroom, slowly turning the doorknob. Page was in first, then Jackie, both watching Karen do her thing. She was putting on an Academy Award performance, sound effects and all. Karen was on top of Sam, riding his pony and rubbing her breasts sensually. "*Oh*, Sam, *oh*, Sam, you feel so good inside of me, baby."

Jackie froze for a minute, letting her fantasies take her away mentally. Page tapped her on the shoulder and snapped her back into reality. Then Jackie slapped Karen upside the head with her gun. Karen screamed, and Sam opened his eyes in shock. Page flicked on the lights, and Sam was now looking down the barrel of a Beretta. "This is a robbery, don't make it a homicide," Page threatened with a stern voice.

"What do you want from me?"

"We want your valuables, old man. If you don't cooperate, we will kill you and your pretty little girlfriend!"

Sam was more than willing to surrender, having never been in a situation like this before. Karen was bleeding from the side of her face, and she moaned from real pain. First things first—Page took out some handcuffs from her pocket, handcuffing them both. Taking the pillowcases off the pillows, Jackie emptied the jewelry box on the dresser into the pillowcase. "Now, Mr. Rich Man, I know you have a safe somewhere." Before he attempted to lie, Jackie's gun was up against Diana's (Karen's) head. "I'll take you to it, my dear." A silent way of letting them know he knew they were women.

To make everything appear real and not staged, they walked Karen along with Sam down the hall to his study. "OK, Mr. Rich Man, open it, and don't try anything funny." Page turned on the light, and Sam lifted the picture off the wall opening the safe door. "Well, well, well, what do we have here?"

One hundred thousand dollars banded in ten-thousand-dollar stacks. A blue velvet drawstring bag with ten beautiful diamonds. A stack of papers, which Page didn't bother to read, and what appeared to be a smoking pipe. "OK, folks, let's move." Jackie waved them back toward the bedroom.

Karen looked at Sam with tears in her eyes. He thought she was scared for her life. Actually, she felt remorse for being a part of the robbery. He had really touched her heart. "So what now?" Sam asked Page.

"Now we tie you up and leave." Page was ready for everything; she had bought some plastic ties and tied their feet, pushing them on their stomachs with force. "Be good people and when we leave, we'll send someone to help you." Sam and Diana (Karen) looked at each other while Jackie and Page walked out the room.

Before leaving the house, Page and Jackie made radio contact with YH. "All is fine, baby, we're rolling up the artwork as we speak."

"OK, good work, hurry up, and be safe coming out." They took down all five of the paintings in the den, rolled them up, and headed for the way they came in. Page thought to herself, *How about if there's something else here of value?* Jackie said, "Let's go, we're already straight." So Page didn't follow her instincts and they headed out the door. Then she turned around and slammed her long-handled flashlight against the glass door, breaking the glass. It had to appear to be a break-in home invasion and not a setup. "We're on our way, Poppa Bear."

They reached the van and pulled off into the night. Once across town, Page stopped and called 911 from a pay phone, telling about a robbery. The only reason they did call police was so Karen wouldn't have to stay tied up for a long time.

"I'm so sorry this had to happen on our special night, Diana."

"Sam, I'm scared, what if they come back?"

"They won't, they have what they wanted—some money and valuables." He didn't seem upset about the money or jewelry. "They left something far more valuable than what they took."

I wonder what that could be, she thought. Smart as Sam was, Diana never crossed his mind as being the infiltrator. One hour later, the police arrived and freed them from bondage and took their statements and notes for a proper investigation. Detective Alex Lopez was the lead detective on the case.

Across town, YH and the women split the money four ways. Forty grand for Karen, who had put in the most and critical work. Then twenty grand apiece for the rest of the team. YH had a fence he would sell the jewelry and artwork to quietly. "You ladies did well, I'm proud of you." This would go down as another plan that came together under his watchful eye. He'd get with Karen in a few days to give her a much deserved share and some good loving. For now it was time to go home, relax for a few, and think about his next move. The game never stops, and to remain on top, you have to keep pushing. Jackie drove away in her Nissan 350Z. YH and Page sped off in his Audi A8 listening to the Miami Player Rick Ross. "Push it to the limit, the world is mine, the world is mine, push it to the limit!"

It had been almost a year that Candice had been gone from home. First on the reality show *Models on the Rise*, now on a nationwide promotional tour for Neon Vodka. As things started to formulate for Candice, Tosha's world was slowly falling apart. She was the complete opposite of Candice. One was driven and wanted to work for her success. The other was lazy and wanted everything handed to her on a silver platter.

She experimented with designer drugs like meth and ecstacy. Breaking curfew and sleeping around was her lifestyle. George and Vanessa grew tired of trying to reach their bad seed of a daughter. The last straw was finding out she dropped out in her senior year of high school. The school's guidance counselor reported Tosha hadn't been to school in months. That was it; she had to go. "No more free rides!" said Mom.

Vanessa called Candice, hoping that maybe she could somehow take Tosha on her tour. Maybe it would jump-start some ambition for success in her daughter. Vanessa loved her daughter and knew she would learn the hard way, hopefully not with her life, dying from AIDS or a drug overdose. Reluctantly Candy agreed, telling her mom to put her on a plane to Clearwater, Florida, which was her next stop on the southeast part of the tour. She loved her family but felt it was a bad idea bringing Tosha along. The lifestyle of her peers was alcohol and parties mixed with sexual escapades, all taking place after long hours of work and travel. Although Candice didn't drink much and didn't do any form of drugs. She was nineteen going on twenty and still very much a virgin. Success was in her eyes, and she was willing to sacrifice to get there even if it meant not dating. Candice was the star of the tour and the most boring by far.

Many guys hit on Candice, but she never fell victim to the game. That made Carl Mills want her even more. He constantly told her if she needed anything, just ask. So naturally it wasn't a problem when she asked if Tosha could come along for the rest of the tour. Carl Mills's assistant, Leslie, was annoyed by Candy's "little miss innocent" ways. However, she knew better than to speak on the issue for job security.

In different cities, they had celebrity guests that performed at the venues. Clearwater was being hosted by comedian Kevin Hart. Candice was so excited to meet him because she was a huge fan. The Florida tour started in Fort Myers where Plies performed. Then Tampa and Clearwater was where they had reserved motel rooms. Two hours after arriving in Clearwater, her phone rang; it was Tosha. She gave her the address to the Sea Captain Resort where they'd be staying and told her to catch a cab to the motel where Candice would be waiting. The Sea Captain Resort was a twenty-nine-unit '50s-era motel with basic room efficiencies and suites. Which meant, of course, Candice stayed in a suite. Part of her contract! The decor was a bit dated, but the place was squeaky clean. The beds and linen were all new, and the grounds were impeccably landscaped. Pool, hot tub, shuffleboard, gas grill, and refrigerator. The resort wasn't for solitude seekers, but it was a great choice for active options. A great place to promote the product and do some awesome photo shoots on the white beach.

Tosha arrived at the resort and couldn't believe how her sister was rolling. She saw the long Neon tour bus and everyone hanging around the resort. The eyes of the men undressed her in those cut-off white shorts with her rear hanging out and short-cut T-shirt revealing her pierced belly button. She walked slowly as she felt the attention being drawn to her.

"Can I help you with your luggage, honey dip?" It was Tymel, the tour's most notorious playboy.

"Sure." She handed him her largest bag.

"What room are you looking for?"

"Room 210, my sister Candy's room."

"You mean Candice—that's your sister?"

"Yes, my older sister."

Tymel had tried to hook Candice with his fishing line, but she hadn't bitten. Maybe he would have better luck with baby sis. "Maybe we could get together sometime soon."

Just when she was about to answer him, Candice opened the door. "Tymel, my sister isn't interested. Thank you for your help." He smiled and walked away, defeated once again.

"Yeah, girl, look at you shining like a star!" They embraced and held hands, looking in each other's eyes. Candice really loved her little sister; she just wanted her to do what was right. Candice went in the fridge and handed Tosha a bottle of water. They sat on the bed and started to talk about the future. Candice told Tosha she expected her to be respectful because this was her job. No drugs or overnight male guests and not too much alcohol.

"Man, sis, you act like Mom, I can't do anything."

Candice tried to explain she had plenty of time for fun, but the right way and with the right people. These years were for building a career and securing the future.

"OK, big sis, I'll behave myself."

"Cool, let's go get something to eat, little sister."

The next day, Candice was scheduled for a photo shoot at 10:00 AM. She was working with a major designer, Diane von Furstenberg, a well-known giant in the game. Candice loved her clothing, but her swimwear didn't exactly fit Candy's body frame. However, with a few alterations, she made it work. She was honored just to wear Ms. Furstenberg's clothes. Candy was really doing her thing, and the tour had been a success thus far. Tosha watched as her sister worked and everyone made a fuss over the star model. Instead of admiration, jealousy and envy got into her heart. In time those true feelings would be revealed.

Tymel, who was one of the tour's labor workers, couldn't keep his eyes off Tosha. They made eye contact several times, and he even licked his tongue. She thought that was sexy and returned the gesture, letting him know she was game for some one-on-one fun. He wrote his cell phone number down, walked past, and dropped it on the white sand. She picked it up and smiled. It was just a matter of time before they would explore each other's bodies.

Like an alert state trooper, Candice watched the two flirt from a distance. She knew a stop had to be put to Tymel's antics. Since she headlined the tour, making her happy was sensible. A call to Carl Mills had Tymel on the first bus back to California. She wasn't trying to cockblock Tosha; she was merely trying to save her life. She didn't feel like she had betrayed her sister; that's what big sisters were for—protection. Protection from the wolves in sheep's clothing.

Club Ukatan was the venue that Neon Vodka and Kevin Hart would work and take pictures. Candice killed the game with a Furstenberg original dress. Tube top, elastic midwaist, and criscross thigh laces. It was beige, and the lace was brown. She wore brown-and-beige suede pumps and a Michael Kors handbag. Tosha wasn't very glamorous; she was more of a Reebok classic and jeans type of girl. Candice twisted her arm to wear a nice Prada dress she had bought in Los Angeles. They wore the same size, 5–6, except Candice was taller. Both had small waists and C-cup breasts, firm and perky. Tosha was welcome to her wardrobe 'cause Candice wanted her sister to look her absolute best. It was a huge turnout, and Kevin Hart killed the audience. *He's definitely the next hot comedian or actor to blow up in Hollywood.* (Those were Candy's thoughts.)

After a long photo shoot, Candice agreed to have a late dinner / early breakfast with Kevin Hart. First she had to make sure Tosha got to the room safely, then she hung out with Kevin. They had a great time talking and laughing uncontrollably. He was a complete gentleman and walked her back to the room. They ended the night with a hug and kiss on the cheek. He promised to look her up when in Los Angeles. Tosha tried to get some juicy details, but there weren't any to tell. "You're no fun, big sister." Candice smiled. "Get some sleep, we're headed to Atlanta tomorrow. The Miami stop was rescheduled, so we're going to Atlanta."

In a few months' time, Candice hit lots of cities (Los Angeles, New Mexico, Las Vegas, Phoenix, Houston Denver, St. Louis, Cincinnati, Louisville, San Antonio, Dallas, and New Orleans.) Now she was headed northeast from Florida. Candice called Mom and Dad to let them know they were fine. It did Vanessa's heart well to know her children were safe. The only question was, how long would Candice be able to contain Tosha?

The tour bus consisted of a hip-hop DJ (DJ Nice) and Silvia and Wanda in charge of merchandising. They sold Neon Vodka hats, T-shirts, shot glasses, mugs, and actual vodka. They gave away promotion samples along with Frisbees and sunglasses. There was the bus driver, Big Hank; the photographer, Pierre; and Mia, Candy's personal stylist. Leslie Clark, Mr. Mills's assistant, doubled as road manager and hair stylist. She was in charge of the models' overall image. Billy was one half of the labor crew; he had extra work since Tymel got sent home. Of course, Candice was the center of all the attention. Mr. Mills had met Leslie while she was in hair school. He took up with her, romanced her, and made Leslie his assistant. When the love affair was over, he kept her on. She proved to be the best assistant he ever had. Everyone made good money and got along for the most part. They weren't actually happy about Tosha tagging along, but Mr. Mills had okayed it, so that was a closed case.

Atlanta was the black Hollywood of the South; everyone was successful in this city. They stayed at the Hilton on Lenox Boulevard; it was only a two-day stay in Atlanta. So lots of work had to be done in record time. Instead of Leslie doing Candy's hair, Derek J, a hair wizard from *The Real Housewives of Atlanta*, was hired. Neon teamed up with the cast members to promote the show and the beverage. In two days, they visited Shark Bar, Majic City, and Stokers. Between photo shoots, wardrobe changes, hair and makeup, and lots of smiling like a politician, Candice was dead tired. Tosha got to see firsthand how demanding a modeling career could be daily.

They did have a few laughs with Hurricane and Shawty—Shawty "What My Name Is" who performed at the venues.

Candice took multivitamins and drank a protein shake every day. She used to drink Red Bull until Big Hank suggested 5-hour ENERGY. She had a lot on her plate, and watching Tosha while she worked didn't make life easier. The crew had the opportunity to eat at Justin's on Peach Street. Before hitting the road, they set up a promo booth in Mid-Town giving out promo merchandise, and a photo shoot to build the Neon portfolio. Next stop was Columbia, South Carolina, then Charlotte, North, Carolina. Tosha's eighteenth birthday was in a week. Candice promised to take her out for a celebration. Leslie had to confirm future tour dates, so they'd be there for a week. Candice didn't see any harm with them hanging out for Tosha's birthday night. She knew baby sister had to get out and spread her wings.

Columbia, South Carolina, was known to everyone as a college town. USC and the HBCU's Benedict and Allen were the pride of the city. Unfortunately the featured club owner cancelled on the last minute. With no venue, Leslie decided to have a promo dinner at Chili's Restaurant, introducing the product to the general manager, giving the newly opened restaurant some much-needed exposure. The photo shoot would go to the Internet and announce Chili's served Neon. After it was all said and done, the general manager ordered several cases and wanted a long-term contract. At the end of the day, it was all about sales and Leslie knew that; she was the best at putting up numbers. Everyone had a good time eating and drinking; it didn't even seem like work. Carl Mills was pleased to hear about the contract and Leslie's ability to adapt to any circumstance. That's why she was his right arm in the business. Leslie made sure everyone was aboard the bus, then they took off for the city called Queen. The Queen City, Charlotte, North Carolina, the little big city of the South.

As they rolled into the city in the evening, the skyline looked purple. The whole city had a purple silhouette in the sky, a beautiful sight. Candice first thought was this was a little big city with character. After living in Los Angeles, it couldn't compare size-wise, but it had a big-city feel. Bank of America signs on the Carolina Panthers stadium stood out.

Then she noticed a mural of Michael Jordan on the side of the Bobcats arena. Wow, she absolutely loved Jordan. Candice always said she wanted to marry a tall dark-skinned brother. The Neon bus pulled into Trade Street; their hotel was on Fourth Street, the Double Tree Inn. They didn't have any more doubles, so Tosha got her own room. Candice wasn't happy about that, but she maintained her composure. She knew Tosha had to have some level of freedom; hell, she'd be eighteen in a few days. She had to eventually trust her because Leslie had planned photo shoots and meet-and-greets all week long. The only day she would get a little slack was Tosha's birthday. Leslie figured it was allowed since the tour was a success, with sales continuing to progress with each city.

Since Tosha been on the road with the crew, she hadn't used any illegal drugs. Some mild drinking with the other girls but nothing major. She wanted some ecstasy for her birthday, and the only way to get it was on her own. With no contacts in the city of Charlotte, she used Candy's laptop to network. She saw the advertisement for BlackPeopleMeet.com, so she created a profile, posted a sexy picture from her Facebook page, and started her mission: to meet a sexy guy that was connected in this little big city. This would be strictly hush-hush, so when Candice was at work, Tosha would be exploring the Net and, hopefully, the city.

The first few days were extremely busy. Candice exercised above-the-board professionalism. That was one thing Leslie admired about the young diva-in-training. She even gave Candice a compliment on her attitude and how she conducted herself during business events. Candice attributed her work ethic to being on the *Models on the Rise* reality show. She had learned so much from the grand diva, Dominique Aroacho. Dominique had taught her so much about fashion, photography, diet, exercise, and networking.

That's why the Diva Dominique was her idol and mentor. The workload for the first two days were several bars and restaurants, Buffalo Wild Wings, Fox n Hound, Iris Pub, Slickers, Hooters, and Club Blue Jazz, followed by the Uptown Cabaret and the Gentlemen's Club. The crew was busy for two days strong. It didn't bother Tosha—gave her time to meet a drug connect and score some ecstasy and maybe some good old-fashioned loving in the process. Hours of screening through losers and wannabe players were taking its toll on Tosha. Just when she was about to throw in the towel, she saw a picture of a guy holding the cutest little Pomeranian dog. So she pulled up his profile. "Mmm." Twenty-six years old, likes R & B and hip-hop and rock. Loves to read, loves animals especially dogs, loves beautiful women of all races. Self-employed. "Mmm, a hustler." Then she browsed his photos. Every picture had a different European car, all with nice rims. He caught her attention with the pictures of the puppy; Tosha loved dogs. If this guy had a little baby like that, he had to be sensitive—most guys had pitt bulls—not to mention those cars screamed some sort of hustler. She sent a message!

Dear Darryl, a.k.a. Young Heat,

I was taken by your pictures and profile. I'm from Cali and here in town for a week, need someone to chill with, if you're interested hit me up. 716-633-1850 Toshatailspin@ yahoo.com

Full day of work. Candice called Tosha to make sure she was fine and had eaten. Then she took a shower and went to bed. She had to be fresh for an early morning commute to the neighboring town of Concord, North Carolina. Leslie was able to land a few more contracts there. She was really a workhorse and expected everyone else to be as well. Tosha told Big Sis she wanted to just chill in the room and watch some movies. Candice was cool with that; plus she was extremely booked all day.

"Baby, do you need anything before I go get my nails and feet done?"
"No, I'm cool, baby girl, go and get fly for Daddy."
With that being said, Page kissed YH and walked out of their bedroom. A few minutes later, he heard the engine to the Acura TL start, then it pulled down the street. Lying in his king-sized bed, YH turned on his laptop to check out the Internet. Nothing new on Facebook. Then he checked his e-mail at Yahoo.com—no new e-mails. Now for Blackpeoplemeet.com.
"Wow, what's this sexy li'l thing Toshatailspin. From Cali, here for a week. Sexy li'l body. OK, how old is she? Hmm. She'll be eighteen in two days. OK, I can wait for two days. Let me call her and see where her head is for an eighteen-year-old cutie!"
YH called, and they immediately hit it off. He had her laughing 'til her stomach started hurting; that was his way of making women feel comfortable with him. She definitely was feeling the conversation. He was the first guy she had talked to since Cali, and Tymel didn't count. After a brief silence, YH asked if he could take her out for her eighteenth birthday. Before she had a chance to think about Candice, she accepted. "You better call me, Young Heat, 'cause I'm feeling your swag!"
"Cool, I'll talk to you, then peace."
Now how can I get rid of Candice on my birthday? she thought.
The next day, Tosha spent the early morning with Candice. They ate breakfast in the hotel's restaurant and shared conversation. Candice was booked for a long day. Tosha said she wanted to catch the city bus or cab to do some sightseeing, maybe go to the mall and do some birthday shopping. Candice was reluctant at first but realized Tosha was turning eighteen. She needed some independence and trust to go along with it. She made

Tosha promise to call during the day, and gave her some money. After their breakfast, Candice was off with the crew to start the business tasks at hand. Tosha took a shower, pressed her hair, and put on some clothes, trying not to seem eager, but the truth was she wanted to kick it with Young Heat. For some strange reason she felt like it was meant for her to meet him. Turning on the computer, she looked over his profile curiously. It was something in his eyes that made her want to know more about him. She had always been attracted to hustlers—the thrill turned her on. Her ring tone was Ace Hood featuring Rick Ross and Lil Wayne, "Hustle Hard," not common for a Cali chick.

While she was browsing the Net, her phone rang. It was YH, and he wanted to take her to lunch then show her his city. Without a thought, Tosha told him the hotel she was staying in and said she'd meet him out front. Twenty minutes later, a sporty 645 coupe pulled in front of the Double Tre Inn. He got out and gave her a polite smile and hug. He opened the car door like a gentleman, and they were off into the midday traffic. YH was dressed like a typical dope boy (Yankee fitted white tee, sweatpants, and Air Force ones). He had an expensive-looking watch and pinky ring; he smelled good and had a fresh haircut. The most impressive thing wasn't his car, jewelry, or iPhone. It was his demeanor. He carried himself as if he were a wealthy, important individual. The ambience had success all in the air, and she was feeling the vibe.

Damn, baby girl is a sexy li'l thing, YH thought to himself.

She was dressed in another one of Candy's Prada dresses—this one a halter top that revealed her firm C-cup breasts—open-toe Prada sandals, and a Prada purse. Her hair was pressed to perfection, and toes were polished the same color of the dress (peach). Her smell was the clincher—Victoria's Secret (passion fruit). The outfit survey told him that her family had and was about their finances. Little did he know her style was borrowed from the older sister.

YH had the best CD and song for the occasion, Keyshia Cole, "Heaven Sent." They smiled at each other and talked while listening to the music in the background. She was feeling the way he accelerated, weaving through the traffic like the city was his own. YH wanted to keep it simple and stray away from being fancy. He took her to the city's best deli, Bedder Bedder & Moore, where they served fresh homemade soup and awesome healthy sandwiches. He ordered an NY-style Reuben, and she had a Turkey Provolone Pita. While eating lunch, the conversation was honest and open. YH told her he made money several different ways illegally but no drugs. That gave her mixed emotions—turned on because he was a moneymaking bad boy, disappointed she couldn't score any ecstasy or anything else. She told him she was from Fresno, California, in town with her older sister, a model for Neon Vodka, on a nationwide promo tour for the company. She figured why not ask about the ecstasy; maybe he'd get some for her b-day. Unfortunately he wasn't willing to give her any drugs. In fact, he talked to Tosha as a friend, explaining that two chemicals that are released in the brain while on the drug were dopamine and serotonin. Once they were depleted, you caused major damage to the brain. She wasn't expecting a biology or chemistry lesson from him. In spite of being a player, he never wanted to see women, especially young women, on drugs.

Just as the conversation really started to get deep, her phone rang. YH couldn't believe her ringtone. It was Candice calling to check on li'l sis. All was well, and they ended the conversation both saying "I love you" to the other. He was touched by the obvious love Big Sis had for Tosha, calling to check on her. Before they left the restaurant, YH asked again if she wanted to hang out on her b-day.

Even if I don't get any X? Thinking about the matter, Tosha decided why not hang out with him. He was a cool guy, and she could get her drink on, hopefully ending up making love on her eighteenth birthday! "OK, YH, on one condition!"

"What's that, baby girl?"

"I want to have a fantasy fulfilled—I want to have a ménage à trois!"

Woot! YH was totally caught off guard with her request. He looked her in the eyes, and she didn't look away or hold her head down—a clear confirmation that she was serious about the contingent indiscretion. His mind ran wild with the possibilities, how wonderful this experience would be. "Hmm" was all he could say. "OK, baby girl, I'll set the whole evening up, just leave it to me. One more question, Tosha—well, actually two. Why me?"

"Because I'm feeling your style, and I've always wanted to do this on my eighteenth birthday."

"OK, cool."

"What's the second question?"

"What kind of girl do you want to experience?"

"As long as she's beautiful and has a flawless body, I'm cool."

"OK, cool, I have just the right person for your eighteenth-birthday ménage à trois!"

YH drove Tosha back to her hotel, gave her a kiss on the lips, and stroked her face with his hand. "I'll call you later, baby girl."

"OK, cool."

She walked into the hotel, and he sped off into the uptown part of the city. There was no other woman that he wanted to experience another ménage à trois with apart from Page. He pulled over at the gas station and texted Page, telling her they needed to talk ASAP. He knew she would be down. She was always down for whatever when it came to his desires. When Tosha got up to her floor, she saw Silvia and Wanda. They were supposed to be at work. Something was wrong; she felt it in the pit of her stomach. Wanda told Tosha she needed to go to Candy's room ASAP! Without any questions, Tosha went directly to her big sister's room. She knocked and Leslie opened the door to see Candice lying on the bed, leg propped up on a pillow with a bag of ice on her ankle.

"What happened, sis?"

"My high heel broke on my pumps, and I twisted my ankle."

Tosha hugged her and held her hand. "Can I do anything for you, Candice?"

"No, I'm fine, just need some rest."

Seems that Candice was rushing trying to change her wardrobe when the accident happened. Leslie felt bad 'cause she was pushing her hard. Well, in the spirit of being fair and honestly concerned for her paid employee, Leslie halted production for two days to give Candice some rest to properly be able to get back on her feet.

Wow, what luck, Tosha thought. Now she didn't have to worry about ducking Candice. She'll be bedridden for two days at least. In a low, soft apologetic voice, Candice told Tosha she would have to take a rain check on the birthday night out. Tosha was theatrical with her acceptance speech. "That's OK, big sis, we'll do it big some other time, maybe Philly or New York!" She stayed in the room with Candice until her pain pills started to kick in and she fell asleep. Tosha went to her room, took a shower, and ordered some room service. YH called and they talked for a few hours, planning to get together the next night, which was her birthday.

YH sat Page down and held her hand while asking if she would fulfill his fantasy. Without even a thought, she agreed to the ménage à trois as he knew she would, then he gave her the rundown on Tosha—how he met her, her age, and her beauty plus body. Since they had an open relationship, there wasn't anything to hide. He didn't even consider Jackie or Karen for the ménage although both were freaky and would have been formidable partners. Tosha was young and tender, so Page was the obvious fit for the intimate moment. Secretly Page had a desire to experiment, so this gave her the perfect opportunity to walk on the wild side.

Tosha woke up bright-eyed and bushy-tailed, feeling proud she was now legally an adult. Mom and Dad called to wish her a happy birthday; she'd get her present once back in Cali. The two sisters had breakfast together in Candy's room. Leslie and Big Hank stopped by to show some concern. Pierre called from his room, and everyone wished Tosha a happy birthday. When the mood was right, Tosha told Candice about her new friend she met two days earlier. Candice didn't seem too alarmed. Tosha figured she wouldn't push the issue too far. So she held back info about going out for her birthday. "Why rock the boat, I'll just let it sail." Tosha spent all day with her big sis watching movies on Netflix. Tosha got a text from YH saying "Be ready, I'm picking you up at eight." (It was 6:30.) Candice would be knocked out soon from her pain medication. Sure enough, at seven she was fast asleep. Tosha kissed her forehead and headed for her room. She took a quick shower, did her hair, and put on one of Candy's favorite dresses, a black lace mini designed by Azzedine Alaia. She finished the look with red pumps that matched her nail polish and a black Louie Vuitton handbag. She looked far beyond her years; it was amazing what clothes can do for one's appearance. Not to mention having a sister that was an up-and-coming supermodel with a wardrobe sitting on top of the fashion pile.

This was a special night, not only for Tosha but everyone involved. YH wanted the evening to be absolutely perfect. He even dressed the part, wearing a Perry Ellis portfolio dress shirt and slacks, Cole Haan casual shoes, white gold diamond earrings, and white gold Rolex watch. Fragrance by Ralph Lauren (Polo Black). He pulled up in front of the hotel driving his mint-green '76 Cadillac Eldorado, complete with T&V spoke rimes and tires. Real pimp status, a show car from his father's run in the '70s. Tosha quickly got inside before any of the crew saw her leave. He didn't even have time to open the door for her to show chivalry wasn't dead. She was turned on by his swagger and pimp persona. He couldn't help but lick his lips, admiring her curvaceous shape in that impeccably fitting minidress, designed specifically for her sister by the great Azzedine Alaia. The CD player had none other than the Isley Brothers's "Footsteps in the Dark" playing—before both of their times, but great music was great music, which always stood the test of time. Fifteen minutes later, they pulled up at the restaurant, Bone Fish Grill. YH parked and opened the car door, leading the way to the fine restaurant. They started the night with a bottle of Kendall Jackson chardonnay. YH hooked her up with one of Page's many fake IDs. Stuffed mushrooms as an appetizer, and two garden salads to follow (balsamic vinaigrette). Tosha had grilled tilapia, wild grain rice, and broccoli. YH ordered grilled Norwegian salmon, rizo, and asparagus garnished with lemon wedges. The meal was extremely well-prepared. They drank another bottle of wine and enjoyed a open, meaningful conversation. YH had dessert brought to the table with the restaurant opera singer singing happy birthday!

A four-layered cappuccino chocolate crème cake made Tosha smile with delight. YH took pictures of the cake and fed her the first bite. At Tosha's young age, she'd never experienced a guy treating her so well. She didn't want to ruin the mood. However, she asked where their other partner for the night was. YH smiled and said, "We'll see her later, just leave the arrangements to me." That she did, continuing to enjoy her evening. Tosha gave YH a huge kiss; this time she slipped him some tongue. "The best is yet to come," she whispered in his ear. YH paid the bill, and they stepped into the warm climate, walking hand-in-hand toward the car. Next stop was Uptown Cabaret, the city's most talked about strip club. He was a regular there; it was where he pulled Karen giving her a better income. All the upper-class dancers knew YH for being a player and a hell of a tipper. He got a VIP booth and a few bottles of Black Spade. The music was pumping, money was dropping, and booties were shaking. YH bought Tosha a table dance from two vets in the game, Strawberry and Stacy Smash. They knew how to drop it like it's hot. Strawberry was actually Jackie's younger sister and one of his sex partners. Tosha was having a ball, and this was all new to her, exciting as well. She found herself being turned on. YH, noticing her arousal, started rubbing her legs and inner thighs. Preparing her for what was in store, he had a night full of treats planned. The funny thing was the dancers Strawberry and Jackie were his first ménage à trois experience. It was tons of fun, but he anticipated Page and Tosha to be better!

Tosha couldn't wait to make her fantasy official. They finished the open bottle, and YH sent the other to the next table. Another player from West Boulevard extending courtesy from player to player. YH grabbed Tosha's hand, and they were out. He wanted to give her a memorable experience for number 18.

The Onyx was the next stop. The who's who of Charlotte would be in attendance tonight. Not waiting in line, YH walked straight to the front and shook the head bouncer's hand. He and Tosha walked in like two celebrities. She was already feeling him, but his respect in this city must really run deep. He and Tosha walked to VIP, where a table was set up with all kinds of bottles—Nuvo, Cîroc, Hennessy, Rémy, Rosé, and bottled water. There was a birthday cake with her name written on it, and next to it was a bottle of Patrón Platinum. Her eyes got big, and she smiled with uncontrollable joy. "Happy birthday, sunshine!" YH shouted out loud. Then Page walked directly to YH and kissed him on the lips. He held her by the waist and whispered in her ear. Turning around, he introduced Tosha to Page. Tosha put it all together, that she was the missing link in the equation. They looked each other up and down and were fascinated by what they saw, imagining what a few hours from now would feel like.

One thing was for sure; the attraction was totally there—that was the most important thing. Attraction, attraction, attraction!

Tosha and Page both thought to themselves what it would be like in the midst of sexual pleasure. YH summoned the photographer, and the three took several pictures together. Then individually changed the airbrushed backdrops. The vibe between the women was positive right from the start. Tosha was feeling the alcohol she'd already drunk. The more she looked at Page, the more she realized the resemblance between her and Candice— same body shape and complexion. Page wore a Gucci body dress, and her head was wrapped in a Gucci scarf. That's what threw her appearance off, but she could pass for her sister. She knew it wasn't Candice, so she chalked it up as a coincidence. Although it was a really weird one—this woman she was about to sleep with favored Candice!

YH was talking to an old friend from the neighborhood, Ricky. So Page asked Tosha to go to the bathroom with her; they both kissed YH and walked away. Ricky gave YH some dap, acknowledging he was a major player. The more Page talked, the more she noticed even more similarities to her sister. Her voice and mannerisms—this was getting spooky. Tosha disregarded the obvious, blaming it on the alcohol. Page pulled out some powder, put it on a piece of toilet tissue, and swallowed it down. Tosha looked puzzled, and before she asked, Page told her it was Molly. The absolute purest form of ecstasy, MDMA. Bingo, that's all Tosha had been waiting on. "May I have some, Page?" "Sure, long as you don't tell Young Heat, he hates women doing drugs of any form!" "OK, it's our little secret, Page."

The two checked their reflections in the mirror then made their exit back to the VIP room. When they returned, YH was waiting all alone; he grabbed both their hands and headed to the dance floor. They danced for at least an hour. Bumping and grinding, enjoying their time together as if no one else was in the club. Now the Molly was in the women's system, and they were feeling groovy, touching and kissing as YH was in the midst of the sensual display. The time was at hand to leave and get comfortable, just the three of them. YH walked them back to VIP, tipped the cocktail waitress, grabbed a few bottles (especially the Patrón), and they were out.

Now Page and Tosha were rolling on the Molly, holding each other's hands while YH directed them out of the club. As always, YH had reserved a suite at the Westin, but Tosha wanted to go back to her hotel room. She needed her birth control even though YH was going to wear a condom. She wanted extra protection—he respected that—and they headed to her hotel. Although it was wise for her to use more protection, she literally forgot for a moment about her sister in the same hotel. Her reasoning was,

I'll have them out before Candice or anybody can see them. All the way back to the hotel, Isley Brothers between the sheets turned all three on in the right spots. Even though YH wasn't on any drugs, he was feeling quite nice from the alcohol. Reaching the hotel lobby, all three held on for dear life, laughing, touching, and teasing each other. Tosha could hardly get the door open because she was so wasted.

Finally the door opened. Walking inside, the two women immediately started to undress. YH followed suit, and within minutes, all parties were in the nude. YH took turns kissing both, tasting both women's tongues; then they kissed each other. YH noticed they were in the mood and seemed passionate with their kisses. He laid both on the bed and poured Patrón on their breasts and stomachs. He started to suck the beverage off their breasts one after another. Both had even-sized C-cup breasts. The nipples were rock-hard, and that made his manhood hard as well. While sucking on Tosha, he tickled Page's clitoris, and the two enjoyed a kiss simultaneously. Everything was done slowly and passionately like playing a violin. Page took the head position and laid YH on his back and started to slowly suck his manhood. While he and Tosha kissed, Page had a fabulous technique she had mastered since becoming his lover. She had mastered the art of deep throating. Before he exploded, she stopped to tease him a little bit with her tongue. Now it was Tosha's turn. Page, again in the driver's seat, laid Tosha down and began sucking her breast, licking her stomach slowly all the way down to her kitty kat. She opened her privates and began licking and sucking tenaciously. Then YH put on a condom and started pumping Page doggy-style, pulling her hair and talking nasty, as he slapped that pretty round ass. The harder he pumped, the more aggressive she licked Tosha's clitoris. Tosha was loving the wet sensation Page's tongue was giving her. She screamed with delight while pinching her nipples. Then YH pulled out before he released, took off that condom, and put a fresh one on.

This time Tosha was getting it doggy-style, and she started licking Page's breast down to her kitty kat. Her long narrow tongue felt amazing to Page as she held her head with both hands. YH spread Tosha's ass cheeks and went deeper inside. She was throwing the juicy ass back at him. He couldn't hold it any longer and let his milkshake go inside the condom. Tosha continued until Page's legs started shaking, and her whole body was trembling from the wonderful orgasm. Now it was Tosha's turn while YH put on another condom. He entered her missionary-style, legs back to her chest. Page was lying on Tosha's stomach letting her lick her from the rear as she sucked on Tosha's clit. They were in a sixty-nine position, and YH was deep inside Tosha. Everyone was being pleased; Tosha couldn't take it any longer. She screamed at the top of her lungs, "Oh yeah, oh yeah, oh yeah, oh my God, oh my God!" *Explode!* She exploded; so did Page, and then Young Heat, one after another. They lay in bed drinking, touching, and talking all night long. The women had never experienced anything more freaky, wild, and sensual. As for what they had just shared together—one word to describe it was *wonderful.* Much as Tosha enjoyed her fantasy, she felt like she had made love to her sister. Page's similarities were just too close to totally ignore them. She humored herself. *Well, they say everyone on this earth has a twin. Maybe it was my sister's. Well, Candice will never know about my encounter with Page, and I'll never tell her either.* All three fell asleep holding each other until daylight. Each wanted an encore but were too tired to handle another round.

That morning, they managed enough strength for another round, each accomplishing their goal, an orgasm for all. YH's phone kept blowing up, and he started to get dressed. He told Page that business called and they had to head out. Tosha kissed both of them and thanked YH for fulfilling her fantasy. She also told him she'd be in touch with him. He gave her a hug and slapped Page's rear. "Let's go, baby!" When he and Page were walking out of the hotel, Hank glimpsed them and thought it was Candice. He figured Candice was back to perfect health and back on her feet. She must have had an overnight guest, which was commonplace on the tour.

Tosha took a long hot shower and thought about the events she had just shared with two lovers. It would be a birthday she would never forget. After putting on some clothes, she went to Candy's room. Surprisingly she was up and about and the swelling on her ankle had gone down. She was ready to get back to work. Looking at her sister made Tosha think about Page and their sexual experience. *Wow, I can't believe how much that stranger looks like Candice.* Her analytical part of the brain started thinking. She knew her sister was adopted; maybe, hypothetically, how about if she was related to Page? Then she quickly dismissed the notion 'cause they were from California. Page was from Charlotte, North Carolina—well, it was just a thought. Leslie called and said they were packing up and heading for Virginia. Charlotte was filled with lots of memories, but it was time to move on.

Since the home invasion, Sam had updated his home security system, taking every precaution for his safety. The police hadn't found any new leads and had no suspects for the burglary. They checked all pawnshops in the county and got no hits. Sam hated that someone took advantage of him, but at least he had the real valuables, which the burglars didn't bother to take. Inside his personal safe was an envelope that contained a map of where he had some priceless gems buried, also a key to a safety deposit box filled with diamonds he had stolen from aristocrats for years, along with a few million dollars. Being a well-respected jeweler, he had access to many wealthy people's heirlooms to clean and reset loose stones from wear and tear. He would switch the stones without anyone ever suspecting him of the crime. He had done so for years, making hundreds of thousands of dollars quietly. If anyone would find out, he would be ruined and thrown in prison. All the good he did for breast cancer and the community wouldn't matter. His reputation and legacy would be permanently destroyed. The only real thing the robbers got of value was look, which to him was peanuts. Several paintings—a Picasso, a Monet, and a Renoir, which would be hard to sell without him finding out who stole the paintings. Art lovers were a very tight circle and always stuck together. The only way they would get it off without a red flag would be in Europe. The diamonds in the safe had major flaws, and he used them to make the switch for naive, unsuspecting customers, pulling the wool over their eyes. He kept them at home so no evidence of foul play would be at the jewelry store.

He was also glad his historic pipe wasn't stolen. It was believed to belong to King James I; he had stolen it from an old theologian who wanted the diamonds reset and the frame cleaned, which was gold. He died, and when the family asked for the heirloom, Sam denied having the pipe. Sam's world could have been turned upside down if the robbers knew what they passed over was worth more than a measly look. The pipe alone with the diamonds and historical value was worth 5.7 million dollars. Well, they would never get a chance to get him again 'cause Sam got a new, improved safe installed.

Every day since the ordeal, Karen spent time with Sam or talked on the phone with him for hours. YH told her to stay on him until the jewelry store caper. She was in waist-deep and found herself developing feelings for the sixty-year-old white man. He treated her like a queen. She was being surrounded by interesting people, and Sam was teaching her a lot about life. She had accompanied him to three black-tie charity events, also the breast cancer awareness dinner he had hosted. She was being noticed by the single women and widows in his circle, all wanting to know who this Diana Colby really was and where she was from. Some of the gossiping women even called Sam's daughters to tell them he was seriously dating a new woman. Rich women had nothing else better to do with their time than gossip.

Karen was enjoying this new way of life with all the perks. Still she wanted to find out what real treasures he had hidden and where. She noticed the robbery didn't really upset him like it should. She knew he was sitting on something rare. It was her curiosity to find out what he had in the stash. It never crossed his mind Karen was a double agent. He was too busy enjoying the young, hot, and steamy loving he was receiving on the regular. She was really positioning herself for the future. She knew being with YH would eventually run its course. She would be loyal to him to a point because he was good to her; he had always looked out and fed her even when she was down and out. It would be a time she had to think for and about herself. So making love to Sam wasn't an order from YH. It was an opportunity for her to get close as possible to that big pot of gold at the end of the rainbow. So if she had to do whatever, then that's what it took. The only question was how long she could keep this act together without her cover being discovered by his nosy friends. Her thought was play the game until the end and play the game to win. At the end of the day, it was all about making and stacking that paper for the future. As a stripper, she had learned dancing was a young woman's hustle. As a woman, she learned stacking that money was every woman's dream. Karen considered herself "every woman" like the diva Chaka Khan!

Keeping his sexual appetite full was just the start of Karen's plot to find out Sam's business. Spending intimate moments was always a way to find out someone's secrets. Her next move was to meet his daughters and form a relationship with them both. Sam's eldest daughter lived in Atlanta and was a housewife. Her husband was on the board of directors for the Atlanta Braves. She met him in her senior year at Georgia Tech, giving up her dream of going to law school to raise a family—two children, a boy and girl, five and six years old. Sam's youngest daughter lived in New York and worked for NBC as a producer. She was married but didn't have any children yet. Karen talked Sam into inviting his children home for the sixty-first birthday party she was having for him. He was so excited by the thought of a woman catering to him. Sam immediately thought it was a great idea. He called both of his girls, and they agreed to come home for nothing more than finding out who this Diana Colby was exactly. Was she a gold digger, or was she financially independent? From the gossip they'd received, she was half their father's age. An incredibly attractive woman climbing the social ladder. Well, they were in for a hell of a visit because Karen had all her bases covered. She couldn't wait for her next theatrical performance, which was going to be an Academy Award performance.

Keri Walters Blackmen and Kelly Walters Phillips took the time to visit their father. However, they traveled alone, leaving their husbands, and for Keri, her kids at home. Sam was excited because he hadn't spent much time with them lately. His daughters were both in their twenties but younger than Karen. He had provided for them immensely, so they were used to the finer things in life. They were always close to Sam, especially since Mom had passed away. Karen knew she was up against two skeptical women looking for the smallest thing to dislike. So her first impression was vital to her plan. Karen was so good at playing her position 'cause she read a lot and watched many educational programs, giving her the ability to converse on many different topics.

When both of the women arrived the day of Sam's birthday, Karen was already in character, cooking on the grill in the backyard. Sam greeted both daughters with hugs and kisses. He took a few minutes to ask them to be respectful to his girlfriend. It was hard for them both to hear that term coming from him, having grown up with both parents and a full family life. For the love of their dad, they agreed to be respectful to Karen. When Keri and Kelly came to the backyard, the aroma was mouthwatering. Sam told Karen both women loved grilled corn on the cob and didn't eat red meat. So she grilled some salmon with her special sweet glaze. The menu was grilled salmon, corn on the cob, and mac and cheese, tiramisu for dessert, and Robert Mondavi White Zin to drink. The backyard was decorated with balloons and ribbons. After dinner, they all spent time talking and enjoying the evening.

Kelly and Diana (Karen) talked about careers and education. Karen gave a falsehood on her stockbroker, financial planner image while Kelly talked about the challenges as a TV producer. Both found the other's story interesting. Keri and she talked about Atlanta, Diana using Spellman University as her undergrad alma mater. She had gone on to Duke Business School, earning her master's degree. The sisters were impressed by her education, as well as her conversation. Noticing her Dior sundress and Chanel frames, she obviously was a woman of class and style. Cleaning the grill and the kitchen, and serving Rum Runners to the sisters while being extremely attentive to Sam proved she could multitask. Accomplishing everything she wanted to, she thanked them for a great day. She said farewell before she wore out her welcome, careful not to overplay her hand, giving her cool points with the daughters. Sam didn't want her to leave, but she insisted he spend quality time with his daughters. Keri and Kelly found that very thoughtful.

Before she left, Karen stepped in the house and came back with a pair of expensive Ping golf clubs. He was red in the face and teary-eyed as he hugged Karen. "Happy birthday, sweetheart, I hope you enjoy them on the course!" He didn't know what to say. Kissing him back, she asked him to walk her to the car. Shaking both sisters' hands, she was out gracefully. She had accomplished her goal. Making the daughters like her made her that much closer to the prize (money). After she left, the sisters said they approved of this Diana Colby to Sam's face. Although Kelly had some investigating work to do to see if Ms. Colby's story checked out. Being a TV producer, she had lots of contacts that could pull strings.

"If I can make it here, I can make it anywhere" were the lyrics to Frank Sinatra's famous *New York, New York* song. The song was famous and a hit record because of the truth the message held. New York, the city that never sleeps, was an oyster for success or failure. Five boroughs with five different styles of living. Eight major league sports teams—basketball, football, baseball, and hockey. Museums, tourist attractions, and historical landmarks. The city was home to some of the world's most elite upscale restaurants. New York literally held the world's economic system in the palm of its hands. The famous Wall Street, where the biggest deals in the world were conducted. New York was the world leader in fashion, and the garment district, lower Manhattan, was the mecca for fashion. New York was among four cities that were immeasurable for fashion—London, Paris, Los Angeles, and New York. Milan, Italy, wasn't far behind. As a designer, if you owned a fresh, unique, marketable style, the chances of making it in New York were great. Eric "Swave" Hawkins was trying desperately to make his mark in the city. His input and hard work helped Ms. Kellia Rogers's personal line become a success at the Harlem Row's fashion show. The creations were all Ms. Rogers's alone, but he helped sew and assemble her vision together. While doing so, he learned a great deal from her and some industry secrets, things a young designer couldn't learn in school. The fashion show was amazing, held at the world-famous Apollo Theater and hosted by the beautiful and stunning Kiki Shepard. Lots of icons in fashion, industry leaders, and celebs were in attendance. It was even apparent that a famous music mogul who also was a fashion designer himself and a native New Yorker was in the house, accompanied by a tall, slender, beautiful supermodel. Seems that opportunity had struck once again for Swave's benefit.

The mogul was at the fashion show with a purpose. He wanted to meet the young designer whose trademark color portfolio he had viewed and liked. The portfolio landed in his hands through industry insiders. A smart business move by Swave, sending his work to fashion execs in New York, taking the advice of his instructor, Lex. Well, the mogul wanted to expand his empire by creating a woman's line. Swave was just the fresh new talent he needed. After the fashion show, the mogul's personal assistant greeted him with a card. It was an invitation to a pool party and cookout at the Hamptons. Overwhelmed was an understatement; he had never thought in a million years he would be personally invited to a private celebrity event. The time was at hand, and his drive toward success had just got shifted from fourth- to fifth-gear turbo drive. It was no time to be silent and passive. It was time to be completely assertive and confident. It was a fine line between arrogance and confidence; Swave possessed the latter. The one thing he learned in school was the true recipe for success, which is when preparation meets opportunity, he had to be prepared. Now opportunity was knocking on his door with a sledgehammer. His next move was to be proactive and allow the miracle to happen. The rapper Curtis "50 Cent" Jackson shot to stardom with his first album, *Get Rich Or Die Tryin'* with lyrics like "My plan is to put the rap game in a choke hold." Well, Swave's plan was to put the fashion world in a choke hold. Build a brand, make lots of money, and become a household name.

Swave wished he could share this moment with his homegirl Kym V. She was in his thoughts, and when he had a solid position somewhere, she was sure to be a part of his staff, keeping his promise. A car was sent to his hotel, the Hilton in downtown Manhattan. As he rode through the city, his thoughts were many. *Am I ready for this? Am I on my A game? Is my cologne too overbearing? Did I dress right for the occasion?* He took a deep breath and prayed silently. He was a walking billboard, an advertisement for himself. If nothing else, maybe someone would like his outfit and order something similar. He wore a tangerine-colored linen short set. The shorts were pleated and cuffed. The shirt was a sailor-style top; he finished the look with Kenneth Cole sandals. His outfit had its signature emblem, Palm Tree, stitched on the shirt pocket. The entire ride to the Hamptons, he told himself, "I'm a great designer worthy of being discovered." Positive reinforcement was the objective.

I can do only what I think I can do.
I can only be what I think I can be.
I can have only what I think I can have.

He chanted this over and over again until it started to set into his thinking. He was trying to be ready mentally for whatever was coming his way. Preparation!

Rolling up to the 25,000 sq. ft. mansion put butterflies in his stomach. Every house along the way was breathtaking, but this one was a tremendous work of art. Extravagant automobiles lined the front driveway. A helicopter sat on the helipad on the side of the estate. The view was like watching *MTV Cribs*. Somehow, fortunately, it wasn't a TV show or even a dream. He was here in the flesh, about to rub elbows with the wealthy folks. The driver stopped at the top of the circular driveway. He refused a gratuity; obviously he was an employee of the host. Stepping out of the car, he was greeted by the same young lady who gave him the invite. She was of Latin descent and very attractive in a librarian type of way. They shook hands, and he followed her into the house. The inside was unbelievable, and furnishings were all modern. Lots of abstract art and sculptures. Large island kitchen equipped with a subzero refrigerator. Stocked bar and center rock fireplace in the living room. As they walked outside to the pool area, it was like walking into a hip-hop video shoot. Lots and lots of attractive women walking around revealing plenty of skin. A- and B-list celebs and music artists, label heads from all genres. Finally meeting the host face-to-face, they shook hands. He handed Swave a drink; he just poured Cîroc and pineapple juice.

"Cheers."

"Cheers."

They toasted, and the two walked away alone to a table and began to talk business.

They exchanged pleasantries, then the mogul got straight to the point. He was a fan of Swave's work and wanted to back him financially in starting a new line for women; actually it would be a joint venture. Fifty-fifty in profits—however, Swave had total creative control. He would basically be a silent partner. As the profits started to come in, Swave could pay back the start-up cost. This was an absolute dream for any up-and-coming designer. Definitely too good to pass on, so he agreed, and they drank to another toast. This one was to the success of the new line, Palm-Tree. They raised Cîroc and pineapple juice in hand to the success of Palm-Tree. Formal, casual, athletic, sleep-, and swimwear—long live Palm-Tree clothing. They shook hands, and his new silent partner said he would have his attorney draw up the paperwork. "Now let's have some fun." He followed the host around, being introduced to the other guests. This was unbelievable, a dream come true even though he didn't officially finish school. He couldn't let this opportunity slip through his fingers. Swave came to New York to work on a project as an apprentice. Now he would be an official designer and head of a company. Not bad for a new jack in the game. Resistance was futile. It was all pedal to the metal, no half-stepping. He excused himself from the crowd and found a bathroom inside the mansion. He humbly kneeled down and thanked God for this blessing and asked him for the strength to make this clothing line a success. "Thank you, God. Thank you, God!"

The next few days, Swave and his silent partner had a series of business meetings. He was finding out that it was much more than designing outfits. He was getting a crash course in the business side of the coin. He had to create a belief and mission statement and conduct business according to the statement. Staff the company, order material, create and produce the merchandise, and advertise and sell the finished product successfully. His partner guided him in the proper direction, but this was a major learning experience. He had his life's work and reputation riding on the success of this clothing line. Also he would be commanding the ship by himself. His partner explained he had several other projects going at the same time in music, film, and real estate. In fact, he was on his way to Europe for a world tour. So the Palm-Tree venture and vision was essentially Swave's success or failure. The first order of business as the company head was to hire an assistant. He got on the phone and called the travel agent for a one-way ticket from LAX to LaGuardia airport. Then he called Kym V and gave her the great news. She was his first employee, and he kept his promise to take her along for the ride to the top.

Toward the last leg of the northeast part of the tour, tension started to rise. Candice was doing more work than originally scheduled. More work and no extra compensation. Not to mention Carl Mills had flown in to a few events, making uncomfortable advances toward her openly. She tried to ignore them at first, but he became more and more aggressive. He was always reminding her of the opportunity he offered and that he allowed her sister a free ride on the tour. Oftentimes she felt like giving it all up and starting from scratch. However, she knew that with great success came sacrifice, but she wasn't prepared to sacrifice her integrity, remembering lessons taught to her by Mom at an early age. "Pray in times of distress, and God will make a way to escape." To make matters even worse, she wasn't getting along with Tosha. She couldn't put her finger on it, but Tosha's behavior was different. She was moody and argumentative. She even started drinking more than usual. What really hurt were comments Tosha let slip out of her mouth, making Candice feel she was jealous of her success as a model. So dealing with an extra workload, a boss who obviously wanted to have sex, and her spoiled-brat little sister, Candice was tremendously stressed out on a daily basis. Now in Philly headed to New Jersey, she was nearing her boiling point. *Maybe because I didn't take Tosha out for a belated birthday she was upset*, was the thought going through Candy's head. Virginia, B-more, and DC were all stressful, and Philly was a heavy workload. *Maybe when I get to New York, I can do something special for my sister*, was her thought as the camera flashes blinded her vision.

Philly was somewhere Candice always wanted to visit. Being a huge NBA fan, she always loved to see Allen Iverson play. The city was alive when he was there. She wished she could come back for an Eagles game to see Michael Vick play ball. The crew did manage to eat at Geno's the world-famous Philly cheesesteaks. Candice was always picky about what she ate, so instead of steak, she had chicken. Chicken cheesesteak was just as good and less for the body to digest. Now on the way to New Jersey, she was enjoying the view on the NJ turnpike. Viewing New York City from a distance was somewhat magical. The only deterrent was Carl Mills, who planned to join the crew in New York. She didn't know how much longer she could stomach his advances. He was a wolf in sheep's clothing with a sinister grin. She wondered if Leslie had to surrender for her current employment. It was a no-brainer, but Candice wasn't conforming to keep her job. Anyway it was only a one-year position, although Carl Mills made promises of more work, and he had contacts in the industry. This was a clear case of why models had to network in this business, always looking toward the future to avoid selling their bodies and souls for income. That was one of the lessons she learned from her mentor. Long-term thinking always made a successful career. So she smiled, appearing to be an extrovert but really being a introvert, plotting and planning her next move. Prayer would turn this situation around, and prayer would keep Mr. Mills's hand out of the cookie jar!

The crew wanted to stop at Atlantic City, but Leslie was on a schedule and had to make it to New York. First stopping in Newark and Jersey City, New York was the last leg of the northeast tour. Then they would head back west, stopping in the Midwest. Candy's strength was weak, but she was willing to stick it out until another opportunity presented itself. She prayed and was remaining optimistic full of faith. While riding through New Jersey, she received a text message from Mr. Mills. He texted, "Hello beautiful just want you to know I have a surprise for you. C U in NYC. CARL." *Great, what is he up to now?* It was becoming an ongoing job trying to read people's minds. From Carl Mills to Leslie and even her little sister Tosha. Wearing all these hats was beginning to slowly wear her out. She was really lonely and wished she had a lover to confide in from time to time. Oftentimes she thought about that sexy chocolate brother she had met back in Los Angeles. She promised herself to call him when back in LA. Now she was able to buy a few outfits and maybe help him get some exposure. It was something about him and his confidence. She was extremely attracted to him, to say the least. There was nothing wrong with having a secret crush or fantasizing about the opposite sex. That was in the head, and a freaky fantasy can't hinder one's success or cause problems with a full workload and busy schedule. So for now, a fantasy was all Candice allowed herself to fall victim to. Climbing to the top was her first and only concern. She tried to pattern herself after all former supermodels. Most or all dated and got married after reaching a certain level of success.

Their careers were more important than drinking, partying, and having sex. So Candice was willing to follow the path set for her by the legends in the industry.

First stop in New Jersey was Newark, a.k.a. Brick City, the city with fast cars and plenty of hustlers. The city had recently built an arena for the New Jersey Nets and the Devils, although the Nets were moving to Brooklyn soon as their new arena was ready. The arena in Newark was used for concerts, college games, and various events. Leslie arranged for the crew to be part of the advertisement market featuring the hottest new beverages and foods to hit the market. She reserved a space to showcase the beverage as well as a photo booth. Consumers would take pictures to post on the Neon Facebook page and critique the product. This was a great opportunity for Candice to shine once again. The entire tour she was completely on her A game. Leslie wasn't entirely fond of her, but she respected the professionalism she displayed consistently. She also knew Candice would be a force to be reckoned with in this industry. Now, her insight being 20/20, she saw what Mr. Mills saw when he hired Candice—a fresh clean face that read "virtuous young lady," which was the perfect look to help sell their product, identifying the product with sophisticated, wholesome, responsible social drinkers. A smooth, clean drink for a clean, fresh person, male or female. The first rule of business is cater to women because they are the biggest consumers. So like her or not, Leslie respected who Candice was (sophisticated, fresh, clean, and wholesome) and what she stood for.

It was showtime after hair and makeup were complete. The Helmut Lang casual collection was her apparel. She also featured the newest nail polish color collection by Ginger Johson and Sara Liz Pickett. Her hands and feet were a matching bright purple. Her thin-strap flared-bottom sundress was lavender and purple. With open-toe Alexander Wang sandals, she once again transcended the average model. She was a star rising to the top. Before the meet and greets, she posed for photos with the consumers. Pierre, of course, was working his magic with the camera lens. Her presence illuminated the film, and brought a certain life to the advertisement. Leslie stood back and watched the spectacular display. Several of the participants were advertising energy drinks. A few others had alcohol, single malt Scotches, and distilled gin. One company had a keg set up with a new microbrewed Amber ale beer. A company out of Greenbay had numerous kinds of cheeses. They set up a fondue display with melted cheese and veggies. There were three different pizza booths and an up-and-coming ice cream vendor. There was even a company that made floral arrangements out of fruit, a very unique concept that appeared to be fresh and tasty. Companies were on the grind and wanted to sell their products. One thing was for sure, a pretty face and clean smile would sell the product every time. Most vendors understood that fact. That's why Candice received business cards from potential clients trying to entice her with employment. Flattered as she was, the next move for Candice had to be a power move. She wanted to be with an est. brand with international appeal. She wanted to travel the world, maybe tour through Europe and learn about other cultures while earning a substantial amount of money. She would establish herself as a supermodel and start to build her brand.

When the photo shoots ended, she did meet-and-greets, talking to potential customers. During that session, she kept Tosha in view; it appeared she was having an in-depth conversation on the phone. Candice wondered who she was talking to. Recently Tosha stayed on the phone for hours at a time. Candy kept her composure and remained professional, thinking of the task at hand, making a mental note to talk to her sister. She was acting peculiar all of a sudden. Even though they were total opposites and really didn't have the same interests, she found it ridiculous to think Tosha had absolutely no goals or ambitions for the future. Unpleasant as the thought was, it was becoming more evident. Tosha was simply not a goal-orientated young woman. There was no misinterpreting her lack of zeal for anything except alcohol and men. This was a horrible thought, but Candice was starting to realize maybe she eventually had to cut tights and let her learn from experience. For now she would hold on to that one piece of hope—that Tosha would become interested in a career and pursue a dream just as she had in fashion and the modeling industry. Determination was the space between an achiever and a dreamer. Candice was determined to be a success and try to help Tosha be one as well.

"Hey, Daddy, how you doing? You know I've been thinking about our episode every day."

"Oh really, have you now, what's been on your mind?"

"Thinking about how you rocked my world. Also the fun Page, you, and I had making love. I miss you, Young Heat, when can we see each other again?"

"I don't know, but I'll make arrangements soon as I get some free time. I posted some pictures from your birthday on Facebook, when you get a chance, give them a look!"

"OK, Daddy, I'll call you later, kisses!" The call ended.

Tosha had been talking to YH every day, several times a day. She was really beginning to have feelings for him. She didn't mention Page too often. Truthfully she wanted to see her again, to see if it was the alcohol that made her think she favored Candice, or if it was a fact. It was a confidential experience with complete anonymity. The only solution to have peace of mind was to look at the pics YH had posted. She tried to minimize the feelings, but she kept having déjà vu. There had to be a connection between Page and Candice. Sitting on the tour bus with the laptop, Tosha went to YH's Facebook account. The pictures were disturbingly what she didn't want to admit. Page and Candice looked identical to each other unmistakably. So Tosha went to YH's friends list and pulled Page's account and profile to see her without her head wrapped in a scarf like the birthday pics. "Oh my gosh." There definitely was no mistake in her sober, thinking mind. These two women looked alike—same age, same birthday, and same hair texture, as if they were from a biracial origin.

She didn't want to assume anything, but this coincidence was rather scary, especially since she had slept with Page—what a mess. OK, these were the facts she made a note of mentally: They both looked like identical twins, same birthday, same hair texture and length. Both had the same body structure, and Candice was adopted! *Hey that's it,* Tosha thought. *I have to call YH and see if Page was adopted and from where.* Now Tosha's mind was racing a mile a minute. One part of her thought she was being irrational, and the whole theory was ridiculous. However, the other part thought nothing was impossible. They could very well be twin sisters and never know the other existed. Well, it was time to dig deep and get to the truth for clarity. Tosha called YH, but he wasn't answering his phone. It kept going to his voice mail. Well she would just wait until he called back later. Until then she was going to wear out the Internet to get some answers. Also Mom would shed some light on this situation and the past. She knew Mom never talked about the adoption, so she had to use tact. That was an issue the whole family never talked about ever, almost as if it were nonexistent. Tosha was now on a mission to prove a hunch. She wanted to have something to hang over Ms. Perfect Candice Gray, her older and more successful sister.

Club Elaganza was the second leg of the Newark tour. After the crew broke down their display, Candice freshened up and had a wardrobe change. The advertising market was another success for the team. Everyone played their position superbly. Pierre really pulled the best out of Candice in the photos. Mia styled and put together another summer look with Givenchy wear. Leslie made sure all ends were tied up and did a marvelous job on Candy's hair. Billy set the display up and broke it down efficiently. Big Hank hung out and ate while doubling as Candy's security. DJ Nice was planning to dramatically showcase his skills on the turntables. The major bottom line was Silvia and Wanda tripled their top sales in merchandise. Also Leslie secured nine contracts for product delivery. So sales were up, and Carl Mills would be delighted. His superiors weren't happy about the tour, but he fought and sold the idea to the CEO. As a result, Carl Mills had generated a 40 percent boost in overall sales. That was a huge number, and he was demonstrating his earning potential in the eyesight of his superiors. Candice was a big part of the company success. Her face was appealing to the younger generation. Carl was putting together something in his head. He wanted to team up with *Spring Break* (MTV) or *Spring Bling* (BET). The sky was the limit, and Candice was the rocket ship to take them there. He was getting thousands of hits on Twitter about the sexy face of the company, Internet likes on Facebook, and hundreds of comments about the brand all saying Candice was exceptional and made them try the brand. In doing so, the brand earned rave reviews from industry proprietors and socialites.

DJ Nice had the club jumping; everyone was having a great time. The whole team was just relaxing while Candice did her routine meet-and-greet. As she worked. Candice kept a watchful eye on little sister. Tosha was texting away like a madwoman. Candice promised she would sit her down later that night. They were going straight to New York; the Jersey City engagement was canceled. Due to a pipe leakage in the club, the property was flooded and couldn't hold the event. So the crew would be able to rest for a day or two until they met Carl Mills in New York. A few hustlers and ballers tried to talk to Tosha to no avail; she wasn't feeling anyone or anything except that phone. The crew stayed till 3:00 AM. DJ Nice lit the house up with his precise cuts and mixes. He also commanded the microphone like a general. Leslie scored again with another account sold to the club owner. They definitely made their mark in the Brick City! All leaving together, they went to eat at IHOP on Springfield Avenue. Then it was off across the Hudson to the city that never sleeps. Candice and Tosha sat together, Candice talking and Tosha staring into outer space. Whatever it was that had Tosha's attention had to be serious. Candice was determined to find out what was on Little Sister's mind. Maybe a shopping spree in New York would soften her up to confide in big sister—just a thought that went through Candy's mind.

Sam Walters was elated by the birthday party his girlfriend Diana (Karen) had for him. He was also pleased his daughters seemed to like Diana. That was a touchy situation, especially as he had never dated since Mary Margret's death. They knew eventually he would go on with his life. Kari and Kelly would've done their dad a disservice, not understanding his human need for female companionship. He was happy, and that's all that mattered, at least for Keri. However Kelly was very skeptical and wanted to make sure Diana Colby was socially acceptable. She would give Diana the benefit of the doubt for now.

Sam surprised Diana with a ten-day getaway along the coast of Louisiana. They sailed on the most opulent and legendary riverboat ever built, the *American Queen*. The steamboat voyage sailed along the old South, leaving from the port in New Orleans, giving a true Southern cultural experience. Extraordinary dining with the world-renowned chef Regina Charboneav. Sam reserved the best suite and all the luxury amenities. When they walked into the suite, he surprised her with chocolate imported from France. Sam was learning how to please Diana, and she was loving the attention. Standing face-to-face after settling in, he stroked her face with the back of his hand, then kissed her forehead, then her nose, then her lips very sensually. She felt so safe and secure with Sam. Karen was having a hard time being Diana because Diana was falling in love with Sam. He was so thoughtful, and unlike Young Heat's thoughtfulness, he didn't want anything in return, just love and companionship.

Being in character was working because Sam started to reveal things. Things like how he made extra finances in the business. At first he was very vague, but eventually he revealed more. She just played along and waited for the proper info that was confidential. Secretly she was fighting with herself, having thoughts about a change of heart. What would YH do if she didn't comply? She was in waist-deep and slowly sinking deeper and deeper. The better Sam treated her, the deeper she sank.

They enjoyed moonlight walks on the open deck and candlelight cuisine on the dining deck. Shuffleboard and skeet shooting by day, lying on the upper deck, and dipping in the hot tub. The quality time was terrific to both parties. Diana was bringing out the tiger in Sam. He was making love like a twenty-five-year old man, with the help of Viagra, of course. Even so, he was delivering dynamic sensations to Diana's body and mind.

The relationship between Sam and Diana went from a casual friendship to dating exclusively to lovers, and now they were inseparable. Sam reconstructed his life and schedule to spend quality time with Diana (Karen). Young Heat always told her she had that red snapper between her legs. This must have been an actual fact because the last night on the steamboat cruise, Sam went against all expectations by proposing marriage. Her face was full of excitement, joy, fear, and disbelief; seeing that twenty-five-carat diamond ring made her a believer. Without even thinking of everything and everyone involved, she said yes, and they hugged, kissed, and made love.

While Sam was dead asleep on the bed, she took her phone to the bathroom and texted YH, told him about the proposal, and her answer, yes. He quickly texted back, "Great, keep working the mark. Great acting Karen. Lol!" What he didn't understand was Karen wasn't acting. She really was thinking about the possibilities of marriage to Sam. Her future would be secure and full as Mrs. Diana Walters. "Oh my God!" The truth hit her—Karen was her name, not Diana. If she married under that alias, the marriage wouldn't be legal. So all the privileges would cease to exist. Now what would she do? She would have to go on with the plan to rob Sam blind. There was no other way, or was there? What lie could she come up with to explain her lying about her name? She needed a lie to be explainable and excusable while being believable.

After all, Sam loved her, so she could just about tell him anything. What about Keri and Kelly? How would she explain to her future stepdaughters. These weren't the kind of people that forgave easy. Usually wealthy people are protective over their fortunes. She didn't want to appear manipulative. The sooner she resolved this situation, the better if she planned to resolve it for a legal marriage. Karen started to dig deep and think about the future as Mrs. Walters if anything were to happen to Sam, provided she was in his will. She could stand to gain a great deal legally. She tried to estimate his net worth. From what he told her and assumptions, she would easily become a millionaire overnight if she played her cards right. The plot just thickened, and a collaboration on YH's part was essential. "Mrs. Walters," she recited to herself. "That has a certain ring to it!" She crawled back in bed with her fiancé, held him tight, and kissed his cheek. The question was, was it a sign of true loving affection or the kiss of death?

A rented brownstone on Lenox between 116th and 117th Street in Harlem was where Swave lived. Kym V rented a loft on the lower East Side. They both were getting used to the New York lifestyle. Working basically seven days a week, getting the company off the ground, Swave multitasked. Being the creative mastermind, he designed, sewed, and oversaw the entire operation. He oversaw every aspect of the business, from minimal to the most important. Kym V assisted Swave in everything, and she was the head of accessories department (creative and production). They spent hours together assembling the premier signature line. He had lots of ensembles in his portfolio, but he wanted to improve everything visually. The Palm-Tree line had to be a breath of fresh air in the fashion world. He was prepared to work night and day to accomplish that goal. The company consisted of ten seamstresses that sewed the patterns together. There was Pamela Orchard, who was a marketing genius with a master's degree in business from Columbia University. She was the former VP of marketing for Harden Clothing Company. She had working relationships with international distributors in Europe and Asia. Kym headed a small team that developed and produced accessories and a packing team that boxed the product. Of course his silent partner handled the financial end. The Palm-Tree company was small, with a large growth potential. The company started off in a renovated warehouse in midtown Manhattan. The first few months of operations were productive, and sales grew from day one. The clothing line appealed to many different cultures.

Having the silent partner, the Mogul, endorse the line increased sales. Pamela Orchard was hard at work, marketing the line in the international market. A few months in business, they had to hire more laborers and expand the offices. Opening a branch in East Rutherford, New Jersey, Swave was hard at work designing a fall fashion line. He, Kym, and Pam were strategically planning a fall fashion show showcasing the fall and winter collections from Palm-Tree. Pam had major connections in the industry, international and nationwide. Company heads, agents, retailers, and distributors were at her fingertips. She knew and had worked with numerous people in the industry for years. Her clout was significant, and she was respected immensely. So Swave trusted her advice and judgment wholeheartedly. She was a proven leader in the fashion industry, a marketing genius who turned a small storefront clothing company (Harden Clothing) into a huge brand name and conglomerate (Harden Enterprises). Swave wanted the same success for Palm-Tree. So when Pam talked, he closed his mouth and listened attentively. Her idea of the fall/winter fashion show was a great business move. Now Pam wanted to employ some up-and-coming models for the show, also hire a face for the Palm-Tree line to market. Someone who was fresh and new and would help catapult the Palm-Tree line to the next level nationally and internationally, with Europe and Asia as the targeted markets. Swave agreed, and he gave Pam all authority to make executive decisions. Now with the creative and production aspects of the line complete for the fall/winter fashions. Pam started looking to secure models. She called her former NCCV classmate, the CEO of Spectacular Looks, Lola Hemmingway, a business associate and friend.

Lola Hemmingway was a former plus-sized model, a very intelligent woman who realized her earning potential as a plus-size model had a cap on her salary. The reality was most clothing companies catered to petite women. So she launched her own modeling agency and was incredibly successful. Lola had a reputation for honesty and equality across the board. She represented her clients well and always conducted business with pride and integrity. In fact, that was the Spectacular Looks mission statement: "We will always conduct business with the highest level of pride and integrity." Not only were Pam and Lola classmates and colleagues in the industry, they both pledged Delta and crossed the line together at North Carolina Central University. Being line and sorority sisters, they trusted each other undoubtedly. Pam knew Lola could suggest the perfect model to kick off their international project, the plan to bring Palm-Tree to Europe and Asia being the goal. The brand was selling well in the States with two locations: the flagship store in Harlem on 125th Street and the other in New Jersey Willowbrook Mall. The vision was to go across seas with strength and dominate the industry. Hong Kong was the first target in expanding. Shanghai and Hong Kong were the New York of China. Already with American stores there (Coach, Calvin Klein, and Esprit), Palm-Tree would also participate in the growing fashion world in China. Pam knew that the difference between success and failure in a foreign market came down to location and presentation.

Their conversation went well, and they promised to link up soon. Both worked full-load schedules and had relationships. Lola assured Pam she had the perfect model to be the face of the Palm-Tree clothing line.

Lola started immediately calling models for the fashion show. She had a dozen or so in mind for the event. The permanent position was a no-brainer. She had the appropriate candidate in mind for the job. After reaching most of the models to confirm their employment, she called her cherry on top of the sundae. Receiving no answer after trying several times, she texted her a message: "Dear Candy, I know your commitment to the current employer is about finished. I have a great opportunity for you call me ASAP. Lola!"

With that being done Lola texted Pam, "Aggie & Eagle classic coming up, let's attend together!"

This was the classic football game for the HBCV, North Carolina A&T against their North Carolina Central Eagles. A famous college rival game, which for years A&T dominated. Win or lose, the Delta sisters always were willing to show their Eagle pride.

Like a fish out of water was how Candy felt without her phone. First time in New York, she learned a valuable lesson. The subways of New York were a thief's playground. The bump and snatch was the oldest trick in the book. Pickpockets were smooth and crafty when it came to this hustle. On the subway A train express, a thief scored an iPhone from an open handbag. Candice would pay a price while learning this valuable lesson. Her entire network and contacts were in that phone. Fortunately her phone and broadband service provider was Verizon so she would be able to retrieve her phone information. All numbers, pictures, and texts would be salvaged.

"Thank God Almighty for small miracles!" Downtown Manhattan, Candice bought another phone from the Verizon store. Manhattan was a different place for Candice and Tosha. Both weren't used to being among that many people at one time. California was large, but Los Angeles wasn't as congested like New York City. Candice took Little Sis on a shopping spree as a late birthday present. They went to the world-famous Macy's on Thirty-Fourth Street on Manhattan Island. Too many bags to catch the subway back, so they took a cab to the Hilton in midtown Manhattan. Much as Candice tried to converse with Tosha, she seemed a thousand miles away. Candy wondered what was so important that made her act distant all of a sudden. True, they weren't interested in the same things. Although they shared most everything growing up, now it was so different. *Have I done anything to offend Tosha? Am I allowing this lifestyle to go to my head?* These were questions she asked herself, trying to figure out Tosha's actions.

Candice started to mentally backtrack, and recall Tosha's behavior changing in Charlotte. She hadn't been the same since the stop in North Carolina. Well, Candice would wait it out to truly find out what was bothering Tosha. Criticism wasn't an option; she needed some understanding. That's what her big sis was willing to give wholeheartedly. Upon returning to the hotel, Leslie and Carl Mills met them in the lobby. Carl hugged Candice as Tosha and Leslie rolled their eyes in unison. Women knew exactly why his wife married him (money).

"We were headed to get a bite to eat, would you like to join us?"

"No thank you."

"Well, let's meet tonight on the fifth floor in the lounge. I have a proposal for you."

"OK, see you then, Mr. Mills." Candice and Tosha turned and headed for the elevator. Mr. Mills watched like a hunter scoping his prey. The sound of her erotic, passionate moans rang in his head. He imagined a fantasy with Candice in nothing but their birthday suits. She knew it was time to move on, but she didn't have an offer or the opportunity she wanted. Candice wanted to soar beyond national exposure. She wanted to be international and work for someone who respected her talent and the professionalism, hard work, and passion she brought to the table, not her outward beauty alone. She needed a change and a chance to shine on a larger playing field.

Candice and Tosha took showers and ate at the hotel restaurant. Later that evening, Candy met Mr. Mills in the bar/lounge on the fifth floor. He greeted her with a dozen red roses and a box of imported chocolate candy. He ordered a Long Island iced tea; she ordered a glass of cranberry juice. Mr. Mills immediately went into his sales pitch, first thanking her for the hard work. Her professional consistency was commendable. The company was pleased with the sales generated from the tour. Next he pointed out the fringe benefits she was receiving as an employee—well, her sister being welcome and taken care of while on tour. He ended his pitch with another opportunity—a contract to represent the company full-time including anticipations of MTV *Spring Break* and BET, *Spring Bling* with national exposure. A handsome salary, car, apartment, and health benefits. The only catch was he wanted her to be his mistress. She slowly sipped her cranberry juice and stood up while walking away. Mr. Mills called her name, but Candice kept walking until she reached the elevator. She turned to face him; he was still seated in the lounge. She waved bye, as if to say bye forever. Mr. Mills felt like he played himself. What was he going to do? They had a few events booked in New York. Hopefully she was still on board until the end. He didn't want to risk another embarrassing moment. So he called Leslie to handle this situation while he tried to save face with an alternate and profitable offer.

Candice was upset and felt disrespected by that scum bucket slimeball Carl Mills. Even though he gave her the opportunity she currently had, his actions made her wonder if she was really talented. Or was she just a personal conquest he wanted to conquer? She contemplated if finishing the tour was wise or if she should count her losses and cut ties with Mr. Mills. There was Tosha to look after, so she had to make the correct decision. She watched Tosha typing away on the laptop, unaware of the present situation. She couldn't call Mom because Mom and Dad would worry. Upsetting them wasn't a pleasant thought. Candice had a nice little nest egg in her savings account. She also knew this industry was about positioning yourself for bigger and better opportunities. She started to wonder, had she been properly doing that? Was she playing the game the way it needed to be played? Maybe she could hang in there a little longer until the right opportunity presented itself. Would he still keep coming at her so strong? Without sleeping with Mr. Mills, would she still be employed? Things that make you say "Hmmm!"

Young Heat finally called Tosha back. She leaped up and headed to the hallway for privacy. He apologized for not calling sooner; he was conducting business. Really he was spending time with Jackie 'cause she had lost her father to diabetes. He was comforting her and spending quality time. Tosha asked about Page's past and her family. YH was curious why all the questions, but he answered, telling Tosha Page was indeed adopted. She was raised in an orphanage and in foster care because her adopted mom died. That was all he knew or was willing to share. He asked why all the questions about Page. Tosha told him she had a hunch that Page was related to her adopted sister. He sighed with disbelief.

"Why do you think they're related?"

"I'll send you proof, just check your computer. I'm sending some pictures to your Facebook account. Tell me what you think, and should I pursue this any further?"

"OK, baby girl, I'll call you back, peace." The line went dead.

Tosha sent pics of Candice to YH's Facebook account and waited for a response.

The new iPhone was charged and ready to go. All Candy's pics, texts, and numbers were restored. She hadn't checked her messages for two days. Surely someone tried to reach her for nothing more than to say hello. Before she had the chance to check the messages, the phone rang; it was Leslie calling to smooth things over. Surprisingly Leslie even offered an increase in salary for the rest of the tour. That in itself let her know she had him over a barrel. Carl Mills especially was between a rock and hard place. If Candice wanted to sue for sexual harassment, she had a case. She needed time to weigh all her options and make an intelligent decision.

Tosha's phone was blowing up as she sat in the tub, enjoying a relaxing hot bubble bath to soothe her nerves. It was YH, and he couldn't believe his eyes. The pics that Tosha sent blew his mind. First he thought the pics were photographically doctored. When he saw the dates and the geographic locations, he knew they were official. YH couldn't believe the resemblance; he literally was looking at twins. There was no denying these two women had to be related. Same birthday, same facial structure, and same hair texture. Body frame was the same—this was truly unbelievable. YH agreed with Tosha; research had to be done. He was willing to help out. YH felt he owed it to Page to help find a long-lost family member.

Candice chatted with Leslie for a while; she all but begged Candice to finish the tour. Honestly she knew if Candice wasn't won over, her job would be in jeopardy as well. They were invited to a fashion show for a young clothing company that was making a huge impact in the industry. Numerous vendors and consumers would be present. It would be a chance to sell some more contracts; as a distributor, that was the goal. Candice would be the key, using her face as the marketing tool. After much thought, she decided to attend the event, which would be two days away. She confirmed the deal with Leslie, proclaiming she'd rather not interact with Mr. Mills unless absolutely necessary. Leslie agreed to the request. Now she knew her next move had to be a power move. She had been networking from day one, and the right opportunity hadn't presented itself. She remained optimistic. The first leg of the tour was awesome, but now it was totally superficial. She didn't enjoy it any longer; she only stayed for Tosha's sake, wanting some stability for her sister and to be a great example of dedication. Candice always put her loved one's concerns above her own. She knew a bad decision would mean a bad environment for her sister. Although above anything else, Candice wasn't prepared to compromise her integrity. Going home to Fresno defeated wasn't even an option.

The conversation with Tosha really made YH think. "Hmm." There was a silver lining to this cloud. Leave it to YH to see things from a monetary standpoint. All he had to do was get Tosha and Page aboard with this gold mine of a plan. He had been chilling since their last heist, which didn't really amount to a great deal. Some cash, however, the diamonds they stole were flawed. Not really worth much what he anticipated. Also his fence was having a hard time selling the paintings. Seems the art world was a tight little community. The heat was all over those stolen paintings. So it was time for a new hustle, and the Walters' jewelry store robbery was moving slow. He was worried that Karen wasn't gathering enough information as quickly as she could. After Sam Walters proposed marriage, seems like something went to Karen's head. He made a mental note to have a chat with his number-one bait woman. She was the face of his operation, and he couldn't afford to lose his goose that laid golden eggs.

The US ports have always been a significant source of financial gain for the underworld, especially the Italian crime families in New York. They controlled the import and export of any necessity or leisure item the city or nation wanted and needed. The East Coast was a major gold mine from New York; Newark, New Jersey; Richmond, Virginia; Wilmington, North Carolina; and Charleston, South Carolina. All these eastern ports were controlled by the Biasi family. Carmine Biasi was a tongue, a no-nonsense type of guy. Third generation from the old country, his ancestors came from Naples, Italy, to Queens, New York (Far Rockaway, Queens). He ran one of the biggest import-export companies in New York. Wine, cigars, clothing, fresh seafood, and jewelry—you name it and Carmine can get it for you at a costly price. He also had a hand in smuggling things the feds would find interesting, eluding the alphabet boys for more than twenty years. He decided to move south and allow his son Lil Carmine (Sonny) to be his figurehead as he silently pulled the strings from a distance. More like a favor to his wife, Francesca "Franny" Biasi, so he wouldn't have to hear her mouth about retiring and spending quality time together. His family consisted of wife Franny, Lil Carmine, and daughters Marie and Bianca "Bambi." His underboss Tommy Two Guns, and head Capo Franky "Ziti" Zimbiti along with his street soldiers. Carmine was a fat, out-of-shape, old-school wise guy. He smoked Cuban cigars and drank Amaretto Disaronno like water along with as much Vino as he could stand.

Now he lived in Wilmington, North Carolina, in a spacious beach house on Wrightsville Beach. He wanted to be close to a major eastern port he controlled. It would be much easier to smuggle certain things in a southern port than out of New York port. He struck a major deal with a businessman from Nigeria to smuggle stolen diamonds. All sorts, sizes, and colors—some more flawed then others. It didn't matter; the important thing was he got them for a steal of a deal then resold them for a major profit. Nato Ogundiran was a Nigerian businessman of sorts, also an international jewel thief with a specialty in diamonds. Carmine met him through his daughter Marie Biasi; they attended the University of Missouri together. He and Marie were graduate gemologists knowledgeable about diamonds, and they worked as appraisers. She worked for Tiffany & Co., also Harry Winston. Now she was employed by her father. As a manager of the Brightest Star jewelry store in downtown Brooklyn, Nato worked for the American Gem Society Gemological Laboratories in Las Vegas before he yielded to temptation and decided to make a fortune as a thief. Returning to his native land, he turned the game upside down. Carmine didn't like doing business with blacks, but he liked the color green more. If he knew Nato was sticking his large Nigerian manhood in his Italian daughter, he would freak out, so Marie and Nato kept their relationship quiet. They spent time in foreign countries keeping it on the down low, enjoying the secret love affair and interracial dating that the Europeans find more socially acceptable.

Some of the merchandise he sold in New York at the Brightest Star. Most was sold in North Carolina. He laundered the diamonds through a highly respected jeweler he met at a Las Vegas jewelry show. This guy could sell a winter coat to a Hawaiian. He had the clientele and the knowledge to sell thousands of diamonds without being questioned. Carmine and Sam Walters made mega bucks together, no one being the wiser. Sam's knowledge went far beyond just diamonds. He was an antique collector and had expertise in rare coins. Sam was a member of the American Numismatic Association. He knew his stuff, and Carmine respected his knowledge. Sam Walters had the perfect image in the community along with the breast cancer work for his foundation, Mary Margret Walters Foundation. He was the perfect man to be in business with, so he thought. Apart from fine jewelry and fine wine, Sam loved the game of outwitting someone who claimed to be brilliant. A chess player, Sam played chess with Carmine's mind, cunningly finding out Nato Ogundiran was Carmine's source by hiring an old friend, Frank Bruno, a private investigator and computer specialist. Hacking into Brightest Star's shipping and receiving files, the name Nato Ogundiran appeared. Sam, a buyer of wholesale jewelry in Las Vegas, remembered Nato as an appraiser. He contacted him via e-mail, requesting a meeting for a side deal. Basically blackmailing him, his private investigator gave him knowledge of a love affair between Marie Biasi and Nato Ogundiran, which would seal his fate if Carmine Biasi found out the obvious deception.

Knowing it was dangerous, Nato agreed, having a history and love for Marie. He couldn't allow her father to find out. He would be murdered, and she would be ostracized. Sam was playing a serious game, making three times as much as Carmine, using his connections and his cargo container to bring the merchandise back to the States.

Kelly Walters Phillips was a skeptic at heart. She inherited that from her late mother, Margret. She felt something in the pit of her stomach about this Diana Colby. She had to check into her background and see what she'd find. Kelly called a longtime friend of her father, Frank Bruno, an ex–dirty cop, now a private investigator for hire. She told Frank her father was blindly in love. Kelly wanted this Diana Colby's life history. He was more than happy to look into her past especially if Diana was trying to take his old friend for a ride. He had to protect him and those finances. Those finances paid Frank's bills in one way or another. He always needed Frank's expertise for many different jobs. So really he'd be protecting his livelihood and his future. Moreover, Frank always had the hots for Kelly; she knew he did. She knew he would be willing to do whatever she asked without a question.

Back from their mini vacation and sporting her twenty-five-carat stone, Karen—or Diana, as she liked to be called—was floating on cloud nine.

She had never felt this way before, being an adult dancer for most of her adult life. She came in contact with all sorts of men, even had a few sugar daddies. She had met and fallen for Darryl, a.k.a. Young Heat, but something was different about Sam. He was warm, caring, and very gentle. He never tried too hard, and she learned a hell of a lot from Sam. This was the first time in her life where she had a significant title. The fiancé to Sam Walters, she would become Mrs. Karen Walters. She liked the sound of that and wanted it to be a reality. The more she thought about the marriage, the more she knew a plan had to be developed. She would tell Sam the truth, at least the partial truth. Her name and alias was made up, to protect her from a raging ex-boyfriend. He abused her so bad she moved to another city, creating a whole new identity for her safety. Hmmm, that sounded good, she even believed it herself. Now the plan was to wear a sexy outfit, cook her fiancé a gourmet meal, then tell him the story and end it making love to him any way he wanted. Until now, she never had him over to the condo she shared with her cousin. Well, no better time than the present time.

Karen gave Sam the directions and invited him over for dinner. She paid her cousin to get lost for the evening. She burned jasmine incense and lit candles all around the apartment. A full stock of his favorite wine, Columbian Crest Merlot. Playing a Sade CD set the stage for the evening.

"Is it a crime, is it a crime." Dinner was grilled lamb chops, green beans, and long-grain rice, everything seasoned with the right herbs and spices. She was dressed in a sheer short-cut robe, revealing her voluptuous breasts, and thong panties. With no perfume, she smelled like baby oil, fresh and clean.

When Sam arrived, she opened the door and pulled him in for a kiss. Immediately he was aroused but tried to pace himself. She handed him a glass of wine and set the table. Soft music, candlelight dining, and her looking so sexy blew Sam's mind enchantingly. She fed him off her plate, which he found sexy. Sade had that effect on a man. "You give me, you give me the sweetest taboo, / that's why I'm in love with you." After dinner, she served a Sara Lee apple pie and caramel French vanilla ice cream. They ate, ate, and ate until both were full. She cleared the table then directed Sam to the couch, took off his shoes, and massaged his feet lovingly. Then it was time. "Sam, I have a confession to make, sweetheart." "What's that, my love?" She told him the made-up story and cried in the process. He dried her tears with his hand and put his finger to her lips. "Shhh. Say no more, you don't have to worry anymore. I'll protect you, you're absolutely safe now." He fell for the story and didn't seem upset that she lied. In fact, he totally understood!

Karen felt so lucky to have a man so understanding even if it was a lie. He had just won her heart sincerely. He looked her in the eye and said, "Karen Matthews, will you marry me?" She cried then said, "Yes, I'll marry you, Sam." The gig was up, and YH would be beyond upset, especially since she had really fallen in love with Sam. She told him her real name but not about the robbery. Young Heat, Jackie, and Page—maybe they'll just let her go free. She knew that was too good to be true, wishful thinking. So eventually the showdown would happen. It was inevitable; their paths would cross sooner or later. Karen didn't plan this; it was how it played out. She forgot she was in the game. Fell in deep and got emotional, forgetting YH's number-one rule. Well, it was too late; the deed was already done. Karen just closed her eyes as her fiancé entered her love tunnel. He felt so good inside of her, gentle and loving. Maybe she was ready to put an end to all the games. Maybe the sound of marriage to a wealthy man touched her heart. Maybe Sam Walters was truly better with age and knew how to please a woman. Whatever it was, she was definitely sprung and didn't care who knew. "He's a smooth operator, smooth operator," Sade sang in the background.

Noticing the blinking light for messages, Candice checked her text messages. She was surprised to see what Lola had written. Lola always had the inside track on a great opportunity. Candice knew it would be in her best interest to respond quickly. Her call went directly to the voice mail, meaning Lola had the phone off. So she left a message saying she was interested in whatever it was, please call her back.

Candice continued to get dressed for the fashion show she and the crew were attending. They weren't officially working; it was a invite to the event. Mr. Mills felt it would be a good look to be among the fashion world's elite, the type of consumers that would inadvertently help promote the product. The gala was held in the Waldorf Astoria ballroom. It wasn't formal but an elegant event, to say the least. Mia and Leslie cooperated on makeup, hair, and wardrobe, turning Candice from a swain to an elegant swain. Her dress was by Dolce & Gabbana, hot pink and gray, shoulderless on one side. Elizabeth Eden peep-toe pumps (hot pink), hands and toes polished (pink), and a D & G clutch handbag. The fragrance she chose was Tresor; she looked like a world-class supermodel. Candice always managed to outshine her colleagues; it was a God-given gift. With everyone assembled and ready to leave, Carl Mills fought hard not to lose his composure. The sight of Candice was like seeing a rainbow after the rain. Even though she and Leslie had an agreement, she allowed Mr. Mills to escort her to the gala strictly for business and appearance's sake of the Neon Vodka company although she was sick to the stomach at the sight of him. Tosha tagged along, looking beautiful in her own right, choosing a Salvatore Ferragamo dress and matching pumps from Candy's wardrobe collection. Candy was still waiting for the ice to break between her and Tosha. She was beginning to feel more and more distant.

All Candice knew was this event was for a fairly new clothing line making huge headlines in the industry, and it was the place to be in New York. Once they arrived, Candice tried to lose Mr. Mills in the crowd; it was futile. His roaming eyes said it all and much more; she felt very uncomfortable. She asked Tosha to stay close to avoid unwanted conversation with Mr. Mills. The Waldorf Astoria was a tourist attraction and well-known upscale landmark. The ballroom was decorated with a sophisticated appeal; the extravagant night was nearly underway. Models, photographers, agents, clothing distributors, and press were all in attendance. Banquet servers walked around with glasses filled with champagne. Mr. Mills took a few glasses off the tray and handed the sisters glasses. Tosha drank the first one down and gestured for another. Candice sipped like a elegant woman, maintaining her poise in a very dignified and self-assured manner. That made Carl want her even more; he loved the way she carried herself. Gently licking her lips after every sip, she had Carl mesmerized. The lights dimmed and the stage lights lit up as the fashion show was about to begin. Everyone took their seats, Candice keeping Tosha close, trying to avoid eye contact with Mr. Mills. She couldn't stand the sight or smell of his cheap cologne. For someone who was a powerful executive, he had the style and demeanor of a ninny.

So many industry heads and behind-the-scenes personnel lingered around. The models were absolutely beautiful; they were serious about their craft. The intense looks on their faces and struts in the walk were professional all the way. The photographers positioned themselves along the catwalk, taking pictures. The wardrobe stylists must have been efficient backstage because the models looked great. The ultimate defining characteristic of the fashion show was the designs. The clothes were absolutely incredible. The big red sign that read Palm-Tree Clothing was appealing to the eye. The unique styles and use of colors were like no other. Candice was impressed and wanted to buy some outfits for herself. The designer was extremely creative and knew how to bridge the gap between casual and sporty with a sexy edge. The models wore the complete fall and winter line. Then the last of the line was the corporate look—exclusive pantsuits, blouses, coats, and scarves. A crew of a dozen models gave an amazing fashion show.

The lights brightened, and the designer walked out. People applauded and cheered, pleased from a wonderful show. He took a bow and gestured for his assistant and marketing director to join him on stage. Kym V and Pam Orchard joined, and the three bowed in unison. When he began to speak, thanking everyone for making Palm-Tree a success, boom, it hit Candice like a ton of bricks. *It's him, it's really, really him.* She couldn't believe her eyes. Hands started sweating, butterflies were in her stomach, and panties got moist. It was that fine-ass guy who gave her a flyer of his designs. He was the one that predicted her winning the Neon contest. She knew leaving without speaking to him wasn't an option. The crowd gave one last round of applause, and the show was over.

There were numerous people standing in line to meet Eric "Swave" Hawkins, designer and CEO of Palm-Tree Clothing. Candice grabbed Tosha by the hand and headed toward the crowd, leaving Carl Mills and the rest of the crew behind. She told Tosha she had to meet the designer even though they already met in the past. The closer Candy got to him, the sexier he appeared to be. Tall, dark, and handsome, and incredibly talented. "Damn, Candice, I've never seen you act this way over a man!" She acted like Tosha didn't even exist; she kept tunnel vision toward the goal. Industry execs and distributors were holding lengthy conversations with him. The line was moving slow, but Candice remained persistent. Carl Mills watched from behind, along with Leslie. Just as doubt started to set in her mind, their eyes met. Swave knew instantly who she was and excused himself from the present conversation. He walked toward Candice, weaving through the crowd with determination. Just before he reached her, Candy's phone started ringing. She realized it was Lola by caller ID. Her eye's stayed on Swave as she answered the phone.

"Candice, this is Lola, I have great news. I have a job for you with an up-and-coming designer who owns Palm-Tree Clothing. His name is—"

"Eric 'Swave' Hawkins," Candice replied.

"How did you know that, Candy?"

"Because I'm watching him stand in front of me at the Waldorf Astoria in New York."

"Are you kidding me, Candice? I supplied that venue with my models. Well, do you want to model for Palm-Tree?"

"Yes, hell yeah, I do. Lola, I'll call you right back." The phone call ended. Swave stood in front of Candice licking his lips and extending his hand. She reached out, and their hands locked, eyes locked, and they began to smile.

"If God made a woman more beautiful than you, he kept her in heaven for himself!"

She smiled. "The last time you told me that, I won that contest!"

"Oh, so you did win."

"Yeah, I did."

"Why didn't you look me up?"

Before she could answer, Tosha cleared her throat. "Ummm." As if to say "Introduce me."

"I'm sorry, this is my sister, Tosha."

He held out his hand, they shook hands, and she winked her eye at him. He turned his attention back to Candice.

"I'm sorry, I've been on tour since we met back in LA."

"What are you doing here in New York?"

"I'm with the Neon crew on the last leg of the tour. We came out to support your fashion line."

"Thank you!"

"Would you like to hang out with me tonight, if you're not busy?"

Tosha gave a look, then Candy replied, "Only if my sister can come along."

"The more the merrier, just hang on until I wrap everything up. I must be a professional. I'm representing the future of Palm-Tree Clothing."

Candice walked back to the crew on cloud nine, it was if she had met Prince Charming. Actually she did; this was the first man Candice ever wanted sexually. A virgin as a young woman, she had a burning desire to be pleased. Not by just anyone—her burning desire was for that chocolate brother Swave. Candice told Mr. Mills and Leslie she and Tosha didn't need a ride back to the hotel. They were hanging out with the designer Swave. Leslie smiled, and Mr. Mills tried to hide his disapproval. He knew he was losing to a much younger, handsome, talented gentleman. The only thing he could say was, "Please be careful, and remember we have a shoot tomorrow at ESPN zone on Forty-Second Street." He turned and walked away; Leslie followed behind submissively, wishing it was her hanging out with the sexy and debonaire Swave.

Taking time to talk to everyone interested in Palm-Tree and its future, Swave made some contacts and took and gave contact information. He networked like his life depended on it, a sign of someone determined to succeed in the business. He took time to thank all the models for a dazzling performance. Fine words were also said to all the photographers and stylists. He made sure to include makeup artists and all the Palm-Tree staff. He hugged Kym V and Pam to show his appreciation for all their hard work. He took a few minutes to text-message his silent partner who was on tour in Europe, telling him the fashion show had been a success.

Kym volunteered to oversee the cleanup and packaging of the clothes. He walked Kym over to Candice and Tosha. They were chatting, having a glass of champagne. He introduced them and gazed into Candy's eyes, asking the banquet server for three more glasses of champagne. He called Pam over and handed her and Kym a glass. He made a toast to the success of the company. Everyone raised their glasses; before drinking, he said, "I couldn't have done this without you helping me, Kym." They drank, and everyone smiled with joy. He turned to Candice and asked, if she and Tosha were ready to go. Again he gave his assistant and marketing director a hug.

Swave, Candice, and Tosha left the hotel. They got into the backseat of the black Cadillac truck (Livery Service) and headed to Sylvia's in Harlem, a great soul food restaurant. He wanted to keep it simple and fun. Even though Swave was making money now, he still remained grounded and humble. So eating in a local spot was second nature to him. Besides, Sylvia's had the best mac and cheese in the city, and he was a huge fan.

Candice and Tosha enjoyed the Southern-style soul food. Both ordered the same entrée, fried chicken (white meat), collard greens, mac and cheese, and corn bread. Swave had country-fried steak, mash potatoes and gravy, mac and cheese, and a biscuit. All three drank Arnold Palmers (iced tea mixed with lemonade). Candice couldn't keep her eyes off Swave. He returned the admiration with a huge smile. Tosha made her attraction obvious by rubbing her foot against his legs. He tried to ignore her affection, but it wasn't easy. They acted as if Tosha wasn't sitting among them. He couldn't believe how beautiful she was, and she thought he was strikingly handsome. Candice gave his work a compliment, expressing her fondness for the line. She asked to purchase the plum-colored pantsuit and beige V-neck blouse. He offered to give her the outfit for free, compliments of the Palm-Tree clothing company. She was flattered but insisted to owe him a favor in the future.

As the conversation went on, she asked Swave if he knew Lola Hemmingway.

He recognized the name from Pam Orchard. "She staffed the event tonight with models from her agency."

Then she explained that Lola was her modeling agent. Also that she was offered the full-time modeling job for his company.

"Wooh." His eyes lit up with amazement. He reached across the table and said, "I couldn't think of anyone I'd like to represent my company more than you. So is it official, will you accept the offer to work with me and Palm-Tree?"

She smiled. "Yes, of course I will, Swave." His hands on hers, they both felt the chemistry with raging hormones running through their bodies.

The intense moment was broken when Tosha cleared her throat. "Ummm, excuse me!"

It was like watching a great action movie, then the screen froze. The moment was ruined from a technical malfunction or, in this case, a dysfunctional little sister who was an irritating third wheel.

They both wished they were alone. He told Candice she would have to meet with Pam to work out the details in her contract (salary and benefits).

One thing he respected—Candice chose to finish out her present contract and tour even though she didn't enjoy working for Carl Mills anymore. She didn't want to leave the rest of the crew hanging. They still had bills and family to take care of daily. Candice became extremely close to Mia, Pierre, Big Hank, Billy, even Leslie. DJ Nice always had parties and clubs he could play. So Swave was cool with that, because after all, he was the boss. So arrangements could be made; he was incredibly flexible. Actually that gave him some additional time to add some extra flair to the line. They finished their food, and he offered to take them to Junior's in Brooklyn for some world-famous NY-style cheesecake. They were thrilled with the idea, and they were off to Brooklyn. The women enjoyed the sites while riding from Manhattan to Brooklyn. Swave texted Kym and Pam to let them know he had just hired the face of Palm-Tree clothing. "Her name is Candice Gray!"

Strawberry-topped cheesecake was Candy's treat. Tosha ordered chocolate cheesecake. Swave had the blueberry topping with whipped cream. He even bought a piece for the driver. They all enjoyed some laughs, and the evening was pleasant. He asked if he could take her out on a real date soon. Candice agreed, and they exchanged numbers to plan around their schedules. He wanted it to be perfectly clear that he was interested, and she told him she was looking forward to the date whenever they could make it happen. Tosha was, and felt like, a true third wheel. She wished it was her who Swave was interested in; she thought how good he would be in bed. Just like everything else, Candice achieved another notch on her goal list. A to-die-for job and a sexy brother who was about his business legally. Tosha was gaining more envious feelings toward her older sister.

The night was fun, and Swave had the driver take the women to their hotel. He got out and escorted them to the hotel lobby. They exchanged farewells. He kissed her hand like a true gentleman, promised to call her, then disappeared out the door. On his way home, he texted Candice: "I've waited my entire life for an angel to enter my life, Thank you Angel. Swave."

When she read the message, a smile attacked her face. She knew in her heart Swave was her future!

When Candice reached her room, she called Leslie to let her know she was fine. She didn't tell her about the job offer, figuring it wasn't her business. Leslie briefed her on the ESPN Zone appearance. They would be leaving the hotel at 9:00 AM sharp. They ended the conversation, and Candice went to bed thinking of her Prince Charming.

Swave had been attracted to certain women in the past, but never like he was toward Candice. He had many opportunities to sleep with dozens of models. However, he wanted his first experience to be special and meaningful. He had a deep desire to hold, kiss, and make love to Candice. It had to be destiny that made their paths cross again. He drifted off to sleep thinking about a future with Candice. He vowed to pursue her with the same passion he had for becoming successful. A great day in the business, a pleasant evening with Candice. Now he would enjoy a much-needed sleep thinking of Candice. He listened to Jagged Edge: "I gotta be the one you love, / I gotta be the one you need. / I'm just telling you that I gotta be."

Off to sleep with Candice on his mind.

The ESPN Zone was not really an official part of the marketing scheme. Carl Mills had a personal agenda that the crew knew nothing about—his side project. Seems Mr. Mills invested in an energy drink called Action. He was advertising the product instead of Neon. He never told Candice so, in essence, she wasn't under contract to promote the energy drink under any circumstance. Just another ridiculous request to prove he was a underhanded snake. Now thinking about it, that's why he offered her more money. It was evident the superiors didn't know about this product. He was having his personal product advertised with the company's money. Very ingenious, as he stood to make huge amounts of currency with the pretty and healthy-looking model as the face of the product.

Guessing this was part of the surprise he promised, along with the mistress proposal, Candice reluctantly agreed to the shoot, first securing a negotiated bonus. She was catching on quickly; nothing in business was free. Although it was a code of ethics she felt bad about breaking, the extra money was to help set Tosha up with a place to stay. Candice was thinking about the near future. She would be traveling nationwide and abroad. This time a traveling companion wasn't in the cards. Honestly she was tired of babysitting and planning her life around li'l sis. Hopefully something rubbed off and Tosha would consider a career in the industry. So for now, Action was a means to an end.

Candice knew as long as she was on board with the project, everyone else made a living. She prayed that the crew did some networking as well, because soon she couldn't think about anyone but herself. Selfish as it sounded, that was the reality in order to get to the next level. So for now, she smiled and played the role of a team player, taking one for the team also to empower her sister. Mr. Mills played his role well, passing out his product like water. The constructed booth was an eyesore and an attraction at the same time on the busy Forty-Second Street in Manhattan. Leslie did what was required, trying to stay employed. Candy's level of professionalism was always above the rest. She was doing her job in the flesh, but her mind was a thousand miles away, thinking about the day she met Swave in LA—what a beautiful day. A smile came on her face thinking about how much of a gentleman he was to her and Tosha. She wondered what life would be like as his girlfriend. She was willing to find out how great that title would feel. So deep in thought, she didn't realize her phone vibrating in her pocket. It finally registered, and she answered the call. "Thank Almighty God!" It was Swave calling to say hello. She felt like a schoolgirl who had her first boyfriend, walking away from the rest of the crew to have some privacy. He wanted to know when they could see each other again. She told him she didn't know when she would be free from work. He asked if he could come down to the venue to say hi. Candice was cool with the idea, then he said to her, "Well, turn around." When she did, he was standing there with a dozen red roses!

He was standing there clean and dapper, smelling like Calvin Klein Eternity. He handed her the roses and gave her a hug. She felt his broad shoulders, realizing how strong and firm a physique he had. Everyone watched as they shared a tender moment. Carl and Leslie were silent, but many thoughts ran through their minds. Tosha watched the two and cleared her throat as usual. Swave spoke to her, Mr. Mills, and Leslie, apologizing for the surprise interruption caused by him. Looking Candice in the eyes, he asked her to have dinner with him at his home. She accepted the invitation but didn't know what time she'd be free. He told her to call when she was available. Then he would come to pick her up from the hotel. He kissed her on the cheek, said good-byes to the crew, and walked away into the crowd. She was totally blown away as she smelled the roses, closing her eyes in a state of euphoria. All eyes were on Candice, and minds were running with all sorts of conclusions. Some were surprised, and some were wondering what will become of their future situations. Mr. Mills knew at that very moment that his days were numbered. He saw the chemistry and attraction the two displayed. His wheels were turning; he had to come up with a plan. He knew she was a virgin and wanted to be the first to put his seed in the delicate, tender young body.

Later that evening after their workload was complete, Candice called Swave; he was awaiting her call. He sent a Livery car to pick her up and bring her to Harlem. He wasn't rich yet but doing well for himself. Instead of spending a load of money on a new car and house, he decided to save for a rainy day. He wanted to bring something to the table when it was time for marriage. Besides, he loved living among the average people. It gave him inspiration and insight on everyday fashion trends. The bottom line was he had a job (self-employed), a bank account, great credit, and a comfortable living space. He greeted her at the door of the brownstone. The house was very similar to the *Cosby Show*'s brownstone. A three-bedroom 2½ bath, kitchen, office, living room, dining room, and sewing studio. He liked to refer to it as the room of creativity. The house was decorated with an Asian appeal. He was very fond of the Japanese culture. His art was from various cultures—African, Asian, and Latin. The combination actually worked for the room. The house was very neat and smelled freshly clean. She could smell the Pine Sol through the aroma from the food he'd prepared.

He cooked an Asian-inspired meal, chicken stir-fry and vegetables made with spicy cayenne pepper and sweet paprika sauce, sautéed in olive oil. He chose a Pinot Noir chardonnay and thought it would be fun eating with chopsticks. They sat shoes off at a Japanese-style dinner table. Close to the floor, the seating arrangement made a much more intimate atmosphere. She was impressed by the meal; it was a different experience—different and also fun to eat, spicy and sweet exploding in her mouth. The conversation was really refreshing and broad. They talked about everything under the sun; she found out he was well-rounded. Swave was knowledgeable about many different cultures. His music taste was wide, and he enjoyed an artist from every genre. The R & B CD that was playing happened to be one of her favorites, Trey Songz. Relationships became the topic, and both admitted to be amateurs in the field. A look of intrigue was apparent to the other when both revealed they were virgins. Wow, each thought the exact same thing, what better person to lose their virginity to. "We must be tailor-made for each other." Candice helped him clean and wash the dishes. Then they moved to the living room couch. He put the movie *Brown Sugar* in, and she was speechless. Shockingly it was her one of her favorite movies. The story of true love that seemed unlikely to find in this society of nonmonogamous free spirits of today.

Working up the courage, Swave seized the moment and kissed Candice on the cheek softly. She turned her head and kissed him back on the lips. He returned the favor, and they kissed passionately. Looking into her eyes, he felt the desire burning from within. Candice was an open, empty, willing vessel wanting to be filled. Without a word, he picked her up into his arms and walked up the stairs to the bedroom. He had the room lit up with candles burning, scented candles that smelled like cinnamon. He laid her down and took off his shirt to reveal a solid chest and ripped abs. She rubbed her hands across his muscular chest. He began to unbutton her blouse, opening up to two perky C-cup breasts. Taking the blouse and bra off, he began sucking her hard nipples. She never thought a wet mouth on her breast could feel so wonderful. Losing all clarity and composure, the animal instincts took over. He reached between her thighs and felt the warm, wet, shaved kitten. Pulling down her skirt and red silk panties, he admired her sculpted body, smooth and sexy. Standing, he took off his pants and Polo boxer brief underwear to expose his naked chocolate body, manhood standing at attention. She froze at the sight of his eight-inch trophy. The words of Trey Songz's "Love Faces" was ringing in her ears. He lay back down with her and kissed on her neck, then the lips. She was breathless, never before having been naked alone with a man. He spread her legs and positioned himself between her hips, pulling a condom from the night table. He opened it and put it on, looking Candice in her eyes. He proceeded to enter into her body. Just before he could penetrate, the doorbell rang several times along with some hard knocking on the door, like it was the NYPD!

What poor timing it was for whoever was at the door. It ruined the moment as the knocking and doorbell continued to be a pest. He jumped to his feet, putting on his pants with no underwear. He told Candice that he'd be right back. He raced to the door, looking out the peephole to find it was Kym V. What could she want at this hour? He opened the door, and she walked in, unaware of his half-dressed body. She was crying and obviously drunk. "Oh boy, what's wrong, Kym?" She told him she really needed to talk and his phone was turned off. Before he could tell her it was bad timing, Candice walked into the room fully dressed. In the distraction, she had a moment of clarity. She felt they were moving too quick. Their attraction to each other got the best of them. Seeing her dressed, he knew the evening had taken a 180-degree turn. Kym finally realized she had just been intrusive. She apologized and headed toward the door. Being a good friend, he stopped her and sat her down. He directed Candice to the kitchen to talk. Swave apologized about his friend's unexpected visit. She understood and figured it had to be something extremely serious. Candice told him she had a wonderful night but wanted to leave before they went any further, explaining they both needed to think things through before taking that big step and losing their virginity. He respected her wishes as a gentleman even though he was ready to take the plunge.

He wanted her so bad that his blood pressure was on overload. She also wanted to feel him deep inside of her. Mainly she wanted to be 100 percent sure that they were tailor-made for each other. Swave gave her a hug and a kiss, looking in her eyes. He asked, "Would you consider being my lady?" She replied, "Only if I'm the only one in your life." He told her he wanted to make a commitment to her and only her. They kissed and she said, "Yes, Eric 'Swave' Hawkins, I would be honored to be your lady and start a relationship with you." They hugged tightly then kissed again.

He called the Livery service to take her back to the hotel. They promised to stay in touch daily and visit when schedules permitted. After a few minutes, a car horn beeped, and he walked her outside to the car, opening the car door for his lady. He said, "Call me when you're at the hotel." They kissed, she got in, and he watched the car drive off. He headed back inside to Kym, wondering what could be so important. She had interrupted him from crossing over to the other side—the side where fantasy and reality meet, where all wishes and desires are filled to the rim. Oh well, she was his friend, and no matter what, he was going to be loyal to their friendship. Swave started a fresh pot of Bustello coffee. He needed to get Kym sober as possible; she wasn't a heavy drinker. So if she was drunk, there was something emotionally wrong.

As she began to tell her story, tears ran down her face. Kym had an "on again, off again" relationship. The guy was from her hometown. Though they had an open relationship, she was madly in love with him. Other men showed interest, but she remained devoted to David. He was an entrepreneur who owned and operated a boutique, a hard worker and visionary in his own right. He cared for Kym but wanted nothing to tie him down. He was a free spirit and wanted to travel at a drop of a dime. Kym was the opposite and wanted a husband and family. Seems that Kym found out she was pregnant. They both planned to be great parents and handle the situation. However, she thought that her pregnancy would hinder her position in the Palm-Tree clothing company. She had worked so hard to become an important part of the company. Kym didn't want to lose her position to an up-and-coming accessory designer. She felt that her decision to have her child would hinder her and Swave's business relationship. He laughed uncontrollably, long and hard, thinking it was funny Kym would think such a ridiculous thought. Truth was, he depended on her for more than the business aspect. He needed her for moral support. Kym's honesty always sustained him in more ways than one. He valued her and the collaboration they shared in fashion. "Are you crazy, Kym? I'll never turn my back on you. You are and will always be a part of Palm-Tree Enterprises. Work until it's time to have the baby, then take a maternity leave. No problem or worries, baby girl, you're my right hand." That brought a smile to Kym's face. She had worried over nothing. It was obvious Swave was her true friend and had her best interests at heart.

Turning his phone back on, it immediately rang. It was Candice calling; they talked as he poured some coffee for Kym. She was obviously too tired to drink anymore. He directed her to the guest bedroom and tucked her in the bed. He continued to talk to his new lady until they both feel asleep. A different night for all parties involved. One thing was for certain, Swave was serious about his new lady, especially the honest and sincere commitment he made to her. She would be headed back to LA to finish the last of the tour. He would be hard at work developing fashion for the international store. They both promised to make time for their new relationship.

Frank Bruno made a decent living being a private investigator. His contacts in the streets generated a significant amount of information. He also was very resourceful in a sinister kind of way. Breaking the rules was common to Bruno and the reason he got kicked off the police force. The major part of his income came from odd jobs for Sam Walters. So doing Kelly a favor meant doing one for Sam. A three-week surveillance of the subject produced some interesting information. Seems Diana Colby was an alias she was using—a deceased young woman whose identity was being used by the fiancée of Sam Walters. Her circle consisted of a male subject and two women whose identities were unknown. Bruno's instincts told him these people were connected to the underworld. This so-called Diana Colby had no job or visible means of income. So foul play was a likely assumption. "Will continue the investigation thoroughly to find out more information. Bottom line, Diana Colby isn't who she claims, and likely participant in love scheme. Will contact you when I have the appropriate proof of a crime. Bruno!"

He sent the e-mail to Kelly, turned off the computer, and started his day, trying to find out what Diana Colby, a.k.a. Karen Matthews, had planned for Sam Walters.

Karen met Darryl (YH) at the Starbucks in the Barnes & Noble in Concord Mills mall. She bought Sam a book about yoga called *The Heart of Yoga* by Desikachar. He noticed a difference in her demeanor; it was obvious. She wasn't the same woman he sent on a mission. They greeted each other with a hug. Her scent made him remember her between the sheets. Unfortunately he hadn't had her amazing sexual talents in a while. He made a mental note to plan a much-needed private session. Young Heat thought he was being summoned for an update on the mark, Sam

Walters. Surprisingly he didn't know Karen was aborting the mission. She had honestly fallen for Sam and wanted to obtain the long-term riches, the benefits and security that came with marriage.

When she told him, silence was between them for five minutes. YH's mind was running, trying to think of what he could counteroffer. Nothing came to mind; he knew he had been defeated. Nevertheless, he had to try something. So with a cruel outburst, he threatened to go ahead with or without her help. She quietly, with a low voice, asked him to forget about Sam and pick another mark. The kicker was she wasn't aboard for any more missions. Karen laid it all out for Young Heat plain and simple. Then she reached in her purse and took out a large envelope filled with money—forty thousand dollars from the last mission. She forfeited her cut of the money to buy a pass for Sam. This raised a real concern in YH's mind. He couldn't understand what Sam had besides money to offer. He had lost his bait chick, the one that set the stage for all the scams, hustles, and robberies. This was too much to wrap his mind around. Well, if he lost her, he'd at least get something out of the deal. So he took the money like a desperate pimp.

Young Heat wasn't a fool, and Sam was still on the menu. YH had to go another direction. "So how about our love life, Karen?" She smiled and said she'd feel better if they broke all ties. That did it; this Sam Walters had to pay. It was one thing that she opted out of the game, but absolutely no more sex—that was totally inconceivable. As he had invested so much in Karen, Sam would pay the ultimate price for his unknown treachery. After robbing him and turning his world upside down, he would see to it that Sam paid with his life.

He thought about the future of his team that committed larceny. He needed another face for future missions. After careful thinking, the answer came to him: Tosha Gray. She was young but very teachable with a wholesome face. If he trained and coached her properly, maybe she could fit the bill. Hopefully he could talk her into joining his crime family. As an incentive, he would give her ten grand to come aboard, which was peanuts compared to what he stood to gain with the jewelry heist. So he placed a call and threw out the bait, hoping she would bite. The one thing he had in his favor was Tosha had a great desire to get away from her sister's shadow. YH was going to make Karen and Sam pay for their acts—Karen for forgetting she was in the game and Sam for blinding her.

YH's call couldn't have come at a better time. Candice and Tosha weren't talking. Ever since she had started dating fly guy Mr. Clothes Designer Swave, Tosha felt like Candice had changed on her considerably. The confrontation happened when Candice told Tosha her days were numbered traveling with her while working. She explained her plans for the future were going to work with Palm-Tree, and she had to focus on her career. It would be time for Tosha to strike out on her own. She gave Tosha four grand to help start her off wherever she wanted to go. She also promised to help her, provided Tosha became goal-orientated. Tosha felt abandoned and left out in the cold. So Young Heat's offer seemed like a golden dream of an opportunity. Tosha felt like this would be her way to make it on her own. Instead of following in her sister's footsteps, she wanted to blaze her own path. She could have tried to start a merchandise company, learn photography, try designing, or even become a model. Candice would've helped her in any honorable career. There was something deep insider her that loved the thrill of the criminal element. So Young Heat's offer called to her spirit, and she answered. With four grand in her pocket and a promise of ten when she arrived, Tosha took the first plane to North Carolina. Without a hug or kiss for her big sister, she left feeling betrayed and angry.

Candice wasn't happy about the situation at all. However, it was time she grew up; it was now or never. Candice was trying to build a career as an international supermodel while helping Swave to make his brand larger than life. It was time for Candice to move to the next level. If Tosha couldn't understand that, it was too bad. The time had come for them to be and live as adult women—separately.

Leaving the mall, Karen felt like she was being watched. She looked behind her and around the mall parking lot, pulling out of the parking deck with her sporty Chevrolet Corvette Z06. She quickly zipped through traffic and jumped on the highway. Bruno had to let her go so he wouldn't blow his cover. He'd pick up her trail again the next day. He had enough evidence for a long day's work. "Subject met Darryl Moffett at the mall. Had coffee, talked for an hour and handed him a huge envelope. If I could guess it would be money." He wrote this on his pad, then headed home to e-mail Kelly.

Karen pulled up at Sam's jewelry store, book in hand. He greeted her with open arms and a kiss. She gave him the book *The Heart of Yoga*. He was pleased, being a yoga fanatic. They talked for a few, then she whispered, "Can we escape to your office for a few?" He expeditiously directed her to the back office. He told his employees Sue and Helen he was taking a break. Once in the office, Karen sat Sam down on his plush leather chair. She unzipped his pants and began sucking on his manhood, slow and precise. While licking his head, she kept her eyes on him. Karen had mastered the technique of sucking and jerking at the same time. His toes started to curl in his shoes. She stood and pulled off her panties. He pulled down his pants and she sat on top of his erection. Kissing Sam and whispering in his ear, "You're the best, Sam, you're the best," she worked the pelvis area and tightened her muscles. He couldn't hold it any longer and released inside her kitten. She sat there and tried to absorb every drop. He said, "I love you, Karen." She replied the same. Karen opened her purse and pulled out a pack of wet wipes. She cleaned Sam's nature, then she cleaned her kitten. As she put her panties back on, Sam got dressed. "I just wanted to give you a midday surprise, honey." "Well, you definitely gave me a surprise and a thrill." They walked out of the office hand-in-hand, in heavenly bliss. They kissed, then she walked out of the store. The women's eyes were all on her like jealous vipers. Helen had been secretly trying to seduce Sam for years subtly. Well, it was a done deal; Karen was the Queen Bee now. Everyone knew it from Sam's newfound attitude. Karen knew the only way to secure a financial future—along with marriage she had to have his child.

So she was on a new mission to get the real long-term rich rewards. She wanted to own something legally without sharing a cut with anyone. Karen knew Sam's daughters were entitled to something, but her unborn child would require more. They were grown, and one thing she could possibly give Sam that the daughters couldn't was a Sam Walters Jr. Yeah, Karen had big plans for the future. The other women and Young Heat would have to understand. Young Heat had showed her the game, but she took the ball and scored. She didn't lose love for YH and the crew, just outgrew the old hustle. Now she saw things out of the box in a major way. A thriving jewelry store, a mansion, and an unrevealed fortune. It was time to make it happen, and Karen was putting in work.

The only bright moments in Candice's days were phone conversations with Swave. They talked several times a day, especially at night. She was depressed about the way Tosha had left her in New York. They were taught as little girls to talk their disagreements out. Now they were grown and weren't following the teachings of Mom. Swave was doing a great job cheering her up; she looked forward to hearing his voice. The tour had become more demanding, doing double the work, promoting the Action energy drink for her scumbag boss. She literally started to dread working on the tour. It was close to being over, and Carl Mills was at his wits' end. Every day he tried to persuade Candice to renew her contract. She still didn't reveal her verbal agreement with Palm-Tree Clothing, so he thought she had no other options. Just as Candice was hard at work fulfilling her contract, Swave was hard at work as well. He was designing signature jeans for the line. This would be the first of the product line Candice would promote. The jeans were called Spices from Palm-Tree Clothing. They would be sizes 4 to 18—boot cut, trouser, super skinny, and pin tuck. He wanted this to be a design for every woman, having the ability to lift and sculpt the body while wearing them. He pitched the idea to Candice, and she absolutely loved his vision. She was so overwhelmed by his brilliant mind. He was fine and a gentleman, as well as being a true genius when it came to fashion. He had an arsenal of ideas; she couldn't wait to officially be part of the team. For now she was happy to have this incredible man in her life, not only as an employer and business partner as he described their working relationship. She was happy to call him her one and only man.

Candice kept playing back in her mind the night they almost consummated their relationship. The thought made her panties wet. As much as she wanted him, she had to admit her fear, fear of the unknown. What would happen after he got the goodies? Candice viewed him as a true gentleman and a true spiritual person although she knew men were subject to change once they reached the mountaintop. Nevertheless, she was willing to take a chance on him. She wondered if he would marry her before they made love. Could he have that much discipline? Just some thoughts that ran through her mind.

Since Swave found out about Kym's pregnancy, he was very protective of his friend. He made sure she ate right and took prenatal vitamins. She still worked alongside him, but he didn't allow her to work over eight hours. Kym felt blessed to have a true friend in her corner. He made good on the promise he made back in fashion school: to take her along toward success in building his brand. Truthfully he knew Kym's input and dedication to the fashion line was genuine. He could count on her for anything at any time. Kym's loyalty meant more to him than one hundred million dollars. Every successful person—or company, for that matter—had a hard worker bee that was the heart, soul, and backbone in the success. The person that worked behind the scenes and was the glue that held everything together. For Swave and Palm-Tree Clothing, that person was Kym V. He knew it and always treated her according to her worth. Good workers were hard to find, as well as friends. He had both in Kym and valued her talents and friendship very much.

Candice tried to reach Tosha at least twice a day. She never answered the phone, which was more than frustrating for Candice; she was worried about her sister. Tosha had never been all alone, on her own before. True, she was legally an adult. Truthfully she was still very much immature. Candice called her mom in Cali to see if she heard from Tosha. Mom hadn't talked to her in weeks. This was becoming more than Tosha being a spoiled brat. She was being extremely inconsiderate and selfish, provided nothing was wrong and she was just being distant. Candice shared her concerns with Swave, who always was an ear for her problems. He was kind and understanding; she couldn't have invented a better boyfriend. She was constantly being surprised with flowers and gifts by overnight delivery. He was always posting poems and inspiring quotes on her Facebook page. They text-messaged and sent pics to each other's phones. The relationship was on a natural high, and both were enjoying the ride. There was no mistaking it; these feelings were growing. Day by day their relationship got stronger and deeper. She even told Mom and Dad about Eric Hawkins—his business savvy, his vision, and the employment opportunity. They were pleased and wanted to meet this guy who had captivated their intelligent daughter. "He must be a real great person," was Mom's reply!

The whole time Swave and Candy chatted on Facebook and Yahoo, Tosha invaded her privacy by using Candy's password. She had known the password for months and always peeked at her account.

Tosha had learned the password by looking over Candy's shoulder while typing. The envy turned into jealousy, and the jealousy turned into rage. Tosha couldn't understand why all the blessings from God flowed Candy's way. In her mind, good things weren't in the cards for someone that wasn't a Goodie Two-shoes. The more Tosha read what Swave posted on Candy's wall, the more she wanted him; he was so caring and compassionate—the makeup of a great lover—and she wanted a taste of his chocolate. Tosha's wheels started to turn; maybe it was time to give Big Sis a call. It was time to implement a plan to knock her sister off that high horse. When it was all said and done, she would sleep with Candy's man. The relationship with Young Heat proved to be a planted seed. Now with the negative roots embedded, she was revealing the fruits. The fruits of treachery and deceit were a part of her anatomy. Tosha turned off YH's laptop and sat back in the chair. "Enjoy your fun for now, my dear sister, 'cause it's coming to an end."

Tosha vowed to turn Candy's world upside down with a vengeance, all because she felt Candice put a man and career over the relationship with her sister.

The Naspus Security Company was an European anticrime unit headed by Inspector Bill Myers, a German ex-police officer known throughout Europe for getting his man. Single, no children or family, he was dedicated to fighting crime. Restoring order to criminal situations was his specialty. Based in Berlin, Germany, the company had the support of all European countries. The security company was founded and ran by Bill. After a wave of high-stakes crime sprees in Europe, Bill decided to use his influence and expertise in helping to solve these crimes. He had an outstanding arrest record and impeccable conduct performance on and off the job. Not to mention numerous high-profile cases he solved. Bill was a decorated officer with more commendations than the chief of police. The level of respect for Bill was high, with the credentials to demand that respect—law enforcement agencies from Spain, Britain, France, Switzerland, Germany, and Ireland. All cooperated with the Naspus Security Company, being in their best interests. He had data of terrorists and thieves internationally. Bill's present investigation was a string of upscale jewelry store robberies (Berlin, Germany; Bern, Switzerland; and Normandy, France). The common factor in all these crimes was the time frame. All were committed at the same time of day (closing time) within two weeks of each other. The other factor was also interesting. When Bill checked the tourist list against passport information, a single name was in all three countries when the crimes occurred. The name Nato Ogunidiran appeared more than once. Bill ran a NCIS background on Mr. Ogunidiran; he had no arrests or criminal history.

Bill learned Nato was a gemologist and worked for the American Gem Society gemological laboratories in Las Vegas, Nevada, America. Nato was a native Nigerian from Lagos, Nigeria. This was the largest city on the continent of Africa, known for its rich natural elements (cocoa, copper, oil, and surprisingly, diamonds). This Mr. Ogunidiran had become a serious person of interest to the Naspus Security Company and Bill Myers. Since Bill took a personal interest in Nato, he was red flagged, putting him on Interpol's Most Watched list, which meant while in Europe, surveillance day and night. This case had become intriguing especially since Nato was flagged entering Dublin, Ireland, with a traveling companion, Ms. Marie Biasi. No criminal history as well, but she was also a gemologist. She managed a jewelry store in Brooklyn, New York—Brightest Star. Bill Myer's intel personnel were fast and efficient. He found out anything about anyone on a dime. Bill was a few steps ahead of Nato, and he was determined to give him the surprise of his life when Nato tried the next jewelry heist. The one detail that really connected all these crimes was the criminal was a masked man. He always dressed and talked as a sophisticated gentleman. He knew exactly what he was looking for, proving he did some homework. He knew what and where the precious stones were kept. He took them and nothing else, a true professional.

Dublin, Ireland, was a lively and fun Irish city. Nato had been there before, but this was the first time for Marie. The two had been there for a week, shopping, touring, and enjoying time together. Marie trained her sister Bambi to watch over Brightest Star while she was away. They dined at several Irish restaurants and frequented the Irish pubs. There was nothing better than drinking Guinness stout in Ireland from a original stout keg. It was different because they served the beer warm instead of cold like in America. Everywhere they went, the Naspus agents were close behind. They even had hotel rooms on the same floor as the couple, Bill, of course, was heading the investigation, taking a hands-on approach to solving the crime. He was assured he was ahead of Nato with the surveillance team. He missed one key element; Nato had another traveling companion. Danril Igelwshi was his first cousin and silent partner in crime. They never talked on the plane and stayed in separate hotels. Both were extremely educated and sophisticated. Different in facial features but identical in height and weight. The whole time in Dublin, Nato knew he was being watched. It was a part of the occupation, knowing your opposition. The whole week, the agents followed Nato. He was conducting countersurveillance to find out who was watching him. While Bill had Nato in his vision daily, Danril was free to roam the streets freely, undetected by the Naspus agents and authorities. As a consequence, the Red Parrot jewelry store was robbed at knifepoint for an exclusive blue onyx diamond, one of a kind. It was worth an estimated two million dollars. The thief knew exactly where the jewel was kept. He was quick and time-efficient, only taking the one stone at closing time, slipping in and out like the great Houdini. There were no witnesses apart from the employees that were present. Security guards were massed and craftily handcuffed, rendering them helpless.

When the silent alarm was activated, he was long gone, disappearing into the streets of Dublin before the police could respond to help the victims. All agents and authorities were alerted to a jewel thief in town. So everyone focused their attention on Nato, which was a mistake. Nato used their intel against them in a brilliant game of cat and mouse. Danril mailed the diamond back to America in a teddy bear wrapped and addressed to Sam Walters's jewelry store in Charlotte, North Carolina. He then rented a car and drove to the next city. He'd stay in a rented safe house for a month, making a full escape from authorities. As expected, when Nato and Marie tried to leave Dublin, they were searched heavily. Bill Myer stood helpless in his confused state of defeat. Nato had outsmarted him, and there was nothing he could do about the scheme. Interpol had to let them go; there was no evidence to arrest him. Nato had the perfect alibi. He was being watched by Naspus Security Team the whole time. Bill went over the statements from the store manager. The thief was tall, neatly dressed, and very eloquent. He spoke English with an African accent and was extremely polite. He wore a mask and only took the one item, the most expensive piece in the store.

"Maybe he had an accomplice? Maybe he was two steps ahead of me?"

Nato Ogunidiran had become more than a lead suspect. He was now a personal target of Bill's. He now saw him as a formidable opponent. He would get Nato if it was the last thing he did. If he came back across international waters, his butt was all Bill Myers's. Bill kept thinking about how Nato smiled mischievously and winked his eye, acknowledging that he was well aware of Bill's presence, presumptuously moving like a true professional criminal. That wink, smile, and face was lodged in Bill's memory bank. He wouldn't be able to rest until Nato was brought to justice.

Nato and Marie arrived at Charlotte Airport on week later, stopping in Nashville, Tennessee, to throw off any additional surveillance, just as a precaution. They took a cab to Walters's jewelry store to meet with Sam. As agreed upon, there was a one-million cash payment for the stone. Sam had already received the exquisite diamond in the mail. He'd make several times that amount by cutting the huge stone. He would cut and set the various pieces in rings, bracelets, and earrings, selling them to his most valued and wealthy clientele. Everyone made out in the scheme, especially Sam. He already had the money in large bills packed in two huge duffel bags. Sue and Helen were curious about the exchange they witnessed but never said a word. Sam walked Nato and Marie out of the store to talk about future projects, which would prove to be a terrible mistake for everyone involved in the conversation. They were unaware that they were being watched by Franky Zimbini and Tommy Two Guns. They were bringing Sam some merchandise at the request of the boss, Carmine. Sam didn't know Carmine was sending some stones to sell. So accidentally, the two Italian wiseguys stumbled across Nato and the boss's daughter, with Sam conducting a side business deal. To make matters worse, Nato and Marie were holding hands and even kissed. Sam went back in the store. Nato and Marie got in the waiting yellow cab as a loving romantic couple. Tommy Two Guns was going to hop into action on the spot, twin Glocks drawn, ready to teach the African some respect. However Franky Ziti kept him calm, insisting they talk to Carmine for the proper instructions since it involved his daughter. Better to be safe than sorry. Tommy agreed to the rational decision; they sped off to meet with the boss, Carmine Biasi.

Obviously Sam and Nato were conducting a side business venture. Clearly Carmine knew nothing about their union. The real smack in the face was a black African having a relationship with the boss's daughter. Franky Ziti knew Carmine would want bloodshed but done the right way. He and Tommy headed back to the boss expeditiously. They had an earful for Fat Carmine, because they had just seen a incredible eyeful.

The living arrangement between the three was unusual but comfortable since Young Heat made Tosha a full-time member of the team. Page had to accommodate her new teammate. The house was a three-bedroom home; everyone had their own room. YH wanted the women to have their own privacy although he spent individual time with them all, each respecting the other and playing her position. Jackie never made an issue about the new living conditions. Honestly she liked her freedom, so no waves were made.

YH sat Page and Tosha down, talking about Karen's betrayal, revealing his strong desire to rob Sam's jewelry store, paying Karen back devilishly in the process. There were several different possible scenarios but nothing concrete. Page found herself feeling uneasy at times around Tosha. Once Page saw the pictures of her sister, she wondered what was going through Tosha's mind. Upset with her older sister, it was clear she wanted to commit some act of vengeance, which was the other plan the three sat and pondered about; however, there was nothing concrete as well. Something had to happen soon 'cause YH was spending more than he was taking in. Taking care of the women and his lavish personal desires made him take an unexpected low amount for the artwork. The fence had trouble selling them without consequences. It was time to make a major score and quick. Now that Karen wasn't aboard, he had to gather info another way. There was nothing more unprofessional then trying to make a heist without the correct intelligence. That was the difference between getting away scot-free and getting caught!

Meanwhile on the other side of the coin, Karen let her cousin have the condo, and she moved in with Sam. She had settled in as a soon-to-be married woman, cooking, cleaning, and making ground-shattering love to her fiancé. Learning about his inside circle of secrets daily, Karen was growing closer to his heart. Her plan was working like a well-oiled chain on a bike. She had keys to all the vehicles and access to the entire house. He even opened a joint bank account for the two. Karen's only concern these days was getting pregnant. She made sure at every possible opportunity she was available to him, wearing revealing clothing, looking ravishing at all times. It didn't take much for Sam, and he couldn't get enough of his tenderloin. With or without Viagra, Karen's kitten kept Sam's manhood at full attention. Not only did Karen have his physical needs under control, she catered to him emotionally, listening to his fears and struggles. She knew sometimes it paid off just to be an ear, along with full-body and feet massages. Sam didn't realize how much he missed having a woman in his life until Karen walked into his life unexpectedly. He honestly fell in love with her and the idea of being a married man again. He hoped that Keri and Kelly would give their full blessing. Sam was the happiest he ever was in years. God took Mary Margret, but now he had Karen!

It took weeks and weeks of trying to time her ovulation period just right. Finally it paid off in a major way, the perfectly planned way. She took a home pregnancy test then went to the doctor to confirm. Karen was a few weeks pregnant. She had achieved her goal, and it would be gold at the end of her rainbow. After years of being extremely careful not to get pregnant, now she planned this to advance in the game. Playing to win—nothing else mattered. Now a son was needed to properly seal the deal. To have Sam's son would ensure that half or more of his wealth would be her own. No one, not even his daughters, could stand in her way.

The next task was breaking the news to Sam and expediting the marriage. To break the news properly, she made his favorite meal (spaghetti with spicy red clam sauce, Italian focaccia bread, and Merlot wine), set the table, and lit some candles for a romantic setting. Karen made sure her appearance was appealing, wearing an Elie Tahari evening dress. She checked her reflection in the mirror, amazed by her evolving appearance. She looked like a respectable woman who was a wife and mother. Well, it wasn't yet definite, but she was doing her part to make it a reality. One thing was for certain—that huge twenty-five-carat ring on her finger was a fact. Also that growing child in her womb was another. All she had to do was get legally married to tie together all loose ends.

Sam walked in the house to a great-smelling aroma. He was half-Italian on his mother's side. He grew up with many authentic Italian meals and knew the smell like the back of his hands. Sam loved Italian food; it was his favorite. He walked into the kitchen to find his loving fiancée standing over the stove. He walked up behind her, kissing the back of her neck. She turned around and kissed him back softly. Looking into each other's eyes, both said "I love you" to the other. Karen guided Sam to the table and poured him a glass of wine, disappearing into and reappearing from the kitchen with two plates of the great-smelling meal. She sat across from him and said grace. They began to eat and converse about their day apart. The food was great, and the wine was sweet. The atmosphere was loving and so peaceful. After the main entrée, Karen served Cannolis and imported cappuccino with Bailey's and Kahlua. Sam was in heaven—his favorite meal and dessert. Reaching over and holding Karen's hand, he said, "Thank you for an excellent dinner, sweetheart." She smiled and stood up and walked over to kiss his balding forehead. Then she took his hand and held it against her stomach, looking into his eyes. It took a minute for his mind to click; when it did, a smile came on his face. She smiled back, knowing he was happy. Karen said, "I'm carrying Samuel Walters Jr." He got to his feet, hugging her with joy, kissing her lips, then kissing her stomach. "You've made me so happy, Karen. I love you so much, darling!"

Inside, Karen was jumping for joy!

The thought of another child was adventurous and appealing, especially the thought of having a son. A Junior, for that matter—it meant another chance at youth for Sam. Married to a beautiful woman half his age and another child basically was him drinking from the fountain of youth. He was so happy the thought overtook everything on his agenda, so much that Sam arranged for him and Karen to elope, to jump the broom in the city of Las Vegas.

He surprised her with first-class seats on Continental Airlines. Once in Las Vegas, they stayed at the MGM Grand Hotel. Karen was overjoyed about getting married. The little white chapel was the place they exchanged marriage vows. He wore a burgundy Pierre Cardin linen suit. She wore a burgundy-and-gray Yves Saint Laurent linen dress. The witness was the wife of the Justice of the Peace. Looking each other in the eyes, they recited their vows. He put a diamond wedding band on her finger, and she put one on his finger. They kissed, and he rubbed her stomach with a smile on his face. It was now official—she was Mrs. Karen Walters. She had played the cards right, played them to win a championship like Michael Jordan. In a short amount of time, she had attached herself to a millionaire. She married him, and now she would have his baby, a large bank account, and access to a fleet of European cars. She would live in a mansion and be able to shop anywhere she wanted. Life was good, and she had visions of it getting even better.

Honeymoon night was a thriller, and Sam didn't spare any expense to make his new bride happy. They stayed in the honeymoon suite complete with a dozen red roses, several bottles of Dom Pérignon, imported chocolate from Belize, strawberries, blueberries, and white grapes. Karen being the bride and pregnant, Sam catered to his queen. He only allowed her to drink a small amount of alcohol (two glasses). He, considering, had sparkling apple cider chilling. She lay on a bed of rose petals as Sam poured baby oil all over her body. He massaged her body from her temples to the soles of her feet, taking his time, then licking her innermost private spot. She screamed with pleasure as her body enjoyed the sensation. His tongue pleased every inch of her sensitive body organs—her breasts, her belly button, her clitoris. This was her day, and Sam was making sure she enjoyed the whole day. Karen wanted to please him as well, so after her second orgasm, Karen returned the favor with a sense of pride. Sam lay on his back, and Karen poured oil all over him, teasing his naked body from head to toe. She started to massage his manhood as it rose to attention. Then she slipped it into her wet mouth, rendering him weak and helpless with each touch of her tongue. Just when he couldn't take it anymore, Karen stopped and allowed the moment to become timeless. She got on top of Sam and began to work her magic. He couldn't last long and released into her already pregnant juicy kitten, finding out for himself that the folktale was true—pregnant loving is the best loving in the world. They made love several times in several different ways. Karen and her husband fed each other fresh fruit. He drank Dom P, and she drank sparkling cider. The night couldn't have been any better. They fell asleep in each other's arms, listening to Toni Braxton's CD, Karen's favorite song, "I Love Me Some Him." They were officially a married couple.

The tour was weeks from coming to an end. The crew had passed through Indiana, Ohio, Illinois, and Michigan and now was in St. Louis, Missouri. Just as promised, Swave caught a flight to St. Louis, surprising Candice with a special visit. She wasn't expecting him to fly to her side for a much-needed visit. In their last phone conversation, she told him they were booked at a venue called Selects in the heart of St. Louis. DJ Nice was rocking the house; Silvia and Wanda were selling lots of merchandise. Pierre was amazing as always, capturing the fun on photo.

Leslie and Mia gave a combined effort in making Candice the absolute standout in the club. She didn't want to wear any other designer except Eric "Swave" Hawkins. Respecting Mia's decision as to wardrobe, she wore a Roberto Cavalli minidress, shoes by Versace, and her hair and nails were impeccably done to perfection. Carl Mills was there to promote his side venture, Action the energy drink. Candice was drinking her traditional cranberry juice, posing for the camera. Everyone was having a ball, talking business and mixing as the song by T-Pain started to play, "Bartender." Swave made his entrance with all eyes on him. He was wearing a Palm-Tree original tailored suit, fragrance by Giorgio Armani (Acqua di Gio). He turned heads headed toward his lady. When Candice noticed him, she put the drink down and ran to give him a hug. They kissed as if no one existed or was around them. He looked into her eyes and whispered, "I miss you."

She whispered back, "I miss you too."

Carl Mills watched from afar, gulping down his drink in an emotionally disappointed rage. Leslie momentarily had a fantasy of her and Swave. Her train of thought was broken when Candice told Leslie she needed a fifteen-minute break to talk to her man. They walked outside the club to have some privacy. Candice began to tell him his surprise visit was special. He asked if she could get away for a mini vacation. It seemed like the timing was perfect. They had already planned to rest for a week then head to the West Coast, a modification made by Carl Mills to save face for the extra workload. Well, it seemed like it would work against his plans of spending time alone with Candice. She smiled at the thought of being alone with Swave for a week. Acting optimistically, he handed her two first-class tickets to Las Vegas. The sound of Las Vegas and this sexy tall, dark, handsome hunk sounded like music to her ears. They walked back inside hand-in–hand, telling Leslie and Carl she would be leaving after the venue.

No luggage, only the clothes on her back, Candice flew with Swave to Las Vegas. He promised to take her shopping once in Sin City. She couldn't care less; just being with him was enough. He reserved a room at the MGM Grand Hotel. They arrived at night when the city was alive. Bright lights and plenty of action, Sin City definitely didn't sleep. This was their first vacation together as a couple. Hearing about the famous MGM Grand and its amenities made it the obvious place to stay as a tourist. The hotel had numerous restaurants, clubs, and clothing stores and round-the-clock action and concerts. Of course, the casino was the biggest attraction. Their first stop after checking into the suite was shopping. She wanted to check out the local boutiques, and of course, Macy's. She loved Macy's and had déjà vu thinking about her shopping trip in New York with Tosha. She shook it off and concentrated on the present. Candice had her own money, but Swave insisted on paying. She bought enough clothes for a week and sexy underwear and lingerie. They went to the nail salon and both got manis and pedis. Candice had the prettiest size-six feet he had ever seen. This was a plus, especially with him having a foot fetish. Just looking at them made Swave want to give her a foot massage. Shopping for clothes always inspired Swave to create the best. He also used the boutiques he shopped at as an inspiring prototype. He knew he would do and be better than his competitors.

Shopping had them both hungry, so they ate at a café in the hotel called Red Café, specializing in organic cuisine. She ordered a portobello mushroom sandwich and mashed potatoes with mushroom gravy. He had a vegetable plate (cucumber, corn, zucchini, squash, okra, and corn bread). They both drank homemade raspberry tea. The meal was great, and the quality time together was endearing. The plan for the first day in Sin City was to enjoy each other. There was no time frame in this beautiful city of lights. Vegas lived up to the much-talked-about hype—Las Vegas, Sin City, the city that never sleeps.

There was a late-night concert by Toni Braxton, who was one of Candy's favorite R & B singers. They planned to go take showers, change, and go see the diva perform. Candice took her shower first, enjoying the violet scented body wash Swave purchased at Bath & Body Works the day prior. While bathing, she rubbed her kitten, thinking how wonderful he'd feel inside her canal. The thought took her away for a moment. She returned to consciousness when he knocked on the door, really wishing he could join her in the shower. She walked out of the bathroom face flushed with emotion and lay on the bed with the sexy underwear he had purchased. He presented her with yet another surprise—a beautiful red one-of-a-kind Palm-Tree dress. It was made by the hands of the designer Swave especially for Candice. A crisscross-strap top, open sides, and fitted waist, length just below the knees—it was absolutely amazing. It was tailor-made just for Candice.

Candice squeezed him tight, and they kissed uncontrollably. Swave hopped in the shower and bath as well. He washed with Giorgio Armani shower gel and shampoo. He walked out wrapped in a towel; her heart skipped a beat. She didn't say a word, euphoria running through her body, directing him to the bed and laying him down. She began to lotion his entire nude body with Armani lotion. Giorgio Armani was his favorite designer outside of himself. His ripped abs and firm chest were so sexy; she wanted to lick every inch of his body. Somehow she held her composure until the right moment. They laughed, knowing it wouldn't be long before the fireworks went off.

They both got dressed viewing each other. She wore the Palm-Tree original with black Versace pumps. He wore a red-and-white silk shirt and red linen pants and black Mauri gators. Of course his outfit was designed and tailored by his mind and his hands. They looked incredibly fabulous together as a couple. Candy took a photo with her digital camera, sending it straight to Facebook for the world to see. The finishing touches were the fragrances: Chanel No. 5 for her, and Armani Acqua di Gio for him. She put the camera in her Chanel handbag. They headed to the concert dressed to kill, stepping like two people with a purpose. Watch out, MGM Grand, here comes the hottest couple in Las Vegas ready to burn the strip to ashes: Ms. Candice Gray and Mr. Eric "Swave" Hawkins!

The moment Karen found out Toni Braxton was at the MGM Grand, it was a no-brainer. The newlyweds would definitely be attending. Having a fabulous time on their honeymoon, Sam was willing to do whatever to please his wife. They had a full day shopping, eating, and playing in the sun. He swam, and she lay out at the pool. Now she wanted to catch a late show by Toni Braxton. So Karen's wish was Sam's command. She went all out with her new black Helmut Lang bodysuit, and a purple blazer, purple pumps by Burberry. Her hair was back in a ponytail, and her nails were polished with a pretty lavender. She looked very stylish, like a Stacy Dash clone. Sam wore his traditional brown single-breasted Brooks Brothers suit, L. L. Bean shoes, and a basic brown-and-tan tie. The only flairs to his outfit were gold cuff links and a Rolex watch. They looked good together in a sugar daddy-mistress kind of way. They headed out to the concert hand-in–hand, Karen swinging her Burberry purse from side to side, and Sam right behind. It would be an evening they wouldn't forget. Honeymoon in Vegas, incredible love making. Now the great and sexy Toni Braxton—what could be any greater than the night ahead of them?

The concert was packed, and every seat was sold out. Swave purchased lower-level seats (E row, seats 5 and 6), which were great seats. They squeezed in through the crowd and found their seats. Candice was so happy to be at the show with her knight in shining armor. They wasting no time taking pictures, which went directly to Facebook. They arrived a half hour early, making sure to find their seats. The seats next to them were empty; she sat her Chanel handbag on the empty seat. Both watched the sea of attractive men and women wearing their best to the show to see the great vocalist. Women tried to outdo each other, and men did the same. Attractive as the many women were, Candice stole the spotlight. The dress Swave designed was a sure headturner. He knew someone would ask Candice where she bought that dress. So it was both a gift and a marketing tool. Swave always thought about business very strategically. This was his passion and how he ate. At the end of the day, it was all about him being successful, becoming a household name no matter what it took. Wherever he was, Swave's mission was to make Palm-Tree Clothing a mega fashion force.

Karen and Sam stopped to play the slot machines before heading to the concert. They had no luck, and Karen started to show her impatience. So they finally went to the concert. It was already in process, and the lights were low. The Braxton sisters were opening for their sister Toni. Once they found the seats, they squeezed in past the already seated viewers to row E, seats 7 and 8. The music was loud, and the lights were rotating.

Reaching the seats, Karen noticed a handbag on her chair. She reached to give it to the woman standing there. The woman attempted to get her bag, and their hands touched. As they looked up into each other's eyes, Karen was speechless. Candice thanked her for handing her the bag. Karen couldn't believe her eyes; it was unanswerable. It was Page, and she looked different; she looked elegant. Why was she here? What was she up to? Who was that fine guy with her? Where were YH and Jackie? These were the thoughts going through Karen's mind. She kept looking at Page or who she thought was Page. Shockingly she didn't look in Karen's direction. Candice was very much into the concert, so Karen tried to talk to her discreetly, to no avail; she was too busy enjoying the show, taking pictures, holding her male friend, and having a ball. Then the thought came to Karen—maybe it wasn't Page; though she looked so much like her, it was impossible that it wasn't. They say everyone had a twin; well, maybe this was Page's twin. Sam noticed Karen's discomfort and asked what was wrong. She smiled and said she was all right. The main event was underway—the sexy diva, Ms. Toni Braxton.

Applause, applause, applause, applause, applause!

One thing was unequivocally certain, Karen had never known Page to dress so stylish. There was a difference between dressing elegantly and just wearing name brands. Moreover, this woman seemed more mature and business-orientated. Judging from her attire, she was a person who did well for herself.

Uncomfortable as Karen was, she tried to enjoy the concert. The concert was going great. Females were singing along with their idol diva Toni. A key clue that let Karen know this woman wasn't Page—as she sang along to the words of the songs, she actually sounded good. Karen remembered Page couldn't carry a note in a paper bag. Karen and Jackie always teased Page about her nonvocal performances. Page didn't have the ability to sing at all; that alone put Karen's mind at ease. Now she could enjoy the show, singing along with her neighbor. The singing women and the gentlemen gave thunderous applause.

While Toni took a break, there was a brief intermission between sets. This was the perfect time to strike up a conversation. Truth was Karen thought her dress was extraordinary. As she brought it to Sam's attention, he was impressed as well. She complimented her on the dress, and Candice thanked her graciously, giving all the credit to her designer and boyfriend. Swave passed Karen a business card: Palm-Tree Clothing, Eric "Swave" Hawkins, designer and CEO. She handed the card to Sam then asked if he minded creating a dress for her. "Sure," he replied. They exchanged information, and she promised to contact him. Then Sam asked if he made custom-tailored suits. Of course he did, so they both were interested in a custom wardrobe.

The two women talked about their admiration for Toni and how much they loved her music. Karen couldn't believe how much she favored Page. She told Candice she favored a friend back home in Charlotte, North Carolina. Candice opened a new conversation about the Neon tour, revealing she was an advertising model of the Neon Vodka company. However, she was soon to be the face for Palm-Tree Clothing. Karen saw the passion of Candice as she spoke about her job as a model, the same passion she felt about getting those long-term riches.

The concert continued, and the crowd went wild. A special surprise guest appeared to sing with Toni. It was the smooth, cool, talented vocalist, the man who gave Toni her start—Babyface. They sang together, and it was sensationally magical. Then he serenaded the crowd with an amazing solo performance, gave a few red roses away to some women, then walked off the stage. Toni came back and sang her complete new album. The finale was her and the Braxton sisters, with a sizzling a cappella ending. The concert was remarkably marvelous, definitely unforgettable. Karen and Sam enjoyed it, as well as Swave and Candice. Before the couples left, Sam and Karen invited Swave and Candice to have a drink. They accepted, and all made their way out of the concert hall. The destination was the Martini Bar inside the hotel.

People making toasts, cigar smoke, and lots of laughter filled the Martini Bar. The ambience was upscale all the way. Sam, being a gentleman and the elder, ordered for all. Candice drank an apple martini, and Karen, a glass of red wine, which would be all the alcohol she was allowed to drink. Swave drank a Long Island iced tea, and Sam, a single-malt scotch on the rocks, Kentel One. The gentlemen shared a conversation as the women shared their own, each talking about business and life in general. Karen found it easy to talk to Candice. They both liked the same R & B artist and had dreams of being diva entrepreneurs. They exchanged cell numbers, making plans to come back to Vegas. Sam was intrigued by Swave's vision for the fashion business world. He saw an opportunity to invest. Trying not to seem overly eager, Sam asked to see Swave's portfolio. He gave him the website Palm-Tree.com, anticipating a substantial custom sale. He invited the couple to their hotel room to be properly measured. Swave always traveled with his tape measure and chalk. They all enjoyed the evening, making plans to have lunch the next day to conduct business. Swave didn't mention the expenses; they weren't even a concern. He knew from experience that people who wanted custom-made clothes definitely could afford to pay top dollar. The couples had a pleasant evening and went their separate ways.

The music that was performed by Toni and Babyface set the stage for the night. The alcohol did contribute to the feelings they both were having. Once in the room, Swave ran a hot bubble bath with baby oil. He took charge and started to undress Candice. The red dress came off easy as she took the pumps off herself. He stood frozen admiring her curvaceous frame. He undressed slowly, giving her a little striptease. He stood in front of her, kissing her neck. She gently turned her face to the side, giving complete access to her neck. Then he kissed her forehead, then her nose, then her soft lips. Both stepped into the hot water, drifting down as the bubbles covered their bodies. He lay back, and she sat between his legs. They chilled, holding each other, enjoying the moment for what it was— the beginning of a true love affair. While sitting in the tub, Swave's hands explored her body. Soft and gentle he touched her breast, hair, neck, and her moist, ripe kitten, moving his index finger in and out of her love canal. She began to open her legs wide to feel his finger totally. Turning her face toward him, their tongues danced together. She whispering in a low sensual voice, "Please, Swave, please make love to me. I can't take it anymore, I want to feel you deep inside me, baby." Without a word, he rose to his feet, picked her up in his arms, stepped out of the tub, and carried her to the bed. Before he started anything else, he played the CD *12 Play* by R. Kelly.

He kissed her passionately, their wet tongues touching each other. He sucked her bottom lip, then her neck. Her nipples hardened as his hot, wet mouth began to suck those firm C-cup breasts. He sucked then circled the nipples with his tongue, slowly licking down to her bellybutton, teasing it with his tongue, kissing her stomach, then down to her shaved kitten. It was wet with juices flowing to her inner thighs. He opened her legs and separated her virgin slit then began to feast slowly, gently, and intensely, licking from top to bottom, in and out, then back to the top again. She was losing all control of her body. She held his head with her hands as he licked her like an ice cream cone, using his tongue like a finger, writing the alphabet on her clitoris. The precision was driving her crazy. He held her thighs with both hands, writing his name on her kitten with his tongue. Before he could finish, her legs began to shake uncontrollably. She couldn't hold it any longer. She tried to push his head away, but he held on to her thighs. As he sucked on her clit even harder, she screamed at the top of her lungs.

Releasing the first orgasm she had ever experienced with a man, her eyes rolled, and she was totally weak. Candice couldn't move trying to gather her senses back. Swave continued to lick down her legs to her feet, sucking her pretty polished toes. All she could say was, "Swave, I love you, baby. I love you."

Now it was time for him to mount himself on her. Opening her legs, he positioned himself then entered her with a strong, firm thrust. Immediately she lost her breath as he went deep inside her, slowly and tenderly, moving to his own unique rhythm. He pumped, and she pumped back, working her pelvic area. Both were amateurs, but making love to each other came naturally. They would remember this day, the day they lost their virginity. As he moved his body in and out of hers, they looked each other in the eyes. As he sucking on her bottom lip, their tongues danced together.

"I love you, Candice. Ever since the first moment we met, I knew something special was going to happen between us."

"I love you too, Swave, I'm glad I waited to share this moment with you."

They held each other tight as R. Kelly sang in their ears. He went deeper inside her canal; she was overwhelmed. The bittersweet feeling took over her body. He moved faster and faster, deeper and deeper until her fingernails dug deep in his back, holding on for dear life as he boldly put his mark on her kitten until they both couldn't hold their insides any longer. Boom—an explosive orgasm occurred simultaneously, leaving their bodies shaking and physically weak. They weren't virgins anymore; they were now lovers involved in a monogamous relationship, looking toward the future, wondering what their destiny will bring.

"I love you, Candice."

"I love you more, Swave."

The next morning, they both were exhausted and hungry. Swave ordered room service to bring them breakfast. Candice lay in bed posting pictures and love notes to Swave from the iPhone to her Facebook wall. "Eric 'Swave' Hawkins, my one and true love." Pictures from the concert and Las Vegas she posted all over her Facebook page. She even posted a picture of Sam, Karen, her, and Swave at the Martini Bar. She was happy and proud to call Swave her boyfriend. She was sincerely happy she waited for the right man to take her virginity.

Pancakes, turkey sausage, eggs, and grits. Orange juice, milk, and coffee. They ate up a storm then lay back in bed, snuggling and watching TV. This was truly a match made in heaven. Her phone rang, and it was Karen calling to confirm their lunch date. She also wanted to come get measured before their lunch date. They agreed on 11:30 AM, then the call ended.

Swave got up to take a shower. He entered the bathroom, turned on the shower, and got in as Candice lay there thinking about what she recalled Silvia telling Wanda. "In order to keep your man, you've got to suck his manhood. If not, another woman will do it." She leaped out of bed and into the shower with Swave. Without saying a word, she lathered his entire body. She rinsed him off with her washcloth. Then she kneeled at his feet and began to suck slowly. Despite being an amateur, she was doing a great job. She did what came naturally and treated it like a lollipop, imagining it was a Charms Sour Apple, and she went to work.

In and out of her mouth she worked her tongue. Swave was so weak, holding her shoulders for support, playing with her hair as she literally rocked the mic. He couldn't have dreamed of a better way to start his day—standing on his tippy toes, trying to hold back the volcano about to erupt. The wet sensation from her mouth and view of her wet hair and body took its toll. With one last slow slurp, he exploded inside her mouth. She swallowed the love juice like a pro. He was weak and almost fell. Candice helped him up, bracing him against the wall. Then she washed his manhood and rubbed his back. Swave's head was in cloud nine. She had just literally rocked his world. First that tasty, wet, and tight kitten. Now her candy mouth was enough to make a man cry. They held each other, letting the hot water massage their bodies. She was his, and he was all hers. A tremendous chain of events had happened. They had met, fell in love, became lovers, and now enjoyed the ride.

After a long sensual shower, they got dressed and waited for Sam and Karen to arrive. Twenty minutes later, there was a knock on the door. Sam and Karen had smiling faces with bubbly attitudes. Candice greeted them as they came in. Swave offered some orange juice as he started to prepare. Watching him was like witnessing a NASCAR pit crew doing their jobs. He worked with care and precision, using his expertise in the craft. He was very professional as he asked questions about every detail. Sam was very impressed with Swave's knowledge on fashion. While being measured, he picked Swave's brain, wanting to see if his knowledge about business was broad. They talked about marketing, merchandising, and product quality. Sam thought Swave was very knowledgeable about all the subjects. Wasting no more time, he told Swave he wanted to expand his empire into fashion. He was silent for a minute, then asked how he could help with the goal. Sam replied, "Simply create a men's line for my company. It wouldn't affect your sales because yours is women's wear. I'll spare no expense in compensating you. I'm very taken by your brilliant mind and eye for fashion. I would love to be a part of your vision!" Swave was very flattered, but the fact of the matter was his silent partner sold men's wear. The mogul might take it as a form of disrespect. He had to consider all things this would affect. However he also wanted another financial partner in case things went sour with the mogul.

It wasn't a bad idea to have an ace in the hole. It was a two-part long-term goal: build a respected and unique quality brand while becoming a household name. There was an old saying, "It's a mighty poor rabbit who only has one hole to run in." Sam represented another option if the current business plan failed. So Swave chose his words carefully, explaining he needed time to think. Maybe they could do some business in the near future. Sam was cool with that, and Swave cleverly changed the subject.

Finished with Sam, he started to measure Karen. Excitedly she told him she wanted a maternity dress. A maternity line by Palm-Tree—as she talked, he envisioned different styles. Karen revealed she was several weeks pregnant. Candice ran to feel her stomach and gave her a hug. Swave congratulated Sam and shook his hand. As a generous gesture, Swave offered to create and produce the dress for free. Karen smiled as a tear ran down her face. Candice knew for sure she had confidently chosen the right man. Asking about colors and materials, he concluded with a handshake. All business was out of the way. They all were hungry and headed to the sushi bar for lunch. The women's choice—of course the men didn't refuse. While on the elevator, Sam handed Swave his business card with his personal number written on the back and instructions to call if he considered doing business. His marketing tool had paid off. The dress he designed for Candice definitely was worth more than the small amount of material it took to make it.

The food and conversation was a learning experience for Swave. He found out Sam was more than a jewelry expert. He was a financial genius, having had a successful business for over thirty years. He also was an antique and art collector. A sharp guy, someone Swave would love to have in his corner. He made a mental note to call him in the near future.

The women grew even closer over lunch. Sam and Swave watched them picking over their sushi. It was a funny feeling for Karen to befriend someone who looked like a past friend. That's exactly what Page was to her now, the past. Karen had a whole new life, with a new set of friends. She considered herself blessed to have met Sam. He taught her how to think outside the box.

Candice also considered herself blessed to have an extraordinary man like Swave. He was smart, hardworking, and going places. Candy knew she loved him and respected what he stood for, hating that the mini vacation would soon come to an end. The other side of the coin was she had just met a new friend in Karen. Things were really coming together in Candy's young life. Soon she would be working with her prince full-time as the face of the company, taking over the fashion world. Palm-Tree Clothing!

It didn't take Tosha long to see Big Sister's pictures in Las Vegas. The more she gazed at the pictures, the more jealousy and deceit set in her heart. "So you're living the fabulous life with your man. Shopping sprees and kicking it in Las Vegas." The anger grew to be something really unhealthy. The desire to sleep with Swave was on an all-time high. Her childish presumptions blinded her eyesight. Tosha couldn't understand that success wasn't all about looks. It was hard work along with the ability and desire to put that work in to accomplish success. She wanted everything handed to her on a silver platter while Candy had a vision, worked hard, and received the fruits of her labor even though her career was still in the infant stage. Tosha must have viewed those pics for hours, looking at Candy's clothing, the scenery, and how happy she appeared. Swave, by her side, looked like a male model.

"Why couldn't I be as glamorous as Candy? Why does she get all the breaks in life? She's adopted and her life is still better than mine!" Wow, she couldn't believe her mind went there although it was abundantly true. Candy made the most of her situation, and being adopted didn't matter. The important thing was she had two loving parents. The Gray family was very proud of the woman she had become. Tosha, on the other hand, was preoccupied with the fast life and all the negativity it included.

She was still viewing the pictures she'd seen numerous times. Young Heat walked in the room. He was there for his daily ritual, sex. The screen on the laptop caught his attention. The pictures of Candy started turning his wheels. She was Page in the face but far more glamorous. A certain je ne sais quoi was the ultimate difference. He couldn't believe how much they looked alike. There had to be a logical explanation to the similarities. YH kept flipping, then there it was—a picture of Karen and Sam seated with Tosha's sister and boyfriend. He couldn't believe his eyes. "How the hell, and what were they doing together?" It was obvious they were having a good time at a social event, having a ball of a time in the exciting Las Vegas city. The plot just thickened, and Young Heat wanted answers. Karen had changed the game plan in the ninth inning. Discombobulated and not knowing what to make of this new development, all he knew was Tosha's sister was now an absolute target of interest. She would be the key to the heist he was slowly planning. Now that Tosha's big sis was friends with Karen and Sam, Tosha's new job was to get acquainted with her sister again. Somehow, some way, some information was bound to leak. Young Heat wanted to be there to catch it and capitalize.

The curiosity was killing him, and he had to know if they were blood relatives. So YH got a pen and pad and questioned Page about her childhood, leaving absolutely no stone unturned, attaining the name of her adopted mother, Stella Meeks. The adoption agency was in Los Angeles, California—Loving Hope. He wasted no time typing in Loving Hope. com on the Internet, found the phone number, and called. The secretary answered, and he asked for the agency's director. He was transferred to Mrs. Evelyn Carter after a few minutes. His cover was he was the nephew of Ms. Stella Meeks. He was trying to find his long-lost cousin. The family hadn't seen her since his auntie had died. He wanted to find her and see if she had other relatives. Mrs. Carter was silent for a few minutes. Typing on the computer, she then said, "*Oh my.* Oh my my." Young Heat wished she would just spit it out. "Seems this is an unusual case, Mr. . . . ?"

"Mr. Meeks—Travis Meeks," he replied. "Well, Mr. Meeks, I'm not supposed to give information out concerning our former clients. Luckily this wasn't a closed adoption, and seeing how you're trying to locate a family member, I don't see why I shouldn't help you."

Young Heat smiled to himself.

"Looks like the only information I have on Page Meeks, was she went to an orphanage after your aunt died. I don't know her whereabouts since she's now over eighteen. However the interesting thing is she was a twin. The other child was adopted by a couple in Fresno, California. Mr. and Mrs. George and Vanessa Gray."

"Thank you, Mrs. Carter, you've been quite a help in my mission to find my cousin."

Funny it was like a story line to a Lifetime movie. Impossible as it had sounded to a skeptic. The fact was that Page Meeks was a twin and her sister was Tosha's adopted sister. Tosha Gray—that last name would explain a lot. Candice Gray, the up-and-coming fashion model. The season 5 contestant of *Models on the Rise* was, in fact, Paige's twin sister given up by a young mother, and father unknown. Candice was adopted by a young couple from Fresno while Page was adopted by a single mother who died. This was definitely a dramatically challenging situation. He didn't know how to break the news to Page. Tosha, however, sat there and listened in disbelief. This information fueled the fire in her, a burning quest to commit a vindictive act against Candice. In her mind, Candice was the family's favorite, always receiving special treatment for her parents. Which wasn't true, but her envy and jealousy were blinding. Young Heat immediately started to form his most brilliant plan—to accumulate riches and long-term wealth for them all, needing all his women to play their roles to the max. Since Karen's departure, Tosha had to be groomed and coached to maintain her composure, putting money over emotions. Even though it was personal for Page and Tosha, for Young Heat, it was all business as usual. The extra satisfaction would be to outsmart Karen and put her back in place—under his control and back in his stable. "Hmm." Page Meeks and Candice Gray, identical twins from two different coasts and two different worlds. Page—a con woman, thief from the underworld. Candice—a fashion model, good citizen, and sophisticated glamour queen. Two total opposites but one origin. Remarkably unbelievable!

Young Heat took a few moments to gather his thoughts then entered the bedroom where Page slept. He turned on the light, waking her from a deep sleep. Sitting on the edge of the bed, he began talking. Page was still half asleep, trying to focus her eyes. He told her the entire story, leaving nothing to the imagination. He finished; she sat up in bed and began crying. One would think they were tears of joy from finding out she had a living relative, a twin sister for that matter. How lucky can a person be? Surprisingly those tears were tears of hurt and resentment. She thought how miserable her upbringing was in childhood—horrible treatment, molestation, and many hungry nights while her sister lived in the lap of luxury with awesome parents. She instantly wanted revenge in a major way, wanted her sister to hurt like she had hurt for years. Young Heat didn't have to convince her to act accordingly. She volunteered to make Candice Gray pay. So it was now a work in progress. Young Heat would call the plays, and his team would play their positions. He was the coach; Tosha was the quarterback; Jackie, the offensive line. Page was the running back, running all over Candice in hopes of scoring a touchdown.

Carmine Biasi was furious to hear he'd been in the dark concerning his daughter's relationship with Nato. To make matters even worse, Nato was conducting business behind his back. Carmine prided himself as being a mastermind, superior to everyone. He disliked black people, especially Africans. So Nato's actions were a double slap in the face. All things considered, Carmine didn't want to lose his extra income generated by Nato's undeniable skill set. The thought of losing hundreds of thousands was worse than the thought of Nato and Marie. He chose to turn a blind eye until he had no further use for Nato. Then he would sleep with the fishes. Sam, on the other hand, was expendable. Before disposing of him, taking over his business would be logical. So for now, he allowed both to go on like their business deals were still undetected. The ultimate result would be both their deaths. The total takeover of Sam's flourishing jewelry business as well as all other hidden assets. The underboss (Tommy Two Guns and Franky Zimbiti) would start Operation Extortion. The plan was to give Sam several authentic exclusive pieces then stage a robbery carried out by the Biasi street soldiers when Sam couldn't produce the valuables to Carmine. He would offer a cash payment, which Carmine would refuse. Instead he would take a portion of Sam's business as payment if he didn't agree to the terms. Tommy and Franky would make him an offer he couldn't refuse. It was the wiseguys' way of doing business. Eventually Carmine would take full control of the store legally. The tactic was called the gradual takeover.

Carmine talked to his daughter Marie about business; it was hard to keep his composure. She was a very efficient manager, always thinking about the family business. Little did Carmine know and understand Marie was quietly building Brightest Star into a small empire. The collaboration between Nato and Marie was more than a physical relationship. Nato was singlehandedly teaching Marie the art of transferring diamonds from the black market to the mainstream market. She knew eventually Brightest Star would be hers. So she was determined to build the business strong. Carmine never questioned how she ran the business. There wasn't any reason with the books always showing profits. Much as he wanted to say something about Nato, the Don of the New York Ports remained silent. It was amazing how money played a key factor in a family affair. Carmine appeared to be his jolly self toward his eldest daughter, Marie. Lil Carmine was kept out of the loop. He was loyal and a good earner for the family. The downside was Lil Carmine was a hothead, reacting quickly without thinking about the big picture. Tommy Two Guns was Carmine's underboss because of Lil Carmine's character flaw, fueling some animosity between the two wiseguys. Lil Carmine didn't act on his feelings toward Tommy. He was a made man and saved Big Carmine's life, preventing an attempt on Carmine's life. A rival crime family wanted control over the ports. However Tommy Two Guns had a lot to say about the takeover. Winning Carmine's love and complete trust. Loyalty ran deep, so Tommy was Mr. Untouchable to any of Carmine's family members, even Lil Carmine.

The file was thick and contained photos and documents. That proved Karen Matthews used Diana Colby as an alias. The reason for a fictitious identity was to avoid authorities. As part of a crew that cashed stolen checks, ran cons, and did home invasions, she was a professional con artist, part of a three-woman crew. The brains behind the criminals was a guy named Darryl Moffitt, a.k.a. Young Heat. Given the statements from Sam Walters robbery / home invasion, these were likely the perpetrators according to their criminal résumé. He handed the case file to Kelly Walters Phillips. Frank Bruno had once again completed an exceptional investigation, never revealing his sources, which didn't matter because he got the job done. Kelly took a few deep breaths then let it out. She loved her father and wanted to protect him, also the family fortune. A manila envelope was handed to Bruno; he stuffed it in his blazer pocket. payment he didn't have to count. On the contrary, Bruno would've done the legwork for free. Well aware of Bruno's attraction toward her, she made sure to compensate him financially. Now that Kelly had the proof she needed to send Karen Matthews, a.k.a. Diana Colby, packing. Kelly had to contact her father immediately. First she called Keri and filled her in, explaining what she had done to find this information out. Keri didn't approve of Kelly's methods, but she was behind Kelly all the way. Saving Daddy's heart was all that's important. The family business and heirlooms were all at risk of being taken by a deceitful and undesirable con woman,

Sam and his new bride made it back to their home from Las Vegas. The sixty-something powerhouse carried his bride across the threshold.

They left on short notice. Sue and Helen from his jewelry store were the only people who knew. Sam gave them a paid mini vacation as well. He and Karen agreed to turn their phones off during the trip to Vegas. He didn't even tell Keri and Kelly about the marriage, figuring he'd break the news to them once back home. There were several messages on his cell and home phone. As he turned the cell on, it began to ring. It was Kelly calling from the airport in Charlotte. She had flown in to talk to Daddy face-to-face. He answered, and she was hysterical!

"Calm down, Kelly."

"Daddy, why haven't you answered or returned my calls?"

"Because I've been out of town. I just came back."

"Well, I'm at the airport on the way to your house. I need to talk to you. It's very important."

"OK, honey, I have a surprise for you and Keri, so I'll see you in a few."

The line went dead.

"Whatever the surprise Daddy has, it couldn't compare to what I have to show and tell him." Kelly went to the rent-a-car office, got a car, and raced over to talk to Sam.

Kelly drove up in the rented Kia Soul, the only car she could get at the time. Sam greeted her at the door; they hugged for a short while. Then she kissed her dad affectionately. Before she could say a word, Karen entered the room. He quickly pulled her to his side lovingly. Suddenly Kelly noticed the couple's wedding rings. "We have a surprise, Kelly!" She was trying to stop the rapid beating in her heart, looking at the wide smiles on both their faces. Then the words came out as if he were talking in slow motion.

"We're married!" Karen held out the twenty-five-carat ring and wedding band.

"Daddy, please tell me you didn't?" She knew his rash decision would be detrimental to the family's future.

"I also have another surprise, Kelly."

Please God, don't tell me there's more!

He put his hand on Karen's belly and rubbed in a circular motion. Kelly immediately knew what he was going to say. "Kelly, you're going to be an older sister!"

She screamed at the top of her lungs. "Daddy, I need to talk to you alone. Please."

Karen knew she'd be upset, but this was entirely too extreme. He kissed Karen. Then she said, "I'll leave and give you two some privacy," looking at Kelly with a sinister grin while leaving the room. This was terrible; Kelly couldn't understand why. The brilliant businessman, her father, could be so naive.

Kelly assertively told her father she disagreed with his decision. Then she took the file out of her purse, starting the display of her obvious disapproval. She even had photos of Karen and Young Heat at Starbucks. He handed them back to her, unconcerned with the pictures. Kelly told her dad that Diana's name was really Karen, including that she was a lowlife con artist.

Sam sternly defended his wife, acknowledging he knew about her real name, explaining there was a valid reason for her alias. Resiliently, she told Sam Karen was a member of a female crew. She believed Karen was part of the home invasion. He shook his head with total disbelief, then held his daughter tight. "Karen Walters is now my wife and mother to my unborn child. I want you to be happy for me and respect Karen. If not, I will ask you to leave."

Kelly couldn't believe what her loving father, who once worshipped the ground she walked on, was saying to her. It was clear that Karen had sunk her claws deep inside his skin. The only way to defuse the ticking time bomb was with extreme care. This was a sensitive matter, and his feelings were involved. Sam had become very emotional, especially thinking of a possible Samuel Jr. She knew her words couldn't compete with what Karen offered. He was old, lonely, and needy. Karen was the answer to his prayers. So Kelly had to retreat and live to fight another day. She kissed her father's forehead and turned and walked away without even a word. Sam didn't know what that meant, but he stood his ground in his wife's defense. He figured she would come around sooner or later. Kelly was a grown woman with a husband and a life. Dad had to live his life on his own terms.

Within a two-month period, Karen had literally turned Sam's life into something wonderfully new and peculiar. He worked fewer hours and didn't frequent the piano bar anymore. He practiced less and less yoga. The charity work for the Mary Margret Breast Cancer foundation had taken a backseat to Karen. He was totally consumed with her and the pregnancy. Sue and Helen were doing extra work, which started to cause resentment. Keri and Kelly hadn't received phone calls like they normally did. Sam was smitten, and Karen had him in the palm of her hand. He took time to go with her to doctors' appointments, making sure she had enough rest and ate properly. This was a second chance for him to be a family man. Keri understood her father's actions, being a former psychology major. She saw things from a psychological standpoint. She knew Sam had lost his beloved wife, and being alone deeply scared him. This was a way to heal his hurting heart, a chance to give him purpose, will, and a desire to live. To live life and have no more regrets. Keri saw things analytically, and Kelly wasn't that type of thinker. At the end of the day, it was his life.

He had the prerogative to live it how he wanted. Karen knew she had him right where she wanted him to be. Karen had single-handedly risen from a stable mare to a pretty and well-manicured show horse in the position of power and dominance. All she had to do now was produce a son, a Samuel Jr. and heir to the family fortune. That would definitely be the nails in the daughters' coffins.

Surprisingly Karen stayed in contact with Candice. They talked at least three times a week. As weird as it seemed at first, Candice favored her old associate. Their friendship grew into a mutual respect. Karen even thought about having Candice as her child's godmother. She was completely overwhelmed, receiving not one but seven stylish maternity dresses from Swave. Different colors and styles, complete with the Palm-Tree emblem. The cost was totally free, only charging for Sam's suit—one thousand dollars, which was an incredibly discounted rate for a signature Swave creation. The olive green blazer had long lapels and four buttons and pants pleated with banker's cuffs. He even made a 100-percent cotton French-cuffed dress shirt and an olive green-and-gold silk tie. The suit was impeccably crafted. Steve Harvey would've loved to wear this work of art. Sam was speechless at the sight of his tailor-made suit. He knew Swave was talented, but this was acute—taking time out of his busy schedule to craft the dresses for his wife and the suit, shirt, and tie for him. It truly made Sam want to do business with him, even more than before. So he decided to use Karen as a mouthpiece in Candy's ear, knowing that with his connections, power, and money and Swave's talents, he could reinvent himself as a fashion mogul. It was never too late to try something new. Creating another line of income, and building a brand—all the more to build and leave to his son and loving wife. Sam was on a mission, and Swave would be the main contributing factor. That is, if he considered going into business with Sam Walters.

Instructing Tosha had become a daily ritual, including physical interaction. Young Heat schooled her on the game; she was getting the con artist lesson 101. He also spent time with Page, making sure she was stable-minded. His finances were being depleted quickly. Taking care of Jackie, Page, and Tosha was very expensive, along with his personal cost of living. So the execution of the plan was very important. He threw together several scenarios in his mind, but nothing was completely appropriate. He didn't know if Tosha was capable of handling the monkey hustle. Jackie and Page weren't really thieves with finesse. They really put the gorilla game in full effect. The cornerstone to the whole operation was Tosha. She had to reinvent herself to Candice; winning back her trust wouldn't be easy. It was imperative that she started somewhere and soon. A better relationship between the two was essential to the plan's success. If Candice could be used as a pawn to manipulate Karen, some useful information about Sam's treasures could be gained. Young Heat's thoughts were that Sam had possession of precious pricey diamonds. That was the main focus; everything else would be secondary. YH didn't want to strike at a bad time. Timing was everything and very sensible. Running a risk of striking when the iron wasn't hot wasn't an option. Careful planning and an inside presence was important. Young Heat was a perfectionist, and that's how he had longevity in the game.

Young Heat realized what to do and how to do it. The only obstacle was talking Tosha into cooperating in this plan. First things first, she had to reestablish her relationship with Candice. It was ironic how things unfolded. For some strange reason, Tosha viewed Page as her sister since her true identity was revealed. Tosha felt bad about sharing a sexual experience with Page. Both were curious but only indulged to please Young Heat even though Tosha was the one who wanted to live her fantasy. Now they were on one accord, planning a horrible act of vengeance against a good-hearted person.

The phone rang several times before Candice picked up. She knew it was Tosha from the caller ID. Answering with a pleasant voice, Tosha tried to hide her attitude by sucking on a Jolly Rancher. Tosha asked how she'd been, telling Candice she was missed.

"Why didn't you return my calls?"

Tosha replied she was still upset about their argument. Candice was still on the last leg of the tour headed to Portland, Oregon; Seattle, Washington; then California, hitting the bay area, then ending in LA. She was busy working double shifts, promoting the Action energy drink and Neon Vodka. Tosha asked Candice if they could spend some time together after the tour. Candice was very vague in her answer saying, "Let's play it by ear 'cause I was headed back to New York to start work at Palm-Tree Clothing." Tosha was hot but wore a mask to conceal her attitude.

When the conversation ended, Candy felt guilty for not planning a visit with Tosha. She wanted to see her sister, but her career was taking off. It wasn't like she'd never spend time with Tosha. The timing just wasn't right for her now. Besides, Tosha never even talked about school or a career path. Even though that was her sister and she loved Tosha, Candy wanted to surround herself with proactive people, a quality that she was going to miss from the Neon staff for their drive and dedication to making the tour a success. She would miss them, but life was about change and evolution. It was time for her to spread those wings and rise to the next level. Candy finally told Mr. Mills, Leslie, and the rest of the crew about her future plans to work for the Palm-Tree Clothing company. She knew some would think her relationship with Swave encouraged the decision. Fact of the matter was Lola Hemmingway endorsed her for the job. Pam Orchard accepted Lola's recommendation. Candy and Swave's seeing each other was a coincidence. She was offered the job before they started to date. Rumors already started to fly, especially after their trip to Las Vegas. It was obvious to everyone that Swave had made love to her. She was a totally different person in attitude and work ethic. Still professional, but the excitement wasn't there anymore. Swave was on her mind noticeably. She relived their romance daily in private, masturbating in the shower, thinking about all the erotic acts they shared. Anyone could see Candy was in love. He was her first and her only.

Progress at Palm-Tree Clothing was really happening quick. Swave's creativity had been elevated since his trip to Vegas. Everyone noticed he was a new man. Actually, he was now a man with a certain someone special. Even Kym teased him about losing his virginity. Most people didn't believe he was still a virgin. Kym knew the truth; she was his best friend, sharing everything with her about his love life.

The flagship stores in New York and New Jersey were flourishing. It was now time to take the company overseas. He was excited about the move to Asia. He couldn't wait until Candy served her term with the vodka company. He and Pam Orchard sat around brainstorming about possible strong marketing techniques. Pam was a wizard in marketing, among other things. That's why she was a part of the team. Swave knew the profitable work she did for Harden Clothing. If she made that small company into a major brand, he knew Palm-Tree would go to the moon under her guidance. Things couldn't be better. His career had taken off, and the company was growing. He remained humble and levelheaded from his upbringing.

Kym was doing fine with her pregnancy going strong. The accessory line had doubled in size and profits. His silent partner was happy with the numbers, earning quick returns on his initial investment.

The biggest plus in his life was an angel. He had every intention of making her his wife one day. It was time to build up the company so he would be able to give her the world. Hustle, hustle, hustle hard and make Palm-Tree bigger than any dream he had conceived.

On the bus headed to Portland, Oregon, Candice was bored, so she called Karen. She answered the phone while lying in the bed, having her feet massaged by Sam. They laughed and talked about movies, music, and fashion. Sam just listened, happy his wife had a friend she could talk to. Candice told Karen how she couldn't wait to get back to her man in New York. They traded erotic stories about their lovemaking. The typical women's talk that they shared was enchanting, filled with intense delight, making Sam start rubbing Karen's kitten. She immediately became horny and wanted to be pleased. Sam slid her panties down and started licking that hot, wet kitten, trying to hide the pleasure she was receiving but couldn't hold her moans. Candice caught the message and told her to call back later. They ended the conversation.

The emotions ran deep, and Candy decided to call Swave. He was in the Gallery with Kym and Pam talking business. Candy asked if he could step away for a minute or two. He did, and she began talking erotic over the phone. He went in his office and sat down, listening to her sexy sensual voice. She wasn't alone, but he was, and he started to massage his shaft along with her seductive voice. He took it out and started to masturbate, thinking of their shower ordeal in Vegas. She told Swave to imagine it in her mouth as she made sucking sounds over the phone. His mind was in the moment, the moment, the memory, and her voice was enough. He couldn't contain the juices that boiled from within. He exploded into a napkin as his breathing grew harder. He opened his eyes, feeling foolish 'cause Pam was standing at the door watching. "Wooh."

He didn't hear her knock, so she had invaded his privacy by walking in his office for a sure surprise, getting an eyeful of the steamy phone-sex episode. Pam had always thought Swave was attractive but not quite her type. Nonetheless, she gladly wouldn't mind having a brief affair with the boss after seeing the size of his magic stick. They locked eyes as he jumped to conceal his self. She smiled and apologized, walking out of the office. How embarrassing was that?

He remembered he still had Candy on the phone. He didn't tell her about Pam, keeping it a secret. He thanked Candy for the momentary escape from reality. Candy told him she couldn't wait to see him. They told each other they loved each other ending the call. Swave felt foolish, but he was satisfied with the release. He was crazy in love with his sweetheart and girlfriend, Candice. He freshened up in the bathroom then walked back to the gallery with his head held high. After all, he was the boss; Pam couldn't fire him. He had never disrespected her or any women he employed. As far as he was concerned, it would be their little secret. That is, if Pam kept it between them. She had no intentions of telling, but she did want some of that chocolate. Too bad for her and fortunately for Candice, Eric "Swave" Hawkins was a one-woman man.

Sitting in his den drinking coffee, reading an investigation file from the Dublin, Ireland, robbery, Inspector Bill Myers started and ended his days consumed with this case. It had become personal because the perpetrator had toyed with him, looking over this case with a fine-toothed comb. Nothing was making a lick of sense. How did this criminal anticipate being under surveillance while in Ireland? Furthermore, how could a thief armed with only a knife casually walk in and out of the jewelry store and have enough time to take the most expensive piece in the store? Was there an inside leak? He knew exactly where and what he came there to get. Bill ran full background checks on all the employees. Nothing out of the ordinary, mostly traffic violations. No felony arrests or convictions for anyone. Then he watched the video surveillance tape a couple dozen times. The perpetrator had the same build as the main suspect, Nato Ogunidiran. However, it wasn't possible for Nato to be in two places at once. He was under heavy around-the-clock surveillance. This case was a brain teaser and the fourth major jewelry robbery in Europe within a short time span. Bill was determined to crack this case, put whoever was responsible for the crimes behind bars. He checked the airline list for international travelers once again. There it was—a needle in the haystack. The name Danril Igelwshi, who had traveled on the same flight. That was it, Bill had to get dressed and head to the office. There was a new break in the case.

The Naspus Security Company had contacts and resources all over Europe. They had access to a black-ops special unit trained in antiterrorism warfare and international criminal affairs. Bill was prepared to use all resources in his arsenal to catch and help convict these clever criminals. He faxed the name Danril Igelwshi to his secretary for a background check. Also his last known address, and anything the system had on this guy. When he arrived, the information was already compiled on his desk.

"Interesting" was all Bill had to say. Mr. Igelwshi had been a recent tourist in Berlin, Germany; Bern, Switzerland; Normandy, France; and Dublin, Ireland. He was a native Nigerian and lived in America. No known means of income but known to live in several expensive properties. What was even more interesting was his mother's maiden name—Ogunidiran! Bingo, that was the connection: Danril Igelwshi and Nato Ogunidiran were cousins. Not just cousins but first cousins. Now he knew who they were; he just needed to catch them red-handed. Since the crimes were in Europe, they were safe in the United States. Bill still didn't have enough for an arrest but wouldn't give up. He vowed to get them if it was the last thing he did. He thumbtacked pictures of the cousins on his bulletin board. His latest focus was the cunning Nigerian jewel thieves.

Nato Ogunidiran was a very intelligent criminal. He didn't steal for the need or greed. It was the thrill and challenge the adventures offered—to outsmart the authorities and toy with them. The one thing he did that his adversaries found foolish was that he traveled under his real name often. Nato was always a few steps ahead and used that against them. Knowing he'd been red-flagged, he used himself as a diversion from the actual crime that was being committed. This was one of the reasons Marie found him attractive. He had a truly brilliant mind and made a prosperous living with his craft, hundreds of thousands in abundance. He lived an opulent lifestyle in several different countries while making large headlines in Europe, so much that the United States started to pay attention. He had a squeaky clean record and flew under the radar in the States. Nato lived very well, having an appetite for the finer things in life. A far cry from his humble beginnings. He had come a long way from the dirt-poor village in Nigeria and was now a well-polished, sophisticated gentleman who spoke six different languages. The huge amount of US currency he made was astonishing. Nato also was a cash cow for Carmine Biasi and Sam Walters. Both men counted on him to seek, steal, and deliver the goods. Little did both men know, Nato was using them as means to direct cash. He was planning to disappear after a few more jobs. He was smart enough to know that both men's greed would eventually turn on him. Sam would want a seventy-thirty split because of the blackmail leverage. Carmine was a fat, greedy crime boss who never was satisfied with what he made.

Marie Biasi was merely a pawn in Nato's chess game. He had used her from the beginning, seducing her in college once he found out she was a daughter of a crime boss, knowing she would be connected to the dark underworld. So he never planned on taking her with him when the game was over. Surprisingly that sweet Italian loving made him have a change of heart.

Carmine Biasi summoned Nato to meet him at the Green Grass golf driving range. Much as Nato hated being in his presence, he knew it was sensible to keep up regular appearances. When he arrived, the normal crew of subordinates was around Carmine like he was the president. He made his way through the soldiers, head held high. They all watched him very closely. Tommy Two Guns and Franky Ziti were both present with very serious looks on their faces. He shook Carmine's hand and was ordered to sit down. Carmine had a golf club in his hand and a Cuban cigar in his mouth. Pointing the club at Nato's face, he told him he needed his skills in acquiring a very special piece of jewelry. It was a brooch worn by Jackie Onassis, given to her by second husband Aristotle Onassis. It had been sold to a jewelry collector from the family estate. The owner, Jesse Palmer, had purchased the jewel for his wife, Beth Palmer, for their fiftieth wedding anniversary. The couple lived in the mountains of North Carolina (Ashville). It's rumored that she admired the piece so much she kept it close at all times. The piece was a beautiful blue diamond set in platinum and worth an untold amount. Of course, it's significance was being priorly owned by Jackie O.

Nato took a deep breath and then exhaled. He knew Carmine wanted that brooch. He also knew if he didn't attempt the caper, Carmine would feel disrespected. Nato always did his dirt out of the country, so this was a change in his pattern. Nato knew Carmine could easily send a soldier to kill him. With several pairs of eyes on him, he replied with the appropriate answer. Carmine smiled and tapped Nato on the face as Italians often did, a sign of approval. Nato told Carmine he'd be in touch. He had to gather information on the job. He walked away scared and even more ready to make a run for the border.

Nato called his partner in crime and cousin, Danril, told him they had a job to do. He needed to gather some info for the job. They agreed to meet later on that night to head for Ashville, North Carolina, to get things started. Nato felt secure when Danril was on a job with him. He was trained in guerilla warfare, a weapons specialist, an electrical engineer, and a computer wizard. Danril was the complete package as a criminal. They had more than enough money to start a business and walk away from the game scot-free. It was the thrill that kept them both on the hint for the next conquest.

From the moment Nato told Danril about the project at hand, he immediately started his research. It was amazing what one could find out from the computer, the Internet. The Palmers were an elderly couple and extremely wealthy, longtime residents of Ashville and known in the community for charity. Same home for more than thirty years. Both retired schoolteachers. Jesse Palmer made his fortune in the stock market among other lucrative investments like commercial real estate. No children, so they spend the bulge of their money as jewelry, antiques, and art collectors. They appeared in the *Art Digest* for their collection, which was held in the American/European Art Gallery in New York. Some of the features were Monet, Pissaro, and Toulouse-Lautrec.

Of the many possible treasures they could steal, only the brooch was on their minds. One thing about Nato that gave him longevity in crime was he was disciplined in taking only what was on the menu. Never wasting aimless time, always moving efficiently. Danril followed his older cousin's command since childhood. Nato was and had always been a leader although Danril was more technical and hands-on. Nato was the clairvoyant thinker and voice of reason. The two had an unbreakable bond. They loved and trusted each other immensely. The loyalty between the two ran deep below the skin. It was a blood bond between two sisters' children. First cousins, partners in crime, and best friends.

The Palmer home was a mini mansion, quaintly modest, not where you would expect people of their wealth to live. They were pleased just being comfortable in their space. The two men watched to see if anyone came to and from the residence. There was no movement for nearly two days and nights. They were alone and didn't interact with many people. Danril brought all sorts of devices for the task at hand.

The third day of surveillance, they decide to test the waters. That night, they parked down the road from the house. The bedroom light gave away which room they slept in. After waiting a reasonable amount of time, both men approached the house cautiously. This was Nato's area of expertise, a skilled locksmith. He pulled out his tools and started to pick the lock. Both wore black clothes and wore masks and gloves. Nato noticed they had an alarm system. Danril assured him it wouldn't be a problem. The door lock clicked when he turned the knob. Danril rushed in with a flashlight, finding the alarm pad. He pulled out an electronic scrambler and attached it to the pad, working his magic expeditiously in a matter of seconds. The security code appeared on the screen. He punched in the numbers to disarm the system. Thumbs up, now they headed toward the bedroom. There were no dogs to hinder the mission. Up the stairs quickly and quietly, they moved in unison, flashlights in hand guiding the way clearly. Nato turned the doorknob opening the door. There they laid the elderly couple sound asleep. It was a large bedroom with a super huge bed. The midnight marauders went straight to the dresser, looking through her jewelry box. Nothing, there were several nice pieces that looked expensive. It didn't matter; they were there for something in particular. He also had a jewelry bow with watches, rings, and coins. They looked at each other, then Nato thought about her nightstand.

He glided over to her side of the bed and opened the drawer to her nightstand. There it was plain as daylight. He grabbed the brooch, giving Danril a thumbs up. They quietly exited the room. Even in the dark, the diamond looked exquisite. They were out of the house without a sound. The mission was a success. Within a half hour, they were headed back to the home front with the diamond in hand. The Palmers didn't even know they had had visitors plundering. She would think, maybe with her aging mind, she had misplaced the jewel and would look for it relentlessly. Another caper in the history books. He would now give Carmine the stone, casually disappearing from existence, cool and quiet. Nato thought about the line Frank Lucas's connect in Asia gave him, from the movie *American Gangsta*: "Quitting while you're ahead is not the same as quitting." That was food for thought as he drove on the highway back home. Maybe one last European score large enough to ride off in the sunset. He would be loaded with enough money to live the extravagant lifestyle he was accustomed to living.

The next day, Nato met with Carmine at an Italian restaurant, Cinelli's. Of course Tommy and Franky were present at his side. Nato handed the brooch to Carmine in a white napkin. Carmine examined the brooch, confirming it was the real deal. Then Carmine told Nato that after the meal, Franky Ziti would give him payment. The sooner the better; Nato wanted to get away from his fat Italian business partner. Danril watched from the bar just in case the men had other plans for Nato. He was prepared to go to war for his cousin. It might be a losing battle, but he still would wage war. Carmine handed the brooch to Tommy, telling him, "Get this to Sam the jeweler, and activate part two of the plan." Tommy left to do his duty for the boss. Franky Ziti walked Nato out of the restaurant to pay him. Carmine sat in front of a big plate of pasta like the world was his own. Now the aim was to take Sam's business, one piece at a time. The name would be the same, but Carmine wanted to secretly control the thriving jewelry store for the Biasi family. He wished Brightest Star did the numbers. The Walters Jewelry store did in a month's time. This way he would repay his enemies for their treason, making money at the same time from their labor, starting with Sam, then Nato to follow. Marie would be assertively reprimanded, but that was about all. After all she was blood, and blood was thicker than water.

Tommy Two Guns walked into Walters Jewelry store toting a huge chip on his shoulder, knowing they would soon control Sam's lucratively successful business. He asked Helen to get Sam, who was in his office.

Sam appeared from the back; Tommy handed the napkin to him. "Carmine said this is very valuable, make a profit." Sam unfolded the napkin; he immediately knew what it was. Being in the jewelry business, he knew the famous Jackie O brooch. He also knew it had to be stolen if it was acquired. The owner would never sell to an uncivilized buffoon like Carmine. So Sam was holding a stolen jewel. It undoubtedly would be hard to sell without consequences, which Carmine had already factored in the plan. Sam was between a rock and a hard place. It didn't matter to Carmine either way 'cause his crew would steal it back from Sam. This gave Carmine the leverage to take a part of Sam's business. Sam shook his head as Tommy lightly tapped Sam's face to imply he wasn't being asked but ordered. To refuse compliance was a complete lost cause. Sam was committed to hold, protect, and/or sell the jewel. Any way the pie was sliced, Sam was in a lose-lose situation. Now he had to think of a way out of this uncomfortable spot he was forced into. The brooch was like a penny with a hole in the middle—useless.

"My whole life has changed since you came in, / I knew right then you were that special one." Those were the words to Ginuwine's song "Differences," being played in Candy's iPod. Missing Swave and thinking about him while on the tour bus, she couldn't wait until this tour was finally over so she could be in the arms of her lover. Also she was tired of smiling while ill on the inside. Being phony wasn't something Candy liked being, and theatrics wasn't her gift. Portland, Oregon, was a big, lively city. Unfortunately they weren't able to visit properly. The owner of the venue had lost his liquor license selling to a minor. Instead of staying to find another venue, Leslie told Big Hank to head for Seattle, Washington. Mr. Mills wasn't there; he had headed back to LA to set the stage for the end of the tour. Candy didn't care; she was looking forward to the end. Her mind and heart were with Swave and Palm-Tree Clothing. She drifted back to the first time she met him and how fine she thought he was, never imagining he would one day be her man. She opened her laptop to view his hot pics on Facebook. Then she posted, "I love you Swave, your lady Candygirl@ yahoo.com." Candy wanted the whole world to know she loved him. She hoped everyone she knew saw the post. Not only did Tosha visit Facebook to see what Candice posted, Leslie started to have an interest in Candice since she revealed her future endeavor.

Candice called Swave just to hear his soothing voice. He answered, and she had butterflies in her stomach. Just hearing his voice made her panties wet. He was always cool and calm while asking about her day. They talked every day, sharing their experiences. Swave told Candy that soon as she was ready, he would arrange a trip to Hong Kong to visit the city, wanting her to get an idea of the market she was going to be attracting. It would just be them two on a business/pleasure vacation. Candice told him after Seattle they would head to Cali, finishing the tour with a few LA promotions. Soon as her obligations to Mr. Mills were over, she planned on flying to New York ASAP. Swave was pleased to hear that, wanting desperately to see his lady. Leslie made eye contact while she was talking to him. Candy was tired of the looks and remarks. Nothing disrespectful, more along the lines of envy. The way Candice viewed the situation, she helped everyone get money from Mr. Mills on down, so not resigning the contract wasn't wrong. It was about trying to make it to the next level. One thing was for certain: Swave was going places, and she wanted to be by his side in business and in a relationship. She was the future face of Palm-Tree Clothing in more ways than one.

Seattle, Washington, was a city with lots of diversity. Especially the music scene in rock, hip-hop, jazz, and R & B. The city was very popular during Prohibition. Bars and clubs were below the city. It was known as the city under the city. Many entertainers and athletes frequented the city for its extraordinary nightlife. The city under the city had a popular restaurant/bar called Scottmans where the crew would be advertising the product. This was a big deal for DJ Nice. This bar was where he had first seen Kurt Cobain and Nirvana play live. Candice was looking beautiful as always, wearing an H&M dress and pumps. Hair was pulled back in a ponytail, and nails were polished to match her sky-blue dress. It was funny; now Candice didn't like to wear any other designer except Swave. Biting the bullet and going along with the program, she respected her colleague Mia's fashion sense, making a mental note to ask Swave to hire Mia at Palm-Tree. Out of everyone on the tour, she talked to Mia the most. Mia was a big part of the reason why Candice hadn't quit months ago. Seattle, the city under the city, was the place to be. The locals were showing their love for the product from the major turnout of future consumers. Men flocked around Candice like bears to honey. She was the main attraction, but never once did she forget about Swave. Their relationship was the greatest thing in her life. One of the highlights of the night—DJ Nice had an open mic in the middle of his set. Locals from all over grabbed their fifteen minutes of fame. While the music played, people sang and rapped. The camera flashes continued, catching Candice in her best light. It was another successful night for the brand. *Another night closer to the end*, was all she could think. "My darling Swave, I'll be all yours very soon."

Leslie racked up a dozen new contracts for the Neon company. The next stop was scheduled to be the bay area. However, Mr. Mills changed the schedule, thinking ahead. He somehow managed to secure four major venues in LA. Mr. Mills wanted to introduce his new model, the young lady who would be taking Candy's spot promoting Neon as well as Action on the next advertising campaign. A young naive target that Mills was using as his latest guest. Someone he was obviously sleeping with and he had promised the contract.

Promises of MTV *Spring Break* and BET *Spring Bling* were the bait to reel her in, along with numerous gifts to secure his place between her legs, continuing to build his repertoire as a sleaze ball.

Ending the tour in LA was like going out with a bang. Candice sincerely hoped the crew would be happy when she left. Mr. Mills wasn't exactly the easiest man to work under. She couldn't promise anything, but her plans were to take Mia along. Mia was far too talented not to be somewhere so she can flourish. Candy decided to enjoy LA and take it for what it was worth, finishing the fulfillment of the contract like a professional. No matter what, Mr. Mills, Leslie, and the entire staff could only respect her for the loyalty to her signed contract.

The tour bus traveled through the night, headed for Southern California. Seattle was a fun time for the crew. Leslie added a few more signed contracts to the already-growing business. Silvia and Wanda did great numbers with merchandising. Pierre's photography skills were at an all-time high. Now it was all about the grand finale. The first stop was Graffton Hotel/Bar in West Hollywood. They would be staying there and using the venue for advertising. The Graffton Hotel had a lounge that was popular among middle-aged professionals. They arrived in LA early morning; the crew was tired and needed showers. Leslie had everyone checked into the hotel and gave the itinerary. They had free time until 6:00 PM, when the ad stand would be set up, the photo booth to follow. Then at 9:00 PM, DJ Nice would start to move the crowd. Candice, of course, would be doing meet-and-greets, advertising the product wonderfully as usual. Soon as she had taken a long, hot shower, she called Swave even though it was a three hours' difference from the western time zone. He was happy to hear her voice. Knowing she was safe did wonders for his entire being; she was that important to him. They wanted to share every moment they could conversing. Even if it was only over the phone, they had each other. He was starting to realize absence makes the heart grow fonder. Swave was definitely fond of Candice; in fact, he was in love. He acknowledged that she was most definitely sent by God just for him.

She was home, so Candice wanted to look elegant. Mia saved the best for last. She dressed Candice in a black Karl Lagerfeld original evening dress. The stilettos and handbag were Lagerfeld as well. She wore basic black from head to toe. The cut of the dress hugged her curves like a glove. Leslie straightened her hair for this event, hanging it right past her shoulders. The styling team was finished; she gave the seal of approval. They all met Pierre in the lounge as he was waiting at the photo booth.

Billy did a good job assembling both photo and merchandising booths. Candice started to meet and greet the potential consumers as Pierre started taking photos. The Graffton Lounge started to get packed. They were only staying until midnight, then off to Fire Fly Lounge in Studio City. Candice was having a good time; she even managed to text Swave just to say she loved him, making her feel connected to her prince emotionally. Men were asking to dance with her; she was flattered. However, getting sweaty wasn't in the cards. Candy really didn't wear much makeup; her natural beauty overrode everything. Nine o'clock came, and DJ Nice started to rock the house. Drinking her usual cranberry juice, she noticed Mr. Mills walking in with a young lady by his side, extremely close. He looked all smiles as if he were trying to compete with someone. The sight made Candice laugh. It must be the young lady who was replacing her on the ad campaign.

Carl walked up to Candice, greeting her with a kiss on the hand. Then he introduced the young lady thinking it would make Candy jealous over the woman he obviously was sleeping with to spite Candice. He introduced her as Maria Cherry. Name didn't sound familiar, but she shook hands with the young lady. Leslie came with haste, and Carl took her to the side for a mini conference. Maria and Candice stood side by side uncomfortably. Candice broke the ice, asking if she was ready to take over the promotions. Smiling, she nodded. Then Maria asked about the routine and the crew. Answering to the best of her ability, Candice was honest and didn't sugarcoat anything. Candice also told Maria she was moving on to greener pastures, going to work for a designer named Swave! Maria's eyes almost came out of her head; she obviously knew the name. Maria started to question the job description. The funny thing was, the questions weren't about Carl Mills and Neon Vodka. They were about Swave and Palm-Tree Clothing. Shockingly, Maria divulged that she had attended fashion school with Swave. Now she was trying her hand at modeling, which was humorous, although she was a cute young lady in a hood-rat kind of way, a round-the-way girl. Definitely not ad material, making it even more clear Carl Mills was using her for more than the advertising arena.

Candice couldn't hold back that Swave was also her man. Maria Cherry really changed colors then. Maria had walked in confident and calm like she was the sh—— until Candice dropped the bomb on her parade. Carl Mills noticed the change in Maria's demeanor. He quickly came to her rescue, to no avail. She was crushed and hurt once again. Swave was someone she desperately wanted. Candice was his girlfriend, and to make matters worse, she was taking over her crappy old job. Maria knew it wasn't all Carl made it out to be. However, it was free clothes and a nice paycheck. Her rent and car payment were due; she had no other options.

So working for Carl by day and being his lover by night was her fate. Of all the irony, she had to be second string to Team Swave's starting receiver. She tried to keep her composure as Carl walked her away from Candice. Then Candice stabbed her in her fast-beating heart. "I'll make sure and tell my boo I met you, Maria." Maria gave a fake smile while walking away. Candice didn't waste any time texting Swave, telling him the hilarious story, continuing with the evening as Carl Mills watched from afar. His whole plan had backfired like an egg all over his face. Respect was due to Candice; she was now a noticeable figure in the industry. From *Models on the Rise* reality show to Neon Vodka promoter, and now the face of an up-and-coming fashion brand. Candice deserved respect, and if she didn't get it, she would take it. Look out, Candygirl.com is coming!

Swave found the text foolishly funny, never thinking about Maria Cherry since his school days. Even then she wasn't on his mind at all. Well, he wrote back, "I hope she'll be successful in her modeling career." Then he wrote back, "Keep your head up Candy. It's almost over!" Candy felt better and stronger just reading those words. The night was going well, but Maria kept her eyes on Candice, imagining what it would be like in front of the camera, wearing those designer clothes and being in the spotlight. Candice told her the truth—with the spotlight comes drama. Nevertheless, Candice wished her the best. Mr. Mills introduced Maria to the rest of the crew. Mia already felt distant from the new model and didn't hide her feelings. She gave Maria a cold stare and an even colder handshake. Silvia and Wanda couldn't have cared less. Big Hank and Billy were glad just to have a job. Pierre wouldn't last much longer. Leslie was stuck in a job she obviously now hated, doing twice the work promoting the Action drink as well for the same salary and no bonus according to sales. Mr. Mills was unaware that his ship was sinking. Soon as Candice was gone, the tour wouldn't be as successful. Leslie knew that in her heart of hearts. She was developing reservations to find work elsewhere.

To show he still was in control, Carl Mills told the crew to pack up to prepare for the next venue. The Fire Fly Lounge was another sophisticated type of crowd. More fashion-driven, it was literally like a fashion show. Candice changed her attire with Mia's direction of course. Mia chose a pineapple-yellow Roberto Cavalli halter-top dress and pumps by Giuseppe. She kept her hair the same. Maria was captivated by Candy's appearance, wishing and waiting for her turn in the spotlight. They didn't set any booths up; they were there just to network, making an appearance for the quickly growing premium vodka brand. The Fire Fly Lounge was rocking, packed from wall to wall. Candice met and greeted people, promoting the brand. An absolute natural, and she did her job well. Mr. Mills figured a shot in the dark was worth trying one last time. He offered Candice the contract once more, this time triple the income. She refused the offer without giving any thought to his new terms. She was happily spoken for, and her new boss was the catch, none other than Eric "Swave" Hawkins. Wild boars couldn't drive her away at this point. Certainly not that lowlife snake, Carl Mills. *One more day* was all Candy could think about. Two more appearances, and it was totally final. Her employment would be over, and she was on the first thing smoking to New York City.

They networked and partied until 4:00 AM, then they set out to get some sleep. Soon as Candy got to the hotel, she got in bed and called her love. He answered as always, this time wide awake. Swave was up working on his new line. He usually worked late nights when designing, saying the creative process was at the height of the thinking chain. He was very intricate with details and colors when he created. Swave took some time off the project to talk to his love, asking about her day and the promo showcase. She expressed the desire to be in New York, in his arms. They both closed their eyes, thinking about that moment. He told Candy all she had to do was show a picture ID. She would be on a flight, American/Continental Airlines, one way to LaGuardia Airport in New York. She smiled at the thought; she would catch the first one available immediately after her last showcase was a wrap. Then she would turn her mantle fully and totally over to Ms. Maria Cherry. Tactfully she asked Swave about a job for her stylist, Mia. He replied, "If you think she'll be a positive addition to the company, I'm all for a new hire." Candice smiled; she couldn't wait to tell Mia. Candice was so pleased to be involved with a man so open-minded and considerate, proving once more to her spirit that Swave was the man designed especially for her by Almighty God.

They told each other how much they were feeling the relationship. She was tired and said she'd call him later. He understood, and they ended the conversation. Now with Mia at her side, she would feel even better entering her new role as the face of Swave's brand. Candy decided to take Mia to lunch to give her the great news. She wouldn't have to work under Carl Mills anymore. Undeniably she was a great stylist, so finding work wouldn't be that hard. Getting in on the ground floor of a burgeoning brand, the expectations of reaching the sky was a blessing. As Candice reached success, she wanted the same for Mia.

The next and final promo showcase was in Beverly Hills since they were free during the day. Candy took Mia to lunch at the Katana restaurant and bar in West Hollywood. They caught a cab and enjoyed getting away from everybody. The Katana was a very popular place in Hollywood. Both dressed casual, using the time to talk about the future. Mia thought this was a way for Candy to say farewell. In fact, it was a way for her to say "Join me." Both women ordered a huge prime rib and baked potatoes, cheating on their diets just for the day. Candy ordered a bottle of champagne, asking the bartender to make mimosas, with fresh-squeezed OJ. Then she toasted to friendship and two new jobs. Mia looked puzzled. Then Candy broke the news of Swave hiring her if she was willing to work for the brand. She raised her glass and, toasting along with Candy, said, "Good-bye, Carl Mills, hello, Swave!"

Mia was so overwhelmed by the job offer, feeling she and Candy had clicked. She never knew Candy felt sincere love like this love, considering it a challenge and a blessing. Candy texted Swave, telling him Mia had accepted the offer. They truly enjoyed the lunch date and talked for nearly three hours. They walked down Sunset to do some sightseeing. Los Angeles was a beautiful city. Mia had been born and raised there but wanted to experience New York life. The brand would take them places they'd only dreamed about visiting. Sunset Boulevard was a diverse location and a tourist attraction. Walking down Sunset made you want to shop. The bug bit both women, and they went into consumer mode. Dolce & Gabbana was their first stop. They must have tried on a dozen dresses between the two. Candy bought herself and Mia two dresses apiece using a credit card she had never used before (Citibank VISA). Mia was touched by the genuine gesture. Next it was the clothing and shoe store called Traffic. Walking in, Candy felt something strange in her spirit like she was having a premonition. There was something profoundly different about this store. She would be here again—if not in body, in her spirit. They tried on many pairs of shoes; finally they bought some Elie Tahari stilettos. The last store was the Armani Exchange. They absolutely lost their minds in the sea of fabulous clothing. Mia didn't splurge much but fell in love with an Armani body-fitting dress. She had to have it. Candy bought a dress, some Armani underwear, and silk PJs and a robe, wanting to look sexy in Asia with her boo.

Hands full, they asked the store manager to call a cab. They rode back to the Graffton Hotel in great spirits, full bellies, and lots of new clothes. It had been an enjoyable day for the two. They bonded even more and couldn't wait till they were in New York. Candy explained she would go ahead first. She and Swave were taking a trip to Asia to secure the boutique and also enjoy a vacation together while working. Then when they came back, she would send for Mia. Fine with her, simply knowing she was a part of the team was enough. Mia respected Candice for being a woman of her word. Hell, she could've quit in the middle of the tour. However, she cared about the crew and honored her contract. Entering the hotel, they ran into Leslie,

Mr. Mills, and Maria Cherry. The two women were all smiles carrying their shopping bags. The look in those eyes while Candy and Mia walked up was priceless. They spoke and continued toward the elevator.

Leslie yelled out, "Ladies, be ready in two hours, we're headed to Beverly Hills to end this tour."

"Not a problem," Candy replied. It had come to this special moment. Leslie and Carl Mills both knew the tour was really over. It was a success with thousands of dollars generated. New customers and the great brand of vodka, Neon, was alive, doing well in the city of Los Angeles where it was born and also well across the country.

Mia decided to wear her new body dress by Armani and pumps by Elie Tahari. She looked totally different from her basic casual wear. Then she assisted Candy in the hair and makeup area. Finally she suggested she wear her new Armani dress. Candy looked like a heaven-sent angel. The dress was silver and black, a minidress with an open back. Silver stilettos by Elie Tahari, simply spectacular. The final touch was a handbag that was universal Armani as well.

The famous Polo Lounge in Beverly Hills Hotel was where they had a reserved VIP section. Mr. Mills really outdid himself with the decor. All the staff were conscious of the meaning of the night. It was the last time Candice would host an event for the company. They all would miss her terribly. She would miss them as well, but all things come to an end. Nothing would keep her away from the future and what it held. Candy was on her way to higher plains. She also thanked Mr. Mills sincerely for giving her the opportunity even if he had hired her with other intentions. He had still given her a chance, and she had turned that one shot into a major life-changing deal to build her legacy. Maria Cherry had hopes of doing the same. Unfortunately she didn't possess the same look or work ethic that got Candy where she was today.

The two scheduled events were held at upscale venues. The Polo Lounge in the Beverly Hills Hotel was an exciting and sophisticated location for the wealthy. The other was the Peninsula Hotel/Lounge in Beverly Hills where the rich socialites in LA came to have a good time. The decor in the Polo Lounge was wild and explosive. It was strictly high-profile people in attendance, drinking vodka martinis, vodka tonics, screwdrivers, and Harvey Wallbangers. All made with Neon Vodka, the gold and silver brands. This wasn't about sales as much as appearance. Carl Mills, being the head of the department, wanted the brand to be associated with success. Candice worked the room like a seasoned professional, meeting and greeting everyone like a gracious hostess. A special surprise made her smile. It was Lola Hemmingway, her modeling agent and CEO of

Spectacular Looks. She had come to personally support Candice and also give her a bonus check for her outstanding job. Candice represented the agency well. Lola was pleased to be affiliated with Candice. They hugged and took a few minutes to talk off the record. Lola congratulated her on the relationship she developed with Swave and Palm-Tree, personal and professional. He was a great catch, and Lola gave her two thumbs up. Lola ordered two cosmopolitans, made with Neon of course. They toasted and drank to the future. The start of the night was a pleasure. Everyone was smiles and enjoying their drinks. In the back of the room, Maria Cherry watched and took notes on how to work the room, learning from the up-and-coming diva Candice!

Candice texted Swave to tell him about her night. She knew he was working hard, so she kept it short and sweet. He texted back, "Let me know which flight you decide to take." So into the night, she almost forgot about her flight to New York. One more appearance to make, she was eager to get the job done. A few hours and several drinks later, the crew and Mr. Mills were ready to go. At the Peninsula Lounge, there was another VIP section reserved for the crew. This was strictly about appearances and positive feedback on the product. Mr. Mills provided the bar with a few cases of the brand. Basically all the vodka drinks were free, compliments of Neon Vodka. So the lounge was filled with industry heads and socialites. All were enjoying drinking the brand. Candice and Mia stayed together throughout the night, chatting quite a bit in their personal space. Leslie thought they were talking about memories of the tour. Truthfully they were making plans for their near future. Candice told Mia to start looking for a residence online. Candice would be living with Swave—that was a no-brainer. Even though she and Swave had never talked about living arrangements, she assumed that he felt the same way (which he did). Leslie walked up to Candice and Mia, telling Mia she would start working with Maria ASAP. The two women looked at each other and smiled. Mia couldn't hold it anymore; she turned to Leslie and said, "I give you my notice, I resign as stylist for the next ad tour." Leslie looked puzzled, then she put it all together, asking what were her plans. She was honest. "I'm a personal stylist to the face of Palm-Tree Clothing." Leslie turned red and walked away furious.

Leslie started to clearly see the beginning of the end. Mia knew fashion and was extremely efficient. She knew how to work within a budget, and resourcefully. It was a major loss for the company. Leslie walked to Mr. Mills, whispering in his ear. Immediately he walked over, asking what he could offer to make Mia stay. She simply said, "I will only work with Candice." He rolled his eyes, trying to remain calm. The silence was broken when the lounge manager came and asked Candice to take a picture with NBA champion Lamar Odom. She agreed, and Pierre walked behind, ready for action. Lamar shook her hand and was a complete gentleman. A line of men followed suit, asking for personal photos. Candy was being blinded by the flashes, one after another. Players from the Lakers, Clippers, Kings, and Dodgers were in attendance. She was amazingly confident, and it showed from the great photos. Everyone in the crew, from Mr. Mills down to Billy, watched and were mesmerized at the way Candice handled the attention. She held the bottle of Neon, endorsing the brand, which was what the evening was all about. Mr. Mills couldn't deny she was the best—an absolute natural at promoting the vodka brand masterfully. He would be losing two top-notch professionals. Candice stole the entire evening and partied at the same time, riding the wave all the way to the top, leaving her name and a lasting impression on the hearts, minds, and souls of everyone she came in contact with that evening. The Peninsula Lounge, Beverly Hills, was a perfect end to a great and financially successful promotional tour. Now that it was finally over, Candy's vision and eyesight were all in Swave's direction. Time to step to the next level and continue to shine.

The night was over; she hugged and kissed the entire crew. DJ Nice, Silvia and Wanda, Big Hank, Billy, Mia, and even Leslie. Candy shook Mr. Mills's hand as well as Maria Cherry's, wishing Maria tremendous success in her new role. Candy walked away respectfully and with an air of humility. She and Mia left together, taking a cab to the West Hollywood Graffton Hotel, totally pleased with how the night had ended. She checked the envelope Lola had given her with the bonus. Candy had given Mia a thousand of the three thousand she made as a gesture for her sincere hard work. Now back at the hotel, she gathered her clothes and started to pack for New York. Candy still had a place in LA but hadn't been there for months. So a little longer wouldn't matter. The rent was paid; she offered it to Mia until the move to New York actually materialized. Candice called the airline and booked a flight (7:00 AM LAX to LaGuardia, New York). It was time to make her dreams happen. Time to be with her man on an everyday basis. She texted Swave and told him when to expect her in New York. Nothing else mattered at this point. She had worked hard to get to this point and was finally seeing the fruits of her labor, which was only the tip of the iceberg. Great things were in store. At least that's what the positive thoughts told her.

Yesterday is history. Tomorrow is a mystery.

Today is a gift; enjoy life daily.

Flight 218 from LAX to New York's LaGuardia Airport was right on time. She scanned through the Internet while traveling, looking at photos from Las Vegas, Los Angeles, and New York. Candice was extremely happy with her life. Things were going great, with expectations of getting better. She was on her way to start her future with the man she loved. There was a little sadness leaving the crew. The thoughts of the future outweighed those emotions. Mia came with her to the airport to see her off, both promising to stay in touch. Mia had become a friend and someone Candy could talk to about anything. There also was Karen in her circle. Although Candy had been so busy, they hadn't talked lately. She promised herself to call Tosha when she made it to New York. Her little sister was still very much on her mind. Maybe she could have Tosha come visit in New York depending on when they were leaving for Asia. The trip was really an exciting anticipation. Swave always managed to bring something fresh and exciting to the table. She loved that about him. She told herself to keep the relationship fresh. He was her first, and Candy planned on keeping him. Closing the laptop, she rested her eyes, thinking of her knight in shining armor. This was the first real rest she took in several days. It felt good.

Sitting a few seats from Candice was a young mother with an eleven-month-old infant. The baby was cute and looked like a Gerber baby. She couldn't keep her mind from thinking about one day having Swave's child. They had only dated a short while. The feelings were sincere and strong. Candy could seriously envision being Mrs. Candice Hawkins, with three children. The thought was satisfying to her brain. She knew she had to bring Swave home to meet her parents. She had told them about him, but it was better meeting face-to-face. She fell asleep thinking about the future, dreaming about being successful and having a family as well. All her dreams were, so far, coming true. She wanted to be in the last ten on *Models on the Rise*. She wanted to land a job to catapult her to a major stage, then model for a brand and become a household name, working and traveling internationally. She was on her way to the top; everything was falling into place. Among all her accomplishments, she was especially proud of the relationship with Swave. He was a great catch, and she thanked God for sending him. In so many ways, Swave reminded her of Daddy. If he was like Dad, respectful and hardworking, she knew Mom and Dad were going to love him. That was the next goal for the near future: bringing Swave home to meet Mom and Dad.

The flight to New York was a six-hour trip. Candy told Swave to be at the airport around 4:00 Eastern time. The flight was scheduled to arrive at 4:25 Eastern time. She texted him again to make sure he'd be there. He texted back he couldn't wait to see her in person. It would be a much-needed break from work. He and his staff had been burning the midnight oil. Things were coming together significantly. They were pushing for everything to be right for Candice. Swave finished the jeans he created, and the fall/winter line was complete. Sales from the new editions were growing between the two locations. They were anticipating even higher sales once in Asia and Europe. He explained the vision to Candy step by step, trying to keep her in the loop as much as possible. She looked at her watch—eleven o'clock Western time, two o'clock Eastern time. Another two hours, so she ordered a cranberry juice from the stewardess. She pulled up Youtube.com to watch her favorite movie, *Brown Sugar*, a loving movie about two friends that fell in love. Candice was a hopeless romantic, and Swave was as well. She started to squirm in her seat thinking about how great he was in bed. The magic would be recaptured, as soon as she had him alone. This time she would be the aggressive one. She was wearing her Armani underwear for him, planning on giving him a fashion show/striptease. Whatever it took to make him satisfied and happy.

Watching the movie brought back memories of their first date alone. They had watched the movie together, and sparks started to fly. He was such a gentleman then and always. Even more reason to take this job. She felt like a piece of meat working under Carl Mills. This was a totally different situation—a win-win. She was the face of a brand she believed in. The greatest fringe benefit was her man was the boss. The movie played its course, and it was time to freshen up. Fifteen minutes till they landed in New York. She went to the bathroom, brushed her teeth, checked her makeup, and tidied her hair. New York looked amazing from this view. Imaging what the skyline looked like at night in the air. Passengers were asked to fasten their seat belts. Within minutes they landed safely. Candy took one final look at the darling baby telling herself, "One day, Candy, one day you'll be a mother." The exit process was almost as slow as the boarding. She walked out of the airplane into the airport, seeing family greet their loved ones. There he was, cool and calm. Dressed casual but dapper, headed toward her with roses. He picked Candice up and spun her around in the air like she was a small child with those strong, ripped biceps. Candy held on to his strong arms for dear life. He put her down, looked her in the eyes, and said, "I love you, boo." She replied, "I love you too." They kissed as if they were totally alone. Perfect way to greet a woman, although the roses were damaged in the passionate physical exchange. It didn't matter; it was the thought that counted.

Swave took charge in a gentleman kind of way, directing her toward the baggage claim center. They retrieved her luggage then headed for their ride outside the airport. Swave still hadn't purchased a car. He had other plans for his money. One thing he did do was start the paperwork on purchasing the brownstone he lived in although he wanted a larger house outside the city one day. Swave had a personal cab chauffer who drove a Lincoln town car. Comfortable, clean, and he was very dependable. Carlos put the bags in the trunk, and they were off to Harlem. He held her hand as they talked about the flight. She then explained about her last two nights as a Neon promotions model, including taking pictures with NBA champion Lamar Odom and several other athletes, which wasn't a big deal. Candy didn't want any secrets in their relationship. Swave realized the honesty and respected her for telling him. He also felt the need to be honest. He told her about Pam walking in on him while he was having phone sex. Now the atmosphere around the office was a little uneasy. She understood and respected his honesty as well. They were off to a great start, building a relationship on a solid foundation. He kissed her hand and held it tight, enjoying the moment for what it truly was, a special tender moment of joy.

Upon reaching the brownstone, Carlos helped with her luggage Swave handed him a hefty gratuity for his speedy service. Opening the door, she was at a loss for words. The house looked like an actual florist shop. Roses red and yellow and all white carnations were everywhere. The house smelled sweet and fruity like candy. He turned to Candice and said, "I wanted this greeting to be special." They embraced for a few minutes, then the doorbell rang. It was a special delivery from FedEx. He signed for the package then opened the box. It was some material flown in from China, Chinese silk made from the finest of the silk bugs in China. He ordered this special silk material to make Candice an authentic nightgown. Once he told her his plans, she was moved by his thoughtfulness. He always managed to keep her guessing on what he had in store next. It was still early, so he asked Candice what she'd like to do. She suggested they take a long hot bath together. He was more than happy to make that happen. Taking her luggage upstairs, he began to run the water. French vanilla bubble bath and baby oil was the recipe for their romantic bath. She followed him, taking off her clothes. She had waited too long to hold him and would be the aggressive one this time around. Swave came back into the bathroom; she was totally nude. He followed suit as she helped him to undress.

Standing there totally naked, the two enjoyed the view of each other. The bath was ready, and they both got into the tub. This time around, Marvin Gaye's music was the setting, "Distant Lover." They sat in the hot bath holding each other tight. She sat between his legs and laid her head on his chest. The hot water, bubbles, music, and tender kisses made the moment sensual. They sat there for an hour then took the romantic setting to the bedroom. He dried her off first then himself, followed by body lotion. He rubbed and massaged her entire body then tenderly kissed her body all over. Her cheeks, then her neck, down to her breast, taking his time, giving each equal attention. Her nipples were hard as she was experiencing pleasure. He continued to her stomach, tickling her belly button, moving down using his tongue to arouse her inner being. She held his head as he performed an intricate act of affection. Top to bottom and side to side continuously. Soft and tender, all so loving until she couldn't take it anymore. She tried to stop him, but it was no use. She yielded to his touches and let herself go totally. Candy hadn't known a pleasure that felt so good. It was wonderfully special, being pleased by the man she loved. She thought she'd be the aggressor but was on the receiving end of joy. They made love over and over until they fell asleep from exhaustion. It was well worth the wait. Marvin sang "Distant Lover."

The two held each other tight through the day.

The next morning he made her breakfast-fresh-cut cantaloupe and cottage cheese, wheat toast, orange juice, and multivitamins. He was starting her off on the right foot. The next few months were going to be about keeping her figure tight. They sat at the breakfast table, Candice eating, Swave drinking coffee. He was on the laptop, sending his staff e-mails for the daily routine. She sat and watched him at work, knowing how serious he took his job to heart. Rightly so, it was his livelihood and reputation on the line. He was eager for Candice to see the office, gallery, and studio called Palm-Tree Clothing along with the warehouse and both flagship locations. He jumped up and told her he was going to take a shower. They had a long day ahead. Also arrangements were made for their trip to China (Hong Kong). Candy's phone rang; it was Karen. They hadn't talked in it seemed like forever. It was a nice surprise hearing from her. They caught up on their lives. Karen told her about the pregnancy and morning sickness. Candy talked about the business and her trip to China. She couldn't leave out how wonderful Swave had been to her thus far. Of course Karen talked about Sam. They were two gossiping women, but the gossip was about their men. Candy was glad to hear Karen was healthy and gaining weight. After a half hour, they ended the conversation, promising not to be so distant. Swave was now drying off, and she went to take a shower to get ready for their full-scheduled day.

Carlos was beeping the horn, waiting for Swave and Candy to appear. He picked Swave up every morning for work like clockwork. He paid Carlos well, so anywhere in the city Swave had to go, the Lincoln was his shuttle to the destination. Today Swave had to go to New Jersey and do inventory at the boutique. He wasn't happy with the numbers in the last few weeks. A serious-minded businessman, he wanted every aspect of the business to be successful. After that task, he would bring her to the home office, the restored warehouse. They later would have dinner with Kym and Pam to discuss the international endeavor. Also Candy would be trying on numerous outfits and having a mini photo shoot later that evening. So the day would be long, but this is what she signed up to do. Pam also had a contract for Candy to read and sign. She was required to look over the contract, Palm-Tree's mission statement, and sign a behavior conduct contract. Swave was sure she was capable of keeping her end of the bargain. It was important to show her that even though they were in a relationship, business was business, and this would protect the prestige and integrity the company operated the business with at all costs. She respected that and prepared to be efficiently professional. Arriving at the store, she was impressed by the appearance and decor. He told Carlos to hang out while he conducted business. His employees were on their toes, knowing Swave ran a tight ship. He introduced the shift workers to Candice, identifying her as the new face of the company. They all recognized her from *Models on the Rise*, the reality show.

He walked around with the store manager, Cindy Rae, going over the inventory and receipts. It was obvious to Candice Swave wasn't about any games pertaining to his business affairs. Two hours of questions and looking over every little detail. He felt confident in his visit. Cindy was an attractive young woman, but she knew he would fire her quickly if the numbers weren't adding up correctly. Swave was about progress, and that came from the head down to the workers. He had to be efficient when it came time to talk with his silent partner.

Swave and Candy were hungry, so he instructed Carlos to head to Newark. He wanted to eat at Cooper's, a well known deli in Newark, New

Jersey, South Orange Avenue. The sandwiches were so huge two people could share one. They ordered a turkey and Swiss on a wheat hoagie. Candy loved the fact Swave wasn't too dignified that he couldn't eat in the hood. He always maintained a level head and humility. Making a great living for himself, he saved more than he spent. Swave had the future on his mind, wanting the real finer things in life. Carlos ordered a Reuben for himself. They ate then headed over the Hudson River to the Big Apple. Part two of the workday was still ahead. Pam and Kym were next for questions and answers about the business.

Fifty-Third Street in midtown Manhattan was where the home office and factory were located. Swave told Carlos he would call if he needed him. The building was split between production, and shipping and receiving. On one side of the building they made clothes. On the other side, they shipped them out to retailers. It had a gallery for the viewing process, the studio for photography, the boardroom for staff and client meetings, the reception area, and executive offices for him, Kym, and Pam. Walking in, his secretary handed him a stack of messages. Sade Jones was fresh out of business school. She conveniently worked well with, and under, the boss. She had far more potential than an average secretary but was willing to start at the bottom. Swave admired her tenacity and was willing to promote her when the time was right. Although they were in a relationship, he made it clear he had high expectations of Candice. He gave her a guided tour of the building while introducing her to his employees. Once again, she was impressed by the company. For a small company, it was structured and professional. He hired twice as many employees, with the sales and demand on the rise. He took Candice to his office, which was his creative capsule. He buzzed Sade, asking her to tell Kym and Pam to meet him in the conference office in ten minutes. It was clear that working for Swave was very challenging and rigorous. His authoritative ways turned Candice on sexually. He was a boss; she was even more attracted to him. She tried to sneak a kiss, but he stopped her firmly. "We're at work, I must maintain a certain level of professionalism." He acted like Andy Garcia in *Ocean's Eleven*. No physical contact with Julia Roberts while working in his casino.

Candice got the message quick and respected his wishes. He wasn't mean but wanted to be professional in the workplace, never wanting his staff to feel he was unable to balance work and pleasure. Swave didn't plan this love; it showed up and knocked at his door. The boardroom was spacious with a long mahogany table and leather chairs. African and Asian artwork, just like in his home. No one understood the collaboration of the two cultures in one place. No one questioned the abstract decor. After all, Swave was the boss, so his decision was final. Kym and Pam were already seated, ready for their daily analysis. He required both women to be aware of every small detail in their departments. Kym, being his assistant, was expected to be on top of the entire business. That was her job, and he depended on her to effectively run things when he was away. The women all spoke, then they went into the meeting. "Wooh . . ." was all Candice could say. Swave asked questions about everything concerning the company. Sales numbers, shipping and receiving numbers. Marketing projections, fabric quality, and future appointments. He was very thorough and serious about the answers. After the women satisfied his inquisitiveness, he gave the floor to Pam. She went over all contracts, salary, bonus plans, benefits, incentives, and business accounts. She was extremely thorough as well, sliding the forms to Candice to sign. Then she handed her a company credit card, an American Express corporate card, along with a check for her first ad and photo shoot, which was later on that evening. There was nothing else on the table requiring his decision, so Swave left the office, giving instructions for Kym to take Candy to a wardrobe fitting.

Kym took Candice to the gallery to pick out some clothes then to the studio to prep for the photo shoot. This is where Mia's expertise was very much needed. There were so many styles and outfits to choose from. Swave's mind was truly brilliant. His designs were on the cutting edge of fashion, pushing the bar with all his spectacular creations. She knew this was the place for her to be. Kym was the figurative head when Swave wasn't around. So everyone gave her an incredible amount of respect. No one said a word while she snacked when working. She was noticeably pregnant. That was a taboo and rule number one—absolutely no eating around the clothing for anyone. He enforced that policy with zero tolerance. However, Swave didn't enforce it in Kym's case. Kym made sure Candice had at least twenty outfits to wear while being photographed, preparing for the photographer who was hired. They didn't have an in-house photographer; she thought about Pierre. Langston Armstrong showed up early with his staff, a sign of a true professional. Him showing up on time was one reason Kym hired him for their shoots. They began the photo shoot. Kym conducted the whole session assertively. Pam and Swave went over international business affairs, the newest direction they wanted the company to head toward. He confirmed his travel arrangements once more. Pam had all the contacts and called ahead for a smooth meeting between the Chinese fashion district. Flight, hotel, and transport were all arranged by Pam. She secretly wished it was her spending the week alone with him. Nevertheless, she didn't reveal her sudden attraction and desire to be touched on the inside by the object she viewed that day.

The day was finally over. Candice earned her first check and got her feet wet in Palm-Tree Clothing. She learned a lot in a course of a few hours, also seeing what it took to be successful in the industry as a designer. Swave had all the qualities of a successful businessman. As the day ended, they all rode with Pam to Philippe Chow, an exclusive Asian restaurant and Pam's favorite. She reserved a private room for the four of them. Philippe Chow was a great dining experience where the service was great, food was great, and it had a soothing environment and amazing drinks. It was the East Coast version of Mr. Chow on the West Coast.

Dinner was wonderful, and Pam took everyone home. They said their farewells until Swave came back from China. The flight was scheduled to leave noon the next day. He knew Kym and Pam would hold down the fort, until he returned. "Vaya con dios," go with God, and they were gone. Before walking into the brownstone, Swave gave Candice a much-needed hug and kiss. She fell into his arms and felt safe. They walked into the house and started their night romance. As if they weren't together all day long.

Lying in bed snug and cozy, Candice was on his chest while he was sound asleep, tired from a long day, hearty meal, and great lovemaking. Candy's phone rang. She tried to ignore the ring but couldn't resist and answered it. Tosha was calling to see when they could spend time together. Candy could hear the disappointment in her voice. When she told her, it was really bad timing. She was headed to China and wouldn't be back for a week. Candy promised as soon as she came back, they would get together, figuring it wouldn't be a problem for Swave. He would understand and openly invite Tosha to stay in their home. Candy already was viewing the house as her own. He asked if Tosha needed any money; she said she'd make it until next week. Candy was wondering what she was doing for money. The few thousand dollars she gave her had to be gone. Hopefully Tosha had decided on a career path. She ended the conversation with "I love you and I'll call soon as I'm back in New York." Since she was up, Candy texted Mia, and Karen, telling both she was flying to China at noon. She'd contact them when she was back home.

"I love you, girlfriend, Candygirl!"

The only thing Candy had to pack was underwear. She was showcasing their apparel, which was already shipped to China, waiting. Swave's bags were packed and loaded in Carlos's car. They were at the airport in record time. Flight would be leaving in an hour. He was thinking, did he handle every detail before leaving? If not, Pam and Kym would have to handle whatever. Baggage checks, passport handy, and laptop and iPhones secure. It was time to head across seas, the first time for both to leave the country. It was exciting and scary at the same time. Then the one thing he thought he'd forgot, in fact, he remembered—a special mouth-dropping surprise for Candice once in China. They boarded the plane and took their seats twenty minutes later, in the sky headed for Southeast Asia. This would be an experience she would never forget. It was business and pleasure. Swave would do his absolute best to make it a trip for the memory book!

Tosha slammed the phone down in the heat of anger. She was tired of being put on hold by Candice. If she had any second thoughts about Young Heat's plan, they now were dismissed. Young Heat held her in his arms and offered his superficial love. Page watched as she thought about her instructions for the plan. She had always done whatever he ordered without doubt or worry, not even so much as a question. However, this time was different. She felt something in her spirit that she couldn't explain. It was a premonition, and it wasn't a good one. She tried to ignore it, but her mind wouldn't allow her to stop thinking negatively. As the leader, everyone else would follow her lead. When it was all over, Darryl promised a vacation in the islands, somewhere in the tropics, just the two of them, when the job was complete. This was a two-part job, and Page's role was vital in each job. At the end of the mission, she would feel a lot better. She would make her twin sister suffer as she did while growing up, a sick and twisted way of thinking. Young Heat encouraged it every chance he got to talk into Page's ear. After this one, maybe he could retire, open a business, and lie on the beach watching Page run around in a two-piece bikini.

Most of the planning was done; it was now an action plan. For various reasons, Young Heat didn't divulge the entire plan to his three team players. He just told them what they needed to know. That's one reason Page was reluctant in her spirit. He tried to call Karen as a last resort for information. Karen never answered her phone. He and Jackie activated Operation Surveillance. They camped out watching the routine of Walter's Jewelry Store. For three days they watched the business. From opening to closing, Young Heat watched and took mental notes. He noticed the store was the slowest in the mornings. Also one employee usually went and got lunch while the others stayed in the store. They took turns eating in the break room. The others were in front handling the clients. So after careful examination, lunch was the best time to strike—while it was slow and they were one less person. They waited for lunch. This would be a job that possibly could change their life. It was Thursday, and Friday would be the day of activation. Young Heat briefed the women and secured all necessary tools for the heist. Everyone except Tosha was involved in this mission. She would be a part of part two of the plan.

The meeting took place at Carmine's favorite Italian restaurant in North Carolina, Cinelli's. Franky Ziti, Tommy Guns, and Lil Carmine flew down from New York. Carmine informed his crew they were taking over Walter's Jewelry Store, keeping Sam Walters as the figurehead to avoid suspicions with the stolen jewels. The Biasi family would secretly control the finances. Nato would be used a few more times for some complicated missions. Then he would meet with a horrible fate when he was no further use to the family. He asked Tommy to pick two soldiers and oversee the Walters Jewelry Store robbery. The goal was to obtain the brooch then use it against Sam to gain power over the jewelry store. He wanted it done on Friday, about closing time. He instructed them not to hurt anyone. Sam was more valuable to him alive and well. If there was any cash, they could take that as well. Carmine felt it was only right since Sam was making money outside the family, going against their agreed-upon business arrangement. Carmine killed people for less. The only reason he and Nato weren't sleeping with the fishes was he wanted to make some extra money off both of them. Carmine learned at a young age that a dead man can't pay what he owes. A scared live man will give his right arm to pay his debts.

The family was all clear about the takeover plan. Everyone knew their roles explicitly. Tommy picked the soldiers and oversaw the mission. Franky Ziti would put the press on Sam about the sale of the brooch, explaining Carmine wanted his money or the brooch. Lil Carmine would contact Nato for another jewel heist and also keep an eye on his sister Marie. He would look over the books at Brightest Star once back in New York. Carmine would do what he always did—eat pasta, drink imported liquor, and spend time with Franny, his wife.

His daughter Bianca "Bambi" had his ear about managing one of the family businesses. After he had controlling interest at Walter's jewelry, he'd make her the manager to watch over Sam. A very well-thought-out plan. Before Sam knew what hit him, his entire world would be upside down. Carmine had taken over several businesses like this before. He was a pro at this tactic, and it always worked. All he needed was his family to execute his plan to perfection. It would be smooth sailing taking over Sam's cash cow.

Friday morning and Sam woke up early. Cooked Karen's breakfast and practiced yoga for a hour. Their relationship had grown stronger since the pregnancy. His daughters still were upset and didn't return any calls. He was hurt but knew he had his own life to live. Since the marriage, he hadn't stolen any more gems from unsuspecting clientele. The side deals with Nato were bringing in a vast amount of currency immensely significant in allowing him to stack money for the future. He had enough, but with his child on the way, he wanted his empire to increasingly keep growing. One could never have enough was his thought pattern. Dressed and armed with a peace of mind from the yoga, Sam started out on his way to work. Kissing Karen, then her belly was his departure ritual. He got in the CLS550 Mercedes-Benz and drove to the jewelry store, always the first there, behind Helen the Sue. He opened the store, and the women began setting the displays. He would bring the jewelry from the safe. Sam was the only one who knew the combination. Once the cabinets were all filled and the display window ready, Sam disarmed the alarm system and opened for the daily business. It was usually slow during the mornings. The women cleaned jewelry and the showcase cabinets. Sam was busy setting stones and repairing broken merchandise. He had the phone headset on, talking to Karen while he worked.

The day was going well, even though only three customers came in all morning. They dropped off some jewelry that needed to be repaired. Sam did repairs only if they bought the merchandise from his store, charging a reasonable rate for the service. Almost lunchtime and they were deciding what they wanted to eat. Sue and Helen wanted burgers from Boardwalk Billy's. Sam decided on a chicken sandwich from there. Sue would pick up their order, and Helen called it in. This gave Helen an opportunity to talk with Sam in private, still very much attracted to him and his status. Sam was blindly unaware of the plot. Kelly offered Helen a substantial amount of money to seduce her father. Kelly wanted the marriage to Karen ended at all costs. Helen saw a financial opportunity, taking Kelly up on the seduction offer. Ironically, Helen already wanted him for some time now, seeing Karen as a gold-digging whore who stole her man. It was hilarious what women thought about each other. While the store was empty, she walked over to Sam, gently brushing her breast against his back. She spontaneously started to massage his shoulders. He was tense, and she knew how to relax him. It had been a while since she had rendered her services to him. Sam felt his nature rising as the mental picture of her breast played in his mind. He always tried to remain professional with Helen. There was a quiet attraction between the two. He loved Karen, but being a man, thoughts came and went daily—it was natural. He closed his eyes, thinking of a way out of this awkward situation.

Young Heat, Page, and Jackie sat outside the Walter's Jewelry Store in the parking lot, watching and waiting for the perfect moment to strike. Sue left the store and got in her Buick LaCrosse, heading to Boardwalk Billy's to get their lunch. Young Heat sat up in the stolen Impala, directing the women on their timing, wanting them to approach the target fast and quietly. The two women dressed in black, put on the masks and gloves, and exited the car. Young Heat stayed outside to watch for police. Within moments, they were inside the store with weapons drawn. Sam was like a deer caught in headlights when he saw the twin Barettas in his face. *Not again*, were his thoughts. He literally had déjà vu. Two women dressed in black with the exact build as the women in the home invasion. Page asked him, "Which way to the safe?" He knew it was the same woman. This time the voice sounded really familiar, like he knew who she was. At least that's what he was thinking. Without a regard for his or Helen's safety, he reached and pulled off Page's mask. His eyes couldn't believe what he was seeing or who he was literally looking at. It was Candice Gray the model, Eric "Swave" Hawkins's girlfriend and face of Palm-Tree Clothing. Page slapped him with the gun, and he fell on the floor. Jackie pointed her gun at Helen; she fell to her knees. Sam cried with pain and fear loudly. "Candice, why are you doing this to me?" Page pointed the gun and told him to rise to his feet and be quiet. "The safe, Sammy, the safe—let's get to it or the woman dies first."

He didn't want Helen hurt, so he complied with the armed woman whom he thought he knew. Jackie double-checked the door, making sure it was locked. Then she pointed the gun at Helen, insisting she start opening the display cases. Helen went to every cabinet, emptying jewelry trays in Jackie's duffel bag. Helen was scared and trembling, never ever having experienced a robbery. In the office, Sam ached from the lump on his head, trying to make sense of the whole ordeal. If Candice was the one who committed the other robbery, then she had to have an inside source watching him from a distance at his home and business. He thought about Vegas—was that all staged? Was she really friends with Karen, or was the meeting a coincidence? His brain was working like an engine in a NASCAR race car. Page's mind was wondering how to handle his misinterpretation of the situation. Maybe it was a good thing, or maybe not. The fact of the matter was her cover was blown. Or maybe not, depending how one looked at the situation. If he thought she was her sister, then she was home free. "Enough of playing around!" shouted Page. He knew she meant business and went directly to the safe. The safe was a large one, filled with precious gems and money. Sam dialed the combination, then stopped, turned to her, and asked candidly, "Candice, does my wife have anything to do with this, or are you working alone?" Page didn't know how to answer the question simply because she didn't have anything against Karen. She chose her road, and secretly Page respected her decision. Ultimately it was one less piece of the pie they didn't have to slice.

Page answered, "If you don't open this safe, you'll be sorry," hitting the back of his head with the gun with a stunning blow. He opened the safe and stepped aside quietly. There were racks of jewelry trays with diamonds, pearls, and gems. Stacks of money neatly banded and a white napkin containing the brooch sitting on the top tray. She motioned for Sam to start filling her duffel bag with the goods. Soon as Sam was finished, Page pulled out plastic band strips, binding his hands, then his legs, pushing him to the floor. Without another word, she made her way to the front. Jackie bound Helen on the floor as well. Both had bags full opening the door as Young Heat pulled in front of the store. Page went back inside and in the backroom to the security monitor, snatched the surveillance tape out, then made a break out of the store energetically. Young Heat was waiting for her. She returned. They pulled off. Page didn't notice the couple standing there, about to enter the store. She ran right past them in a haste. They made a clean getaway. Now they were on the highway headed to the Audi A8, with Tosha behind the wheel waiting for the team to show. The first part of the plan was profitable.

Reaching the homestead, everyone calmed down and changed clothes. The women gave Young Heat the valuables. He had connections to sell the items. The cash came to another look to split. The real money was in the jewels and how he planned to sell them. The women weren't overly concerned because Young Heat always played fair, especially when it came to finances. For the moment he was content. The second part of the plan would bring the real big money. Before things got too far gone, Page told Young Heat about Sam assuming she was Candice, him pulling of her mask and calling her by Candy's name, the reason she went back for the surveillance disc. Young Heat thought long and hard, then a smile graced his face. The random act of stupidity on Sam's part had actually played right into Young Heat's hand. It was perfect and made his future tactic much easier to accomplish. He opened a bottle of Rosé, pouring all the women a glass, then toasted to a not-perfect but well-executed performance. He wanted them to get some rest and enjoy the celebration. Soon they were going on a road trip for phase two.

Sue returned from Boardwalk Billy's with the lunch. The police were already at the scene; the couple had called them. They noticed Helen bound by plastic and were witnesses to the perpetrators escaping in a black Chevy Impala. Sam and Helen were seated, being questioned by the police. Sue tried to console them, but she was glad she wasn't there for the drama. The couple described Page as best they possibly could. Jackie, still having on her mask, couldn't be identified. The driver wasn't noticeable, but they knew he was a black man. Sam told the officers he didn't remember the female's face. Helen wondered why he would lie. She had heard him call her Candice, as if he knew who she was personally. She figured there had to be a reason for his deception. The surveillance disc was gone, wisely taken by the culprit. Sam could kick himself for not updating the security system to Internet. There was also the thought of something important in the safe—the brooch. He had a two-million-dollar insurance policy on the stolen jewels. That wasn't a problem, but Carmines personal property was an issue. Especially since he had never appraised the brooch, never knew the true value of the piece. It also had some historical value. Undoubtedly this would be an issue down the line. After all the questioning, Sam closed the store and sent the women home. The police stayed around to help fight the news reporters off. Sam Walters was a known and respected business owner and community leader. Any injustice against him was major news.

Sam was hurting, tired, and wanted to go home. The police gave him a ride home. He was clearly in no condition to drive himself. Never revealing this to the police, he knew he'd been robbed twice by the same crew. He started to think about what Kelly said to him, trying to make sense of the whole equation. He was careful not to jump to any assumptions until he was sure, giving no indication of what he was thinking.

Karen greeted him at the door, worried when she saw the police car. He obviously was in pain. She helped him to his favorite chair. Sam told Karen what happened, watching her facial expressions. She couldn't have been that great an actress, 'cause she sincerely was concerned. He felt and knew she was moved while holding her stomach. He continued to say he knew it was the same female from the home invasion. "In fact, it was Candice Gray." Her eyes almost popped out of her head. Once he described the scene, Karen knew it was YH, Jackie, and Page. She should've known they would finish what they started. Her hands were tied at the risk of incriminating herself. "Hmm Candice, hmm Page." She knew it was Page, having met Candice and them favoring each other. This was really becoming scary. Karen remembered the text from Candice saying she was going to China with Swave. It had to be Page; they had to be related, maybe even twins. That was one thing she thought of, and Sam thinking Page was Candice was confirmation.

Karen didn't know what to say or do; her brain was working on overdrive. She knew her old crew had committed the crime. Telling the truth would surely reveal her past. So she would play it by ear until Young Heat called, which he would. She'd answer. Sam took a long hot shower after several shots of Johnnie Walker Red Label Scotch then lay down on their king-sized bed. Karen was the ever-caring devoted wife, tending to his afflictions and making him feel comfortable. All he wanted to do was relax and have peace of mind. This was a case for his workhorse Frank Bruno. He wanted to know everything there was to know about the crime team. He planned to keep the store closed for a while. Maybe take a vacation, just him and Karen. There were a lot of coincidences and unexplainable events. However, he would remain positive in his relationship with Karen, giving her the benefit of the doubt, although he was going to contact Kelly for a chat. Karen felt like she was treading on thin ice. One false move or wrong statement could end her entire lifestyle along with all her hopes and dreams for the future. The only security was the unborn child she was carrying. She was faced with a tough dilemma that had to be addressed: Tell Sam the absolute truth or come up with a counter story to protect her and the child's future inheritance.

Carmine couldn't believe his eyes and ears while watching the evening news. Sam Walters, a noted anti breast cancer activist and business owner, was robbed today at gunpoint in his jewelry store. Carmine almost spilled his drink. He was agitated because he and Tommy agreed to cancel the mission until Monday. So whoever did the robbery wasn't part of the Biasi family. He frantically got on the phone. Tommy was quiet while Carmine gave him an earful, demanding he find out who did the robbery, also if the prized brooch was stolen, and find out ASAP. He hung the phone up and drank a shot of amaretto.

The phone rang, and Sam refused to answer, looking at the number. Seeing it was Tommy, he figured now or later he had to answer to Carmine about his property. Tommy got straight to the point about the brooch, uncompassionate about what he'd gone through earlier that day. He asked questions about the whole ordeal. Sam angrily answered, and it was obvious to Tommy now wasn't the time; Sam was still shaken up from the robbery. Tommy got the answer to the bottom line—the loss of the Jackie O brooch. He would relay that to Carmine. Sam, eager to get off the phone, told Tommy he'd call Carmine tomorrow. He desperately needed to get some rest. The line went dead. This was a problem Sam really didn't need, but the confrontation was inevitable.

The Walters Jewelry Store robbery was a big topic of discussion in the Mecklenburg County Police Department. Detective Alex Lopez was assigned to the case since he was the lead detective on the Walters home invasion. He sat at his desk going over all the facts. He was a proven expert at finding most perpetrators. The crime team had obviously worked together for a while. Reading over several unsolved crimes in the city, he knew it was the same team. Two women armed and knowledgeable about their victims, a sign that they studied the prey. The more Detective Lopez went over the cases, he found a lot in common. Two things he had to do—contact Sam Walters for a face-to-face interview to see if there was anything he wasn't mentioning. The second was work the streets adamantly to get some info, see if his confidential informant had some information. Lopez was well-known and known to pay cash for any info leading to an arrest. He was also known for busting heads for false leads, rarely having any problems in the streets of Charlotte. He'd also give his old buddy Frank Bruno a call, aware that Bruno was the cities most popular and reliable PI. Usually Bruno had some info to sell 'cause everything had a price when dealing with hardnose Frank Bruno. They had gone through the police academy together, maintaining a personal friendship after Bruno was kicked off the force. Lopez had a lot of work to do, and it was cut out for him. It didn't matter; he was committed to solving this case, bringing some justice to the disrupted life of Mr. Sam Walters.

The next morning, Sam felt a little better but had a swollen lump on his head, a mild headache, and his nerves were shot. He was still wondering about Candice and how she stole a large fortune from him. She was so cold, and her eyes looked like death. The intense look had him scared for his life. Calling Carmine was the first thing on his to-do list. Biting the bullet, he got it over with in a respectful tone. Carmine answered. He could hear the coldness on the other end of the phone. Sam explained everything in perfect detail, trying to play the victim to the fullest with absolutely no sympathy. Carmine wanted compensation for his loss. Sam assumed as much but didn't think it would be a partnership. Carmine wanted a piece of his business legally. Too scared to bargain, he folded and agreed to the terms. They would finalize the terms in a few days. Then Carmine asked if he somehow knew the bandits. Without thinking and scared, he told Carmine it was two women, the leader being someone his wife befriended. She possibly committed the home invasion and had his expensive brooch. He told him he saw her face, and it was definite. She was the perpetrator in both crimes. Candice Gray. *Models on the Rise* reality show season 5, model and face of Palm-Tree Clothing Company. The girlfriend of clothing designer Eric "Swave" Hawkins. Carmine took the information; that made no sense to him. Why would a model rob him? Nevertheless, he knew Sam wouldn't lie to him. So Carmine would investigate, wanting the gem back, which had cost him a lot of money. The more Carmine thought about the story Sam gave him, the more he realized it made no sense. Looking up both Candice Gray and Eric "Swave" Hawkins, they weren't criminals and were in the fashion industry. He learned Swave was a hardworking young designer with flagship stores in New York, New Jersey. Very respected in the fashion district in New York. So he wouldn't be a likely suspect to commit the crime. His girlfriend was an up-and-coming model. Who made a small ripple in the pool of fashion modeling. One thing he knew, young women were an easy target to be manipulated. Wisdom wouldn't leave anything to chance, and no stone must be left unturned. Even if it was illogical, it was very possible. The bottom line was he wanted that brooch back at any cost. He wouldn't allow his investment to be taken away. He had paid Nato a handsome fee to acquire the brooch. Now it was gone, and he needed it back. Not only was the brooch gone but Lil Carmine was having trouble contacting Nato. He wasn't returning any phone calls or messages. The condo he lived in was suddenly empty. It was like he had vanished into thin air. Things weren't going well for the Biasi family. The one bright part of the saga was Sam agreeing to the partnership. A small stake of interest at first. Eventually the Biasi family would take control. Carmine called a mandatory meeting of the minds. The entire family would sit down and get implicit directions on how the boss wanted them to handle the situation. Commanding with or without force, the brooch would be retrieved. There would be bloodshed, and the family didn't want theirs to be the blood spilled.

The doorbell rang, and Karen slowly made her way to answer it. Sam was relaxing in the den, trying to rid his head of a headache. She answered the door, and it was Detective Alex Lopez. Karen remembered him, but he showed his badge anyway. He asked to talk with Sam Walters. She offered a drink and directed him towards the den. Sam saw Detective Lopez; he stood and greeted him. It was an informal visit to talk about the robbery and the culprits. Sam was careful not to implicate Candice. He wanted to handle that himself. If he got the chance, his big mouth would foolishly give Carmine the lead. So Sam danced around the truth and sent Lopez on a wild goose chase. Sam's mind-set was with Bruno's help, he could hopefully get the brooch back. Then he wouldn't have to share his business with a crime boss. After a series of questions, Lopez closed his pad shaking Sam's hand. Sam thought it went well; little did he know Lopez was clever, already forming an opinion about his sexy young pregnant wife. He made a point to look into her past, Sam's as well to see if he was as squeaky clean as he appeared. Maybe these crimes were a consequence of something Sam had done unlawfully. Maybe it was an act of vengeance from a business associate. Lopez didn't believe it was a random act or an unplanned robbery. He had a lot to look into. Luckily he was a man with strength and determination. He walked out of the house with several theories to consider.

All the information Bruno had on the crime team he faxed to Sam. The names and known hangouts in Charlotte. The head was Darryl Moffitt, a.k.a. Young Heat. He even had a picture of him and Karen at Starbucks before their marriage. These were the suspects: Young Heat and two women, Jackie Bright and Page Meeks. He didn't have their photos, but the three were known to have committed a number of high-profile crimes. Sam would carefully go over the information before making a decision. Maybe Karen had a valid explanation on why she met with this Young Heat. Maybe this wasn't the crew that robbed him. Definitely something to look into. If Kelly would call him back, they could talk. He desperately needed to feel better about the situation. Karen entered the den. He put the info away and rubbed her belly. No matter what, he vowed to be there for his son. He loved Karen and his unborn child. She handed him a sandwich, some juice, and two Tylenols. She kissed his balding head and walked out the door. Extremely kind and loving, no way could she be a part of this drama. Sam wanted to think positive. His heart was involved, and he was waist-deep in the trickery. Karen was playing by ear, and she was playing to win.

This was his decree, and he wanted his ordinance carried out to the fullest. Candice Gray was to be found and questioned about the robbery. Retrieve the brooch at all costs. Find out where and who the accomplices are. Use every resource in the city of New York. He gave Swave's work and home address, which was in Harlem. They would have a hard time blending in there. It was for the cause, so they had to demonstrate patience. Bring her back to Carmine and make her tell or be tortured.

Next was the disappearance of Nato. He was to be found and given another assignment in order to make 100 percent profit through Sam's store. After he accomplished what Carmine had in mind, he was to be eliminated. Then the complete takeover concerning Walter's Jewelry, extorting Sam for the insurance payment. The Biasi family would control every aspect of the business, giving him only a small portion of the policy payoff. These three projects were to be up and operational ASAP. Tommy and Franky would oversee every detail, then report to Carmine.

Hong Kong was in the eastern part of Asia bordering the South China Sea. For years, Hong Kong was occupied by the United Kingdom until the nineteenth century. In 1984, Hong Kong became part of the Republic of China. For centuries, China stood as a leading civilization, outpacing the rest of the world in arts and science. The Chinese economy had changed from centrally planned to largely international trade. They became more market-orientated and imported and exported with numerous countries, thus becoming a major player in the global economy. The recent boom in the economy made room for more Western fashions. The Chinese who once were known for more traditional native garments amazingly were changing in business as well as fashion. The capital, Beijing, and the port city of Shanghai were making great strides. However they were light-years behind the land of Hong Kong. Japan, Taiwan, and Singapore traded with Hong Kong, creating a demand for American fashion. Hong Kong, the New York of Asia, was on the fast pace to becoming the fashion leader in Asia, promoting American products and flagship stores like Gap, Coach, Calvin Klein, and Esprit. Swave felt he had an unbelievable chance to flourish in Asia. He and Candy arrived, excited about their vacation/ business trip. They stayed at the Hong Kong Mandarin Towers, which was a prestigious hotel. Pam reserved the hotel room on the company credit card. Upon checking into the hotel, the manager told Swave there was a package awaiting his arrival. He signed for the oversized box, and the bellhop carried the box to their room. The view from the seventeenth floor was breathtaking. He tipped the bellhop, and they were finally alone.

Candice started to look around the colorful room as Swave opened the box and unpacked the clothing. The package consisted of clothes from the line Candy would be wearing and modeling. While her back was turned, he put a small box in his pocket, something he had sent to surprise Candy.

As he took the clothing out, she was astonished by the never-before-seen ensembles. Colors and styles were specifically designed to her tastes. Candice couldn't understand how he created clothing according to her personality. There were twenty outfits neatly folded. A portable steamer was packed to release wrinkles in the clothes. She stood and watched Swave piece together outfits like a puzzle. He was so passionate about his craft. She had never seen anyone so particular and professional. His creations were elaborate, and the intricate detailing were precise with every stitch. Kym had done an excellent job with the designing of the accessories for the exclusive line named Candy Girl Wear by Swave, one of the surprises he had for Candy. She was overwhelmingly stunned when she saw the emblem on the blouses, shirts, and dresses reading Candy Girl. Swave was full of surprises and kept them coming. Aggressively she pushed him on the bed. She straddled him; they began kissing, leading to making love. The episode lasted the entire first night in Hong Kong.

As they lay in bed holding each other, Candy thought to herself life couldn't get any better than the present. Hungry, they ordered room service to revitalize their strength. Surprisingly the hotel served traditional American cuisine. They ate sausage, eggs, hash browns, and wheat toast. Orange juice to drink and a newspaper to read. Unbelievably the *New York Times* was available in Hong Kong. Swave read the local Hong Kong newspaper to get a feel of the city. He made sure Pam called Verizon phone company to broaden his cell phone service to include international networks. Candice didn't, so she'd talk to her network of people upon her return to the States. His first full day in Hong Kong, and the sky was the limit. His meeting with the importers of the garment district wasn't for a few days. He was free to take Candy sightseeing. Later on in the week, he had a meeting with a real estate developer. He would bid on the property, where the store would be located. They took a long hot shower together then got dressed. This was a casual day, so they dressed comfortably to move around and take in the sights. Swave wore khakis, a shirt, and loafers from his company of course. Candy wore a halter-top minidress and open-toe sandals from her Candy Girl line, starting their day of fun and adventure.

Leaving the hotel and going into the public was surreal, seeing the diversity in the city, a mixture of Asia and the western part of the world. Hong Kong was fast-paced and resembled a modern city in the United States. Of course, there was still a small section of native traditional Chinese businesses. Bathhouses, herb stores, restaurants, and clothing stores. A great deal of modern businesses were monopolizing the city. One of the must-see tourist attractions was the Hong Kong historical museum, featuring the history of Hong Kong before it became the property of the

Republic of China. Also the strides they'd made in the last twenty-five years. They took the tour around the museum and were truly amazed at the cultural artifacts. Weapons and uniforms from the ancient army, native-land clothes, and masks worn by the Chinese in the fourteenth and fifteenth century. The museum also featured the ancient red dragon the natives used while dancing their ritual tai chi dances. They observed and studied as much as possible, receiving a history lesson from another culture. Once again, Swave had shown Candy something new and educational. The facility was probably the most interesting place she'd ever visited. After the tour of the museum, they were hungry, wanting to try some Hong Kong Chinese cuisine. Right outside the museum was a local restaurant, Wong Tow Kitchen. They stopped and ate some fried rice, vegetables, and egg rolls just to hold them until later. Candy had taken pictures all morning and had a week's worth of photos to take.

The Mandarin Towers were mostly occupied by tourists. The hotel had several luxury amenities to offer—bar, restaurant, gym, spa, hot tubs, and yoga meditation sessions. The city was busy and contained many different attractions. Candy was more than ready to experience Hong Kong in its entirety. Swave was a huge fan of the Asian culture. So this was a perfect place for a vacation. They relaxed in the comfort of their plush room. Swave used this time to check his e-mails while Candy massaged his shoulders and neck methodically. Seems Pam talked to the real estate owner via e-mail. He looked forward to doing business with Palm-Tree in hopes of leasing other properties to future fashion proprietors. The meeting was moved up, and this was a very important appointment that affected more than just him. He had to remember this wasn't just a pleasure trip. There was a lot riding on his performance as a stable businessman. Once the store was secured, he would advertise with a billboard, a much-needed expense to give consumers a face. The face would be Candice; her looks and allure would make sales soar. He had a lot of work to do in a short amount of time. He decided to spectate at the fireworks display the city was having to honor the Chinese basketball team, hiring Yao Ming as VP of operations. He was a huge sports icon there. Candice, being a sports fan, wanted to see the festivities.

The streets were filled with people and fireworks everywhere. There was a large billboard with Yao Ming's face. The celebration was equivalent to New Year's Eve in Times Square. Swave and Candy strolled the streets holding hands, absorbing the energy and taking pictures for memories. Swave didn't know Chinese people were fond of basketball. He even saw teenagers wearing Michael Jordans on their feet. He surveyed the crowd, making mental notes about the clothes they wore, realizing his clothing line had to also accommodate men. A spin-off men's line would be a smart business move. Starting one in the future was the plan, but now Candy Girl was the focus. He knew Candy Girl apparel would take off dramatically. After two hours of watching and walking down the streets of the city, they decided to go back to the hotel. Candy enjoyed the day and relaxed in a nice hot bath with her iPod, listening to Keyshia Cole's second album, vibing hard. Swave was stuck on his laptop, preparing for his two meetings. After he handled the business part of the trip, he could fully concentrate on giving Candy her much-needed vacation. Swave had something extraordinary planned for Candy. First thing was his business sales pitch of a lifetime. Undressing, he joined Candy in the bath tub. They sat and held each other, wishing the moment would never end. She smiled while listening to Keyshia Cole's song, "Sent from Heaven," thanking God for sending Swave her way. He had made a difference in her life tremendously. As she sang the lyrics, she squeezed his biceps, singing, "Sent from heaven, sent from heaven."

Mr. Kim Lee, one of Hong Kong's largest and most successful real estate developers, sent a car to pick Swave and Candice up for the meeting. They were greeted at the location by his assistant. The location was equivalent to a strip mall. The store Swave was interested in was a 2,500-square-foot prime location. Ming Sue guided the guests to her employer, Mr. Lee. The two gentlemen shook hands. Mr. Lee bowed his head and kissed Candy's hand as a sign of respect. Once the pleasantries were over, they walked around the future home of Palm-Tree. Swave liked the structure and the architectural design of the building. Mr. Lee quoted a price before Swave had a chance to haggle. Honestly it was a more than fair price. Mr. Lee offered the property at the price for one year. The logic behind the deal was Mr. Lee wanted Palm-Tree as a tenant. He wanted Swave to be successful 'cause the more successful he was, the more Mr. Lee could charge in the future. Also he wanted other proprietors to do business with him. Basically Mr. Lee made an offer Swave couldn't refuse. Swave pulled out the Palm-Tree company checkbook, writing a check to Mr. Lee for a one year's lease. They shook hands, and Mr. Lee gave Swave the keys. After the signing of the lease, he gave him the security code to the property. The first international business transaction was a success. Now the next order of business, was to secure the merchandise, shipping through the people who controlled the importing in Hong Kong. One business hurdle jumped, now Swave was running to jump the next one. Candy watched as her man operated with precision, the right amount of business savvy. She respected him and how he conducted business. He was a master in the bedroom and boardroom.

Mr. Lee's driver drove them back to the hotel. Two hours later, he met with the Chin brothers. The two brothers controlled the majority of American-imported merchandise. They also wanted to make a deal, thinking of the future possibilities. Swave learned from the last meeting to be quiet, allowing the Chinese to talk, which was effective, because after a brief conversation, they offered a low standard fee for importing. Knowing enough not to offend them by trying to haggle for less, the business deal was sealed with a contract and a handshake. All parties were pleased with the outcome. He assured the Chin brothers they would have a full and prosperous business relationship. They toasted with some warm Honjozo sake, the Japanese joy juice most sophisticated Asians drank, also a ritual for doing business with the Chinese. The Chin brothers couldn't keep their eyes off Candice. It was obvious that she had their attention. Swave saw she was a lucky charm in both business ventures. He had chosen wisely. He knew the next decision would be the best choice of all. The meeting was over, and they went back to the room for some quality time. One more hurdle to jump, a photo shoot to get her face on a billboard with the name Candy Girl wear by Palm-Tree.

This would be the day Swave concentrated on Candice. The entire day was dedicated to her in more ways than one. In a few hours, he would meet with the city officials that rented the advertisement space. There was a space available for Palm-Tree. He made the connection through the photography agency. Pam was the key to the entire photo and advertising exploit. She had many connections in the industry that made Swave's job considerably easier. It was all about having a resourceful team to help. The space would be expensive, but that was to be expected. The photo shoot would be a very important event. The head of advertising would be there to make a deal for the city. Hong Kong was particular on who they did business with concerning advertising. Not just anyone could be featured in the city of Hong Kong. So Swave explained the situation to Candice to make sure the photo shoot was exceptional, although Candice was a perfectionist, always rising to the occasion. Her wardrobe would be several ensembles from the Candy Girl collection, the first of which was a denim jean outfit, super skinny cut, and polo-style shirt with the Candy Girl emblem. Also featuring the sizzling hot Candy Girl sneakers. Swave wanted to advertise with simplicity. He felt that was the best way to sell the line to teenagers and young adults, the preferred target market for the line. Candice had the wholesome look and appeal to sell the line. Then with the other styles, like the dresses, she would appeal to a older group of consumers. That was the beauty of Candice. She attracted different age groups and cultures with her look, the reason Lola Hemmingway jumped at a chance to represent her at Spectacular Looks.

The wardrobe was packed and ready to go. They boarded the travel service reserved by Pam. She was many miles away, still handling business appropriately, taking up the slack that Kym's pregnancy caused. Swave was dressed like a serious-minded businessman. Single-breasted gray suit, white shirt, and blue-and-gray striped tie, the suit from his signature Swave line. He wore Salvatore Ferragamo shoes to complete the look. Ready to sell the face that was going to change the game in the city of Hong Kong. They arrived at the photography agency, Blendz Photography. All eyes were on the power couple. Swave walked with his head up and squared shoulders, looking like an important figure in the industry. Even dressed in jeans, Candy walked like the trained model she was, exhibiting true poise and grace. The photographer was a Chinese legend in the game, Ken Sun. He greeted them with handshakes as his staff offered coffee and juice. Swave immediately started to talk business, explaining to Mr. Sun exactly what he wanted with the company photos. Ken Sun took it all in and said, "Let's begin." His staff started to set up backgrounds, lights, and cameras. Mr. Sun gave Candice a compliment. "Your look is truly a work of art, I'm impressed." She smiled and started to lay the wardrobe out for various photos. While the session was in play, Swave greeted Mr. Lang, the advertising rep for the city of Hong Kong. Firm handshakes from the start told Swave this wasn't going to be easy. He guided Mr. Lang over to the photo shoot in action. Blendz had a makeup artist touch Candy's angel face up. It was hard to improve sheer perfection.

Mr. Lang was stunned by Candy's beauty, and Swave noticed the interest. Candice worked with grace as she modeled the denim line. Several pictures were going to be reviewed for the ad. Then it was wardrobe change. Candy really missed her stylist Mia while she was changing clothes. Swave talked to Mr. Lang about his vision for Palm-Tree, also how Hong Kong's vision and his could help each other win. Mr. Lang wanted to help the Chinese economy by increasing foreign sales in his country. Swave wanted to create an international following of his brand. The two wanted the success of Palm-Tree to blossom. The question was how much would it cost. More importantly, was the brand marketable in Hong Kong? The two gentlemen tossed several figures at each other but nothing concrete. Then Candice came back in the studio, wearing a royal-blue minidress. A V-neckline necklace and bracelets for accessories (a matching pair). She wore rust and navy-blue stilettos, looking absolutely stunning. Mr. Lang told Swave Candice would look great on the billboard. So that question was answered. Now it was a matter of how much and how long. Candice started to pour it on as Swave winked at her. She went into perfection mode like the diva Tyra Banks. Mr. Sun was loving the session, and his camera was working magic. Candice stole the show, seizing the moment like a champion. Swave watched with admiration as his girlfriend and employee worked extra hard to secure the contract. Mr. Lang called his assistant, whispering something in her ear. She was a pint-sized young Asian lady with a bad case of acne.

Excitedly Mr. Lang invited Swave and Candice to an early dinner as soon as the shoot concluded. Swave accepted the offer, smiling at Candice. She continued to be professional, working through the entire wardrobe sequence. Finally the shoot was over, and Mr. Ken Sun kissed Candice on the hand, showing his appreciation for her participation in the photo shoot. Bad as Swave wanted to show her some affection, he held his composure for a one-on-one tender moment, remaining in business mode, being completely professional. She noticed the twinkle in his eye, knowing they were going to have a great night together. Swave thanked Ken Sun with a check and handshake. The photo shoot was a success. Mr. Sun told Swave he'd load the photos on the company e-mail address, also send color prints to his office in New York. The both anticipated doing future business together. Mr. Lang was obviously impressed with Swave as well as Candice. Now it was time to work out a deal that would compliment both parties. The determination was intense on both sides. This deal was major for the city of Hong Kong. Bringing exclusive Western-world fashions to Hong Kong was economically brilliant. For Swave, it was a stepping stone for his brand to catapult his brand into the fashion world's stratosphere.

The Spicy Pepper was a world-renowned restaurant specializing in Asian cuisine, a major tourist attraction in Hong Kong. Mr. Lang must have been a regular there. His party was immediately seated before a two-hour waiting list. People stood patiently waiting to be seated in the popular restaurant. The dinner party consisted of the four: Mr. Lang and his assistant, Swave and Candice. Mr. Lang ordered a round of drinks for the table. Pam instructed Swave to never refuse a drink while conducting business with the Chinese. It would be considered an act of disrespect. So he and Candice drank vodka martinis Mr. Lang ordered, having a good time with pleasant conversations. Swave was eager to put this deal behind him but remained patient. The two women talked among themselves as Swave tried to remain calm. Suling complimented Candice on her beauty, and she smiled. Candice complimented her as well; Suling put her head down. Candice lifted it up from her chin, looking Suling in the eyes.

"Have confidence in yourself." Then she gave her a beauty secret on how to reduce acne using lemons, oatmeal, and alcohol as ingredients for a facial. Suling was honored that this beautiful model took the time to encourage her. They held hands as women often do as a gesture of endearment. That was the moment Mr. Lang knew he couldn't let them get away without doing a deal. They briefly talked in their native Chinese language. Then Mr. Lang pulled a contract and pen out. He wrote a figure on a napkin, handing it to Swave. The number was high but fair. They shook hands, and Swave signed the contract.

As a measure of good faith and to celebrate the union, Mr. Lang ordered a bottle of Ty Ku Junmai Daiginjo, the most expensive bottle of sake Spicy Pepper carried. Everyone drank to the financial success of the brand. It became perfectly clear that Mr. Lang was personal friends with the head chef. Without even a menu, food appeared at the table. The waiters brought out a variety of food. Sweet and sour chicken with snap and snow peas, peppers, and onions. Roast Peking duck, which was a Chinese delicacy, stuffed with red and green peppers. They all ate to hearts' content, enjoying every bite. The meal was eaten with chopsticks, adding another twist and memory of their first date. Their feet and hands touched under the table, both bodies wanting to be touched and held. Swave was turned on by Candy's entire being. He couldn't wait to have her all alone. She had really been a lucky charm in his business deals. He couldn't help but notice the appeal she had on the Chinese, another indication that he had chosen well. He had one last surprise for her to fully make this day special. He respectfully sat through the rest of the dinner with his host. The day went well, and the evening was going to be even better. A great meal with a pleasant host. Swave saw dollar signs in his eyes although he wasn't in the industry just for money. Creating and producing clothes was his calling. Passion, purpose, and pleasure were why he was a designer. They finished the evening on a high note. Then Mr. Lang's driver took them back to the hotel.

Once inside the hotel room, they immediately lost control, kissing and touching passionately, all while undressing each other rapidly. Standing totally nude, Swave looked into Candy's eyes. He stroked her cheek with the back of his hand. Then he told her he loved everything about her being. She smiled. The moment was very intense, then he ran to get a gift in his luggage. It was a small black box. Walter's Jewelry was printed on the top, giving away its origin. Kneeling down on one knee, he said, "Candice, I'm in love with you, I have been since the first time me met. You're heaven-sent to me from God. You're my first, my only, and my everything. I can't go a day without talking to you, and I can't live without you. You're the woman I want to have my children and grow old together with. Will you do me the honor of becoming my wife? Because you're for me and I'm for you, and we're both tailor-made for each other."

He then opened the box to a beautiful fifteen-carat engagement ring. He was emotional with tears rolling down his face. She took the ring and held it to her heart. Swave then placed it on her left ring finger. "Yes, Swave, I would love to be your wife." They embraced tightly, both crying with joy standing totally naked. Overwhelmingly happy, she never expected this to happen so soon. Once again, Swave had surprised her in abundance. This was the happiest day of her life. She was now an engaged woman with a great fiancé. Life couldn't be any better than it was right now. They both were experiencing success in their professional and personal lives.

He lifted her in his strong muscular arms and carried her to the bed. The intensity had been boiling all day. Now they were finally all alone to express their love and affection for each other without hesitation. While she lay on the bed, Swave took a moment to look at her piercingly, looking through to her spirit, taking in her beauty totally. Captivated by her curvaceous body, shaved kitten, and pretty polished toes. He made love to her before, but this time would be different. This time she was the woman who would bear his children and last name. He slipped his tongue into her mouth. They enjoyed tasting each other's tongues. He then started sucking on her neck, and his hands discovered her body. "I love you, Candice." "I love you more, Swave." He sucked her breasts, slow and sensual, taking turns on each, giving equivalent affection, licking her nipples as they grew harder, circling them with his tongue, then licking down to her bellybutton. The touches with his wet tongue drove her wild. There it was, her wet, tight, shaved kitten waiting to be tasted and fondled. With a caressing motion, he opened her kitten with his right thumb and index finger, licking her kitten up and down to start the serenade. She opened her legs wide as he continued to perform. The fresh, clean taste had his mouth water for another and another taste. She was at the top of her lungs moaning with approval; he slowly and meticulously worked his magic. Candice never thought this could feel so good, and Swave was proving that point, sucking on her clitoris and writing his name on her kitten with his tongue. Shivering, trying to hold back the orgasm that was coming in dynamic form like a waterfall, she tried to push his head away, but to no avail. He continued until she released and screamed at the top of her lungs, "SWAVE!"

He opened her legs wider and inserted his long, thick manhood inside her tight, slippery love canal, stroking deep and deeper as she fought to catch her breath. He looked in her eyes as he made sweet love to his fiancée. Candice sucked his bottom lip, holding him tight as he went in and out, her legs in the buck position, feet to her ears. He drove strong and firm slow stroking. She worked her kitten muscles and gripped his shaft. The tightness felt great to him entering and exiting her canal, scratching his back in the midst of the sensual sequel. Without a warning, his muscles locked and he exploded inside Candy's womb. He collapsed on top of her body, breathing uncontrollably. She kissed his forehead and held him in her arms. They had made love before, but never this intense. It was really making love, and they truly loved each other. They would be husband and wife for life. The pair were lovers, friends, business colleagues, and soul mates. Candy wanted to get up, but he was sound asleep on top of her. So she cuddled and went to sleep as well, drifting away to the thought of the song by Ashanti, "Baby, baby, baby, baby, baby 'cause you're my baby!" They both slept the night away in a state of euphoric bliss.

The next two days were spent seeing the sights of Hong Kong by day, making wild, passionate love at night like bunny rabbits, strolling the streets like teenagers in love, holding hands and kissing as if it were not tomorrow. Shopping at novelty shops, buying artwork for his collection of Asian art. Eating at every restaurant that featured traditional Chinese food. Swave wasn't too eager to eat many delicacies. Their vacation was relaxing, especially since the business was handled. He did e-mail Pam and Kym, letting them know about the rental space, billboard, and photo shoot. The next couple of days were going to be spent enjoying engaged life. Candice kept looking at her ring with amazement. She was so proud of the rock on her finger. He called Sam and sent him a blank check to pay for the engagement ring, which was remarkably made. Sam took the same pride Swave did making clothes into making jewelry. Candice thought about all the people in her life that would be surprised about her engagement. Her parents, Tosha, Mia, and Karen—they all would be the first people she contacted. She also made a vow to spend some time with Tosha, try to rekindle their relationship because it meant a lot to her heart. Now it was time to enjoy her vacation and her fiancé. They lived life to the fullest in a foreign country, building the Palm-Tree brand, securing their future together.

Business, pleasure, shopping, and dining out were the exploits of the past week. Swave felt invincible reaching heights that would make him an international name. His brand was on its way to the top. The United States, now Asia, and before it was over, Europe would be the next target to conquer. Swave knew his silent partner would be pleased with the growth of the company. All accomplished with honest hard work and talent. Swave was a natural, and that's why the mogul invested in him. In turn, it was a brilliant investment that was paying off tremendously. Swave texted the mogul telling him about the international expansion. The mogul was delighted! Even more when he viewed Candy's photos Swave had sent via e-mail. Things were really looking great for the business. Swave knew the mogul, Pam, and Kym would be shocked about the engagement. Shocked but happy for him. He wildly thought if they started a family soon, his child and Kym's could grow up together. (What a thought.) Now the vacation was over, and it was time to head back to New York, work hard for this international transition. Tons of work ahead of him to make this go smoothly. A meeting with his lawyer, accountant, and marketing director, Pam, to make sure the merger with the Chinese would be a success. Candice also had some work ahead, promoting the Candy Girl line for national retailers. He agreed to give her a week or so off to spend time with Tosha because she was worried about her welfare. He also promised when he had time, he'd go meet her parents to properly proclaim their engagement.

He was cool with her taking some time to spend with Tosha, witnessing she was about business when it was time to work. Also he looked forward to meeting his future in-laws, making a mental note to bring her meet his mom. Well, Hong Kong was a blast. Now they boarded a flight back to New York, heads held high and all smiles. Swave confident and ready for his next challenge, Candy happy and proud of her new title and ring on her finger. They sent everything they bought to New York by parcel service. Lightly traveling on the plane was more convenient. Candy watched her favorite movie again, *Brown Sugar*. It was something that reminded her of their love affair. He sat quietly with her iPod, listening to Michael Jackson's song, "The Lady in my Life," thinking about his journey to get to where he was now. He worked hard and avoided the streets, drugs, and loose women. He invested in himself and believed in his own vision. Now finally he was seeing his vision of an international store. He was on the right track to total success, seeing the fruits of his labor materialize. Out of all the great accomplishments, the relationship with Candice was the highlight. He knew she was sent by God above, the Almighty Creator and ultimate tailor who made her just for him as a reward for his faithfulness. He sang to himself the great Michael Jackson's song, "You will always be the lady in my life."

The next step to a well-thought-out plan was to bring the women to New York. They traveled to the city in two vehicles: Jackie and Tosha in a Dodge Durango, Young Heat and Page in a Chrysler Town country van with tinted windows. Young Heat chose to travel in two cars for countersurveillance. He told the women only what he wanted them to know. Of course he had the whole mission mapped in his head. His word was sufficient to them; that was all they required to act. In their minds the end justified the means. YH was engineering a major payday. Page and Tosha would be paying Candice back for selfish reasons. Jackie was just going along for the ride, taking the opportunity to talk with Page while traveling, telling her about the plan to kidnap Candice and assume her identity. Then they would call Karen and get her man, Sam, to buy back the stolen jewels at 75 percent of the retail value. Sam would make 25 percent profit when the insurance paid off. They would blackmail Karen into persuading Sam into the deal. Failure to do so would blow her cover. Everyone would make out on the deal. Actually it was a brilliant plan to make an easy 75 percent on all the jewels at one time then make some major money from Swave's company. They would have Page impersonate her biological sister, extracting valuable company information from Swave using her special manipulating tactics, clearing out his bank account, maxing credit cards, and writing company checks. Young Heat had all the angles covered, or at least he thought so. If the women played their positions as instructed, the plan would take them to the promised land, which was plenty of money and vacationing on exotic islands.

Tommy Two Guns and Franky Ziti were taking this intrusive act on Candice's part seriously. The result of not finding her or the brooch would be detrimental to their health. Carmine made it very clear that he wanted bloodshed. Tommy, knowing him well, assumed it would be a family member if they incompetently failed to produce results. Before leaving to New York, they handled business with Sam, at least started the process. Sam told Tommy he had his attorney drawing up paperwork. Also he was waiting for the insurance adjuster to clear the claim. It was a waiting game, and they knew he was being honest. He could've given Carmine money from his personal stash. Money wasn't an issue for Carmine. He was after ownership and control over the cash-cow business. Next order of business was Nato and his whereabouts. They checked his last known address, resulting in no information on him at all. Every number they had just kept ringing. No one in the circle had seen him since the brooch heist. They left their subordinates in charge of finding Nato. It was essential that he reappear to plan and participate in a jewelry heist Carmine had on the back burner. Their plan was to kill two birds with one stone, head back home to New York, and see if Marie knew where Nato was by conducting a secret surveillance operation. Then they would snatch Candice Gray up, finding out where the brooch was. They had their work cut out for them. The major incentive was to make Carmine happy. To fail wasn't explainable, nor was it excusable.

Karen was Sitting and listening on the other end of the phone as Sam had a long conversation with Kelly. His daughter gave Sam an earful, whether he wanted it or not. She felt Karen was a bad influence and a gold-digging tramp. The only concrete evidence she had on Karen was the picture of her and Young Heat. Karen's mind was thinking the whole time. She knew it was a major hurdle she was up against. Kelly even tried to implicate her in the home invasion although she had no proof that Karen was involved. The allegations were all circumstantial evidence, which was the loophole Karen needed to wiggle out of her appearance of guilt. Going into high defense mode to protect her future, she was thinking of what she could tell her husband to ease his inquisitive mind. Whatever she said had to be believable. This was for all the marbles, and the stakes were high. She rubbed her stomach, trying to soothe the pain from the kicking baby. That was all she needed to feel, snapping her back into action. She had come too far to stop or be defeated by a nosy little Daddy's girl. She reminded herself she was superior and held all the cards. The baby in her stomach made the advantage shift in her direction. Whatever Kelly said, she would refute it using a sensible and logical explanation. Knowing what she was up against was half the battle. Quietly hanging up the phone, she mentally prepared herself to do battle for her place in the Walters family. Aware of all consequences and intended purposes, her determination and perseverance could put all suspicions to rest.

Sam hung up the phone with a splitting headache from the stress. He knew his daughter was overprotective. Nevertheless, there still were questions that needed to be answered. He wanted to believe the best about his wife. Honestly Kelly raised some doubt in his mind about Karen. Before he could leave the study, Karen appeared. She had some pain medication and a cup of hot tea spiked with a shot of Scotch. It was perfect timing, like she was reading his mind, Sam thought to himself. Karen kissed his forehead and started to leave the room.

"Please, sweetheart, sit down for a minute," he asked politely. This was it; she'd have to be theatrical to come out of this on top of the game. He asked her if she had ever been unfaithful to him. She answered quickly, "No." Then he asked if she had a male friend he didn't know about. She again answered, "No." Then he opened the desk drawer and handed her a picture, Young Heat and her having coffee. Karen started to laugh uncontrollably about the suspicion. He looked at her very seriously, wondering what was so funny. She held his hand and said, "Sweetheart, you don't have to worry about any other man." Then she started to explain about the picture, why she was having an innocent cup of coffee with a man.

Karen told Sam she was indeed involved with the man in the picture. However, she ended the relationship before starting a new one with him. He wouldn't take no for an answer, persistently kept calling her on the cell phone. She had met with him face-to-face, telling him about Sam. "I didn't tell you about this matter because he is in my past. You and our child I'm carrying is the present and future." She kissed him; he relaxed and was at ease. Sam believed her wholeheartedly. She painted a picture of a bitter ex-lover who would do anything to get her back, explaining she didn't want him to hurt Sam. So she threatened him with plans of going to the police, taking out a restraining order against him. Hearing talk of police, he agreed to leave her alone. She was concerned for Sam's safety because her ex-lover was a street guy with lots of connections. She revealed he was the first friend she had met in the city of Charlotte. Trying to start a new life with a new identity, this guy helped her with the transition. Coming from an abusive relationship, she was broken, scared, lonely, and broke. She went to work in a strip club to get back on her feet. That's where she met her ex-lover. He helped her out in finding an apartment, even let her borrow some extra money. Karen laid it on thick, and Sam fell for it because of love. He loved her and wanted a second chance at romance in his life.

Tears were running down her face like a river. Turning on the theatrics, she looked Sam in his eyes, saying, "Honey, when I said my vows, I meant them totally." Feeling her sincerity, he started to cry as well. Then he hugged her and kissed the belly carrying his child. He apologized for doubting her love for him. Sam had a few more questions like how did she make money after quitting her job as a dancer? However, he left well enough alone, thinking of the stress he might cause his pregnant wife. He believed her, and far as he was concerned, it was in the past; they were living for the future. The matter was water under the bridge. Karen had convinced her husband and once again beat Kelly. She knew there would be one more hurdle to jump. It wasn't over, but she had Sam's love and devotion. That was the most important thing to Karen. His love for his unborn child was a major factor in his emotions. Playing right into Karen's hand for power, the husband was eating out of the palm of the wife's hand. Working too hard to turn back now, the reward was right within her grasp. All she had to do was deliver a healthy baby boy. Their future would definitely be secure, mother and child. Now she would relax and take care of her health. The delivery of Samuel Walters Jr. was the most important thing in her life. She needed him to be alive and well.

Detective Alex Lopez wasn't one to sleep when he had a case to solve. The whole Walters case puzzled him for more than one reason. He felt there had to be an inside source. The information had to be leaked by someone. It was a gut instinct, but Lopez felt Karen had something to do with both robberies. He found it too much of a coincidence that Sam Walters's troubles had started when he got involved with his wife. Mrs. Karen Walters had become a person of interest to the Mecklenburg Police department. A personal guest to Detective Alex Lopez, to find out answers. Knowing Frank Bruno and his connections in the streets, he found it unbelievable he didn't have more to share, specifically about the robberies and the crew who committed them. So Lopez started to wonder what he was hiding. His favorite part of the job was hitting the streets for leads. The thing that interested Alex about this case were the perpetrators, a team of women working together skillfully. There had been a dozen or more crimes committed by women. All unsolved, and Lopez knew these crimes were related somehow. Who was the mastermind? These women weren't amateurs at their craft. Why Sam Walters? Questions kept popping into the detective's head. Maybe he needed to dig deeper into the Walters affairs to see what exactly he could find illegal. Karen Walters was already an unofficial suspect. "With a little digging, who knows what I might find?"

The life of a tough, no-nonsense street detective wasn't easy. Always watching your back on the street and in the department of internal affairs. Lots of times Lopez acquired information from confidential informants (CIs), who were used throughout law enforcement nationwide. These street guys were often criminals trying to get a break. Trading a favor for not being arrested, street-labeled as snitches, from drugs, murder, robbery, or any other crime. Every hardnose detective had a CI in his corner. For Detective Alex Lopez, Cornbread was his eyes and ears in the street, his own personal snitch. Cornbread was a lowlife crackhead thief. He made a living running cons, pickpocketing, and shoplifting to get his daily drug of choice, crack cocaine. Known as a con man to the Charlotte law enforcement, he lasted in the game so long by only committing petty cons. Usually police didn't want to do the paperwork, or he'd spill his guts to have freedom. There wasn't much of anything illegal in the city old Cornbread didn't know about. He was a drug addict, but his information was official, always leading to a major arrest and conviction. He was a modern-day Huggie Bear from the '70s police drama *Starsky and Hutch*. Detective Lopez rode around town until he found his source of information. Cornbread was walking in the notorious drug area, Betty's Ford Road, known as the Ford. They made eye contact, then Lopez drove to the shopping center at LaSalle, and Betty's Ford parked and waited for Cornbread. A system they used to avoid Cornbread's cover as CI being blown.

Much as Detective Lopez hated drugs and those that used them, he had a tolerance for being around and doing business with Cornbread. His usual payment of twenty dollars bought him an earful. Cornbread was in the streets and had his ear to them. He knew every con artist and crew that committed larceny. Cornbread told Lopez that an unnamed female from the West Side had been involved with a few high-stakes robberies. She was linked to a guy who was well-known in the streets of Charlotte. The name Young Heat didn't ring a bell to the detective. However, his government name, Darryl Moffitt Jr., did. Lopez had arrested Darryl Moffitt Sr. If he was anything like his father, he was a handful. Young Heat was known to be a pimp in his own right. He kept a stable of women who committed crime at his command. This young lady was one of his loyal women. Ran her mouth about these robberies while getting her hair braided. The beautician's boyfriend got the information from her. It spread like a wild forest fire. The crew was also known for credit card and check scams. That was all the detective needed to hear; he had a name and suspects. Amazing what a twenty-dollar bill could buy these days. Cornbread was worth his weight in gold. Once again he gave the star detective enough to lead a proper investigation, almost nearly a sure arrest. Darryl Moffitt Jr. was his target, and he would turn the heat up on the streets until someone gave him up for questioning or he caught the mastermind and his stable attempting another one.

After a series of small investigations, Darryl Moffitt Jr. turned out to be a very interesting guy. Someone with his street credibility almost always had a criminal record. Surprisingly he didn't, and to make his life even more interesting, Darryl Moffitt Jr. rented a house in Ballantyne according to the utility bills in his name. Lopez still didn't know who the female was, but he was working on it. Lopez wondered if Bruno knew about this Young Heat. If he did, why wouldn't he reveal this information? Were he and Sam Walters planning an act of revenge? Furthermore, was Sam Walters involved in some criminal acts concerning this Darryl Moffitt Jr., a.k.a. Young Heat? These questions and many more were going to be answered in time. The major one was, how can Young Heat afford his lifestyle? He rented a huge home in an extremely wealthy community. There were several expensive cars in his name. The only visible means of income was vending machines. Young Heat apparently had a business license. Lopez ran across a flyer claiming he sold clothing at retail prices and owned vending machines. A smart move on his part showing some amount of income. Lopez knew it was a front for his real source of income, larceny.

Until Lopez could prove anything solid, Young Heat was only an unofficial suspect in these crimes. Lopez would activate surveillance to watch Young Heat's house.

Back from their business trip and vacation, the power couple was happy to be back in New York. They wanted to put things in forward progress. Swave had a long list of things to do, and Candy vowed to spend time with Tosha before things started to roll toward traveling. Still tired and jetlagged from the long flight, Swave sat down to breakfast that Candy prepared. She was putting her mother's teaching to practice. Mom had taught her from a young age to cater to her man in more ways than one. The French toast, scrambled eggs, and turkey bacon was filling. Multivitamins and fresh-squeezed orange juice to wash it all down. It was a balanced nutritional formula for the day. Swave ate his breakfast pleasingly, thinking how great life would be married to Candy. He read his *Wall Street Journal* and *USA Today*, checked his e-mails, then called Carlos to pick him up. He thanked Candy with a kiss for breakfast, also the incredible lovemaking session they shared that morning. He told her he'd be gone all day busy with work. Afterward he, Kym, and Pam were having a dinner meeting to discuss the international store and marketing. She understood, telling him she'd be home waiting for his return. Candy told Swave she was going to fly Tosha to New York, inviting her to stay with them for a week. He didn't veto the plans 'cause after all, she was her sister. Also she was going to be his sister-in-law. Might as well get used to her being around. Carlos blew the horn, and Swave kissed his fiancée and left for work.

Candy took this time alone to answer all her messages from the last week. First on the list was Mia. She called, but there was no answer. Then Candy remembered Mia was on the West Coast. It was probable that she was still sleep. She'd call her later on in the evening. Next she called Karen; the phone rang but there was no answer. Funny, because she left several messages asking Candice to call ASAP. Candice wondered what was wrong and why she wasn't answering the phone. Before calling Tosha, she decided to call Mom first to tell her about the engagement. Mom didn't mind what time Candy called. Early in the morning or late at night, Mom was always willing to talk to her daughter. Mom answered and was happy to hear Candy's voice. Not beating around the bush, Candy told Mom she was engaged to Swave. Mom screamed happily into the phone. Seems George and Vanessa Gray had looked Swave's company up on the Internet after reading an article in *Black Enterprise* magazine about Eric "Swave" Hawkins and his growing clothing company. He was featured in the "Company to Watch" sequence. So naturally Mom and Dad were pleased that she was involved professionally and personally with this young entrepreneur. Mom handed the phone to Dad, as he gave his blessings. Even though they had never met Swave, he accumulated a good reputation for being a respectable, honest gentleman according to the article in *Black Enterprise* magazine.

Mom and Dad made her promise to bring Swave to Fresno as soon as they had time. Candy explained that it was a busy time for the company, but she promised. Then Mom asked if she had heard from Tosha. Candy told her mother she planned to fly her to New York for a visit. She would call Tosha after their phone call ended. Mon expressed how worried she was about Tosha. Candy told her mother all they could do was pray. The women talked for an hour then ended the call. The last phone call was to Tosha to give her the invitation to New York. Candy poured some cranberry juice while waiting for the line to connect. Just when she put the phone down, it rang. It was Tosha calling her back; they greeted with pleasantries. Then Tosha told Candice she was in New York and wanted to visit as soon as possible. Candice was overjoyed; now she didn't have to fly her to New York. Tosha told Candice she had caught a ride with some friends. All she needed was the address, and she'd be there in a few hours. That was great, giving Candy a few hours to exercise then freshen up. She gave Tosha the address, then she told Tosha to expect a surprise. Tosha tried not to feed into any emotions, remembering why she was there—to make Candice pay, taking what she wanted, and not settling for what Candice had to give. This was a well-thought-out plan, and Tosha had to play her position.

"Great, I can't wait to see you, sister!"

Tosha ended the call; Young Heat gave her a kiss. "You did great, baby girl, now stay focused." They were staying in a motel in New Jersey on Route 1-9, which was only a half-hour drive to New York City. Young Heat had everything planned and all the necessities they needed. Jackie and Page were ready to move into action. Page still felt like this wasn't a smart move. For some strange reason, she was against this plan. Deep down in her gut, she didn't want to do it. Not wanting to disappoint Young Heat, she was willing to go along with the plan. Never before had she felt like this in her spirit in all the hundreds of jobs they pulled together. The one thing that kept her somewhat grounded was the opportunity to see Candice face-to-face. the chance to claim a life that could've been her very own. When that thought played in her mind, she was more than willing for an act of vengeance even though Candice didn't directly do anything to her nor even know she existed. Someone had to pay for the years of abuse she had to endure. Page shook off the guilty conscience and put on her game face, the face that said she was an elite soldier, ready and willing to fight for the cause. Even die for it, if that's what it took. She looked at Young Heat as if he knew what was playing in her head. He knew she was ready and didn't have to be briefed anymore. It was game time, Michael Jordan in the fourth quarter.

Driving through the Lincoln Tunnel from New Jersey into New York actually was a nerve-racking experience for Tosha and Page. Both were dealing with their own demons. Page was thinking to herself, after this last job they would go off somewhere and retire from the game, a picture that Young Heat painted to keep her focused on the prize. As for as Tosha, no one could understand why, why she'd betray her only sister. One thing was for sure, if she would stab her sister in the back, anyone was fair game for her betrayal. Young Heat kept that in the back of his mind. Crossing the New York state line and into Manhattan, Young Heat's GPS directed him to the Fifty-Ninth Street bridge to head to uptown Harlem. They reached 116th Street, got off, and drove slowly down the street. Now Tosha called Candice, and she answered immediately. Tosha asked Candice to describe her brownstone and for a landmark. Tosha told Candice she was right down the street. They parked across from the brownstone. It was time to put the plan into action. Tosha stayed in the Durango behind the wheel. Young Heat, Page, and Jackie headed toward the brownstone. He signaled, and Tosha called Candice again, telling her to come outside while Young Heat and Jackie stood to the side of the door. Candice opened the door; her eyes almost jumped out of her head. It was like she looked into a mirror, but a live one. She stepped outside to gather her thoughts. Before she realized what was happening, Young Heat covered her nose and mouth with a cloth napkin containing the knockout chemical, chloroform.

Within seconds, she was knocked out. He picked up Candice like an infant and carried her to the van. Once she was in there, Jackie duct-taped her mouth, hands, and legs. They closed the van and went back to the brownstone. Tosha sat and watched without moving an inch. Page couldn't believe it was really her sister. A weird feeling overtook her, and she couldn't say a word. Young Heat gave Page her final instructions before he left. Page picked up Candy's phone that had fallen to the ground. He kissed Page and told her to stay in character, looking around before leaving, making sure she was alone and safe. Then he and Jackie headed to the van, Tosha behind them in the Durango;. they sped off into the city's traffic. There was so much moving and going on in Harlem. No one seemed to notice the kidnapping. If they did, people minded their business as people in New York often do. Especially in Harlem, an old and cardinal rule. Jackie was in the front seat with Young Heat and Candice in the rear. Tinted windows, so she was unseen and on her way to another state. Page was left behind to assume her biological twin's identity. So far, Young Heat's plan had been absolutely perfect in terms of accomplishing what he wanted in record time. Now part three of the master plan was in full effect.

Page took her time and looked around the house, intimidated by the situation. By the look of the house and the decor, along with Candy's wardrobe, Page knew she was out of her league. The willingness to please Young Heat kept her in character. She was paralyzed in her spirit, knowing this was morally wrong. Honestly she was frightened by the unknown, vulnerable to whatever came her way. In spite of her reservations and fear, there was no time for procrastination now. The plan was in full effect, no turning back now. Page was in the bedroom going through Candy's belongings. All designer names along with Palm-Tree. She felt like a kid in a candy store trying on different clothing, feeling a magnetic force while wearing her sister's clothes as if she knew what was happening at that moment. She viewed the pictures on the dresser and wall. They looked like a very happy couple. The more she viewed them, and noticed their loving smiles, the more Page wanted her sister's life. Candy had it easy all these years. Great family, modeling career, and a handsome chocolate fly guy boyfriend. Page's mind went back to every crime she had to commit to live the life she was living in the present. The more she thought, the more she wanted a change. It was too late for virtue; she was a female thug. There was no way out of this trap of a lifestyle. In Page's mind, she was in waist-deep and couldn't get out.

Page tried to take in Candy's spirit in order to properly assume her identity. Pretending was the easy part; being able to stomach it was the hard part. Even though Candice was a stranger to her, the emotions ran deep. Much as she fought it, Page felt remorseful about what she was doing. Nevertheless, Young Heat was her family, and he'd been there for her daily, taking her out of the homeless shelter into a huge comfortable house. It was the least she could do for all he did to help. She laid in the king-sized bed, and her mind ran away in a fantasy, a daydream about what life would be like as Candice Gray. A warm and full feeling ran through her veins, thinking about all the possibilities that were available. While brainstorming, she scrolled through Candy's pictures in her iPhone. They were lots of different backgrounds and foreign landscapes. One of the backgrounds read Hong Kong Mandarin Inn. Clearly they were in the city of Hong Kong. Then she noticed something very important: Candice had an engagement ring on her finger. She flashed it proudly in the pictures, hand held out. How would she explain to Swave the absence of the ring? Page frantically called Young Heat on her phone. He answered and calmed her down. It was a fixable setback; he told her to chill. The deal was to tell Swave she took it off while washing dishes, misplacing it in the process. Young Heat would take the ring off Candy's finger then mail it to her by Fed-Ex next-day mail. After hearing the rational explanation, she felt better.

Truly electrifying, the joy on their faces in the pictures. The two looked like a match made in heaven. Page only dreamed about being that happy. She enjoyed and respected what she had with Young Heat, but it wasn't true love. Honestly it was becoming progressively redundant, to say the least. Page was feeling different lately, and her mind often thought maybe Karen felt the same way. Maybe she wanted something different for her life. Is that why she weighed her options? Going with security versus being a blind opportunist. Page had never thought about the future before. Everything in her life revolved around Young Heat and his bright ideas. Even though they'd been successful thus far, what about the one time things didn't go according to the plans? The thought made her extremely uncomfortable. Horrible thoughts of failure set in her mind and spirit. She knew deep down inside this was the wrong thing to do. The powers of the universe would release an extreme case of karma. Page looked around the house for some alcohol, needing something to ease her internal pain. If she could just make it until this was over, the life of crime was over as well. At that very moment, she decided to finish this job then move on to greener pastures, somewhere peace of mind dwells. Page wanted the best but suddenly wasn't prepared to pay the cost to achieve monetary gain.

Candice started to come out of her state of unconsciousness. Eyes blurred, and she had an extreme headache. Once her eyes focused clearly, she saw a man and woman. She felt her hands, mouth, and legs duct-taped. Young Heat greeted her by giving Candice her situation. "Well, well, Ms. Gray, so glad you could join us today. Who I am is unimportant, but what I am isn't. I'm the man who has kidnapped you and your sister Tosha. You're here for a purpose. That is to help me achieve a goal. You'll find out soon enough. If you cooperate, then you save the lives of your sister and yourself. If not, the rest is self-explanatory. I see you have on an engagement ring. If you ever want to see that smooth designer, you call your fiancé again. Then you'll do what I ask." She responded by nodding her head in agreement, clueless to what this man in power had in mind. Young Heat thought this out long and hard. He wanted Candice to think Tosha was in danger as leverage to use against her and a rebellious mind. Little did Candice know her sister was alive and well, riding in a vehicle behind them. Candy's mind was sliced in many different layers, wondering who this man was and how he knew Tosha and Swave. Obviously serious—just the fact of the kidnapping was proof that he meant business and wasn't playing any games. Candice agreed to play along until she could form a plan or try to escape, which would be a long shot; she didn't want to risk Tosha's life, or hers for that matter.

Late in the evening, Swave finally called to check in. At first it was hard answering to another name. Then Page thought about Young Heat's last command, "Stay in character." So she took a long, deep breath and played her role, unaware if they had pet- or nicknames for each other. She called him sweetheart, an appropriate term of endearment. He proceeded to tell her he just had a dinner meeting. He'd be home within the hour and Kym and Pam sent congratulation wishes. She thought for a minute, then it dawned on her—the engagement. She sent her gratitude for their wishes, blowing him kisses over the phone, and they ended the phone call. "OK, Page, it's time to act accordingly," she whispered as she started to freshen up. The bathroom was full of beauty products, body lotions, and perfumes. Then a very important factor became a major issue, one that they didn't think about, or at least she didn't. Swave would most likely want to make love to her consistently. He was irresistibly attractive, tall, dark, and muscular. She toyed with the thought for a few minutes. Page was only physically involved with one man, Young Heat. She was faithful to what they shared. He was a decent-looking guy, but Swave was drop-dead gorgeous. A magnificent physique, smooth chocolate skin tone, and a clean white smile. Equivalent to sunshine after a rainy day. It would be an experience she would welcome and never forget. The question is, would she allow her body to be explored?

She looked in the mirror and tried to coach herself. Finding a bottle of Blue Riesling wine, she poured a glass of wine and talked to herself. The more she drank, the more an affair with Swave sounded appealing. Sleeping with her biological sister's fiancé was an exciting part of this mission, taking her mind away from her futile way of thinking. Young Heat was a good lover, but he had become very predictable. This was an opportunity to spice up her sexual appetite. Then she started to justify her thoughts. "Young Heat did tell me to stay in character." That would include making love to her fiancé as if she were Candice. Then she heard the door open and close. A voice from downstairs called out, "Candice, I'm home, where are you, baby?" This was it—a performance to solidify her future. Not only hers, but the entire. This theatrical display was for all the marbles. A lot was riding on her shoulders, requiring her to perform up to par. He walked into the bedroom and met her in the bathroom, gave her a hug and a kiss lovingly. So far, so good. Damn, he looked and smelled irresistible. Tailor-made suit from his personal line. Solid back with a crew-neck French-cuffed dress shirt, cufflinks, and Louis Vuitton shoes. The fragrance was Bond No. 9. He was looking like a model for Neiman Marcus. She couldn't speak, like a deer caught in high-beam headlights. He kissed her and held her tight while running his hand across her rear end. Page was instantly wet between her legs. The fact that she was wearing thongs didn't help. She wanted some affection, and she wanted it from Swave.

Before she could gather her thoughts, Swave had her in his strong arms, headed toward the king-sized canopy bed. Paralyzed by his touch, her heart beating fast and hard, vocal cords weak and squeaky, she couldn't utter a word. He moved in for the kill, undressing her slowly. She tried to resist, but the temptation was to strong. Within a matter of minutes, she was completely naked. He stood and undressed quickly, standing at attention with his manhood hard. The view almost made Page swallow her tongue. She had seen porn tapes with men that were well-endowed. Never had she seen something so large in person. Page couldn't believe her eyes, mesmerized by his appearance. His touch was sensual and his kisses endearing. His smell was irresistible, and she yielded to her desires, starting to kiss his chest and hold his broad shoulders. He had drunk a few drinks with his colleagues. She was feeling the effects of the Blue Riesling wine. Both were experiencing the effects of the alcohol, wanting and needing the touches of each other. The he rolled on top and opened her legs wide, about to insert his manhood inside her kitten. He noticed the bright-colored horrific scene. Her eyes were closed, not aware that her monthly visitor had arrived. The sheets were soaked with blood from her womb. He gently rose from the bed and went to the bathroom to get a towel. She was extremely embarrassed and upset at the same time. If it wasn't for bad luck, she wouldn't have any luck at all. Like a good fiancé and gentleman, Swave ran her a hot bath so she could soak and feel clean.

Swave didn't know it, but he had just dodged a big bullet. Making love to her would've started an emotional dialogue between their bodies. So after her long bubble bath, Swave was loving and compassionate, holding her all night. Page had never experienced intimacy so excessive and sensual, wishing the night had turned out far more physical. Still she enjoyed the tender touches on her body. As they lay, Swave felt for the ring on her finger. Realizing it wasn't there, she whispered in his ear. "Sweetheart, don't be angry with me, but while doing the dishes I removed my ring. I can't seem to find it, but I'm sure I'll find it. I just misplaced it." He didn't make a big deal out of it, 'cause after all, where could it have gone? It was definitely somewhere in the house. Amazed at his attitude about a ring that cost a pretty penny, she assumed it was a sign he was in love with Candice. He held her tight and said, "We'll find it tomorrow together." Page's mind again split into layers; she wished she were Candice, engaged to this amazing hunk of a man. Staying in character was very enjoyable as well as an act of turmoil. It was a catch-22 to the fullest. She enjoyed playing this role but knew it would come to an end. Feeling his erect manhood against her rear while snuggled under the cover, Page wanted this fantasy to play out to her benefit and never ever end.

Morning came quickly, and Swave was up early on his computer. He had a busy schedule lined up the next few days. Drinking coffee, looking at marketing reports, Pam e-mailed him. His fiancée woke to granola cereal and fresh-cut grapefruit. He was conscious of her diet. Swave sat across from her, watching his love eat, then asked about Tosha coming to New York. She replied it would be a few more days before she came. He was fine with that as long as she was happy. He planned all her photo shoots for two weeks ahead. She'd be free to enjoy her sister's company. He explained that the next few days would be hectic, a heavily busy time for him and the company. On the grind, putting together the international marketing plan. She kissed his forehead, saying, "Do your very best, baby." Swave couldn't put his finger on it, but she seemed different that morning. He dismissed it as just being her time of the month. However, it was definitely something different. She asked Swave if he wanted anything specific for dinner. "Nothing at all, I'll grab a bite while working." She didn't argue because the truth was Page couldn't cook. She was planning to get takeout and try to pass it off as a home-cooked meal. Hopefully he wasn't the type that required a hot meal every day. *So far so good,* she thought to herself. Now Young Heat's next pair of instructions needed to come quick.

He was dressed for the business day ahead of him—dress slacks, dress shirt, and a formal tie, casual Prada shoes to complete the look. Swave was ready for a long day in the field of fashion. The time on his Royal Oak timepiece read nine o'clock. Carlos would be beeping any minute. He took a few moments to look her in the eyes. While talking, he noticed something distant in her eyes. Once again, maybe it was her emotions getting the best. She felt him studying her deeply. So she tried to change the subject of whatever he was thinking. The easiest way was with a wet kiss. He kissed her back, then the car horn beeped. It was Carlos, right on time as usual. He put his index finger to her lips. "We'll finish this chat when I come home." They kissed passionately, exploring each other's mouths with their tongues. He grabbed his briefcase, laptop, and cell phone, turned, and said, "I love you, I'll see you later on tonight." She stood in the doorway watching him get into the Lincoln. Page felt herself enjoying the theatrics and feeling deeper into her character as the diva Candice Gray.

As soon as Swave was gone, Page called Young Heat for further instructions. He answered immediately, making sure she was OK, He was already back in Charlotte driving almost nonstop, stopping once for gas and the restroom. Jackie released Candy from the duct tape and accompanied her to the bathroom. The fear of Tosha's life kept Candice in proper control. After she used the bathroom, Jackie duct-taped her again, this time blindfolding her in order to allow Tosha to gas up and use the bathroom. Now at a safe house in Charlotte, Young Heat kept a watchful eye on the prize guest. He commanded his troops with a stern hand, known as the pimp hand. Calling the plays through the phone. He informed Page of the plan at hand. She was to call Karen on Candy's phone, insisting on her full cooperation in the scheme to sell the jewels. Sam thought it was Candice that robbed him; that's the way it would stay unless Karen didn't want to play ball. Then he told her to collect credit cards and checks for additional cash flow. She was clear on her duties and more than willing to carry out his instructions. As soon as they ended the call, the phone rang—it was a call from Karen. Page quickly answered the line. Karen's voice made her freeze for a short moment, considering which character she would play. Without any more thought, she answered as Page. Karen was able to distinguish her voice from Candy's. They sounded similar, but there was something distinctive about Page's voice. Karen was able to discern between the two.

Karen's face was red from the shock. Page announced she was going into the blackmail scheme. Karen's head was totally screwed up by this unexpected chain of events. Seems like every time she was in the clear, there had to be another lie told. Karen began to wonder if meeting Candice in Las Vegas was a planned occurrence directed by Young Heat. Too much of a coincidence not to be a planned encounter. Page ran the whole plan down to Karen, along with her role to encourage her husband to buy back the jewels. She just listened to the other end of the phone, knowing there was nothing she could do but confirm and play her role. Karen was pregnant and tired of all the lies she told. She had to be at peace and stress-free for the welfare of her child.

The birth of a healthy baby boy was her only main concern. She had come too far to allow Young Heat and crew to destroy her in the process of achieving long-term wealth. Without a moment's hesitation, Karen told Page she'd go along with the plan, only on one condition: "Tell Young Heat after this is concluded, leave me and Sam alone." Page assured Karen she would pass the message on to Young Heat.

They sat in the Con Ed power truck across the street from the brownstone, watching and plotting on the female who now was alone. They saw Swave leave the residence and get into a Lincoln town car carrying a briefcase, obviously headed to work. It was time, and Tommy Two Guns and Franky Ziti were equipped with the necessary tools for the trade, down to power company uniforms. Franky walked on the side of the house, flipping down the old-style circuit breaker to the brownstone. Then they both stood on the porch, knocking on the door, clipboards in hand to appear realistic. Page came running to the door after the power went out. Using the peephole, she saw it was the power company. She asked who it was anyway. They replied, "The power company, there's a problem with the power on this block. We need to check your fuse box please." She opened the door, and two men with smiling faces stood in the doorway with clipboards. Tommy reached out his hand and shook Page's hand. They seemed official, and she needed the power back on. She welcomed them into the house, directing them to the fuse box in the kitchen. She turned around, and Tommy slapped her so hard she flew a few feet, landing on the kitchen table. Ziti locked the door and started his search for the brooch. Page didn't know what hit her; she was in a state of shock. Finally she came back to consciousness, realizing she was in trouble. Tommy picked her up and started to yell, asking for the brooch that was stolen from Walter's Jewelry Store.

She was stunned and didn't know what to make of the ordeal. One thing she knew, they were serious and she was in trouble. He slapped her again, this time holding her by the hair. "Don't let me ask you again, you bitch." Page started to cry, feeling helpless and scared. Ziti kept going through the house uncontrollably. Page yelled for them to leave her alone. Then Tommy slapped her again; this time she flew into the wall. "I want that brooch you and your crew stole from the jewelry store. If you don't cooperate, this will be the last face you see." She knew he meant business, and protecting Young Heat wasn't an option. Looking at the gun as he twisted on the silencer, she yelled out Young Heat's name, telling Tommy he was the mastermind behind the robbery. He also had all the jewels that were stolen. Tommy stopped for a moment, instructing her to call this Young Heat. Of course she agreed, and he walked with her to the upstairs bedroom. While she dialed Young Heat, she wiped the blood from her mouth from a busted lip. The connection was made; Tommy grabbed the phone, putting it on speaker so Page could hear. Young Heat didn't understand why Page wasn't answering his greeting. Then it all made perfect sense when Tommy threatened her life if the brooch wasn't handed over. Young Heat calmly asked who he was talking to. Tommy replied, "Your worst nightmare if you don't return my property." Young Heat heard Page screaming as Tommy slapped her around with pistol in hand. She screamed, "Young Heat, please give them what they want."

He was suddenly in an uncomfortable position. Page was his all-star on a winning team. They had been together through many tough times. She was his homie, lover, friend. He cared about her dearly, but to return the jewel that obviously was worth a lot wasn't in the cards. If whoever went through finding the crew for that jewel, it must be worth a large sum of money. The logic Young Heat came up with while thinking about what options he had, it was clear to him they didn't really know him nor where he was if they had Page. They obviously thought they had Candice. Page had got caught in the crossfire tracking Candice. Then he decided much as he would miss Page, she would be a missed casualty of war. Thus the price of that brooch just went up in value. He screamed out to the adversaries, "You'll never get that jewel back. Kill her if you want." Young Heat ended the call by hanging up the phone. Page started to scream and cry uncontrollably. She knew Young Heat had just sealed her fate. How could he have turned on her for a stupid piece of jewelry? Tommy looked at her with eyes of death, pissed off and tired of this whole ordeal. He slapped her again, sending her to the bed. Then he jumped on her and started to choke her tightly. Her face was red, and she was gasping for air. He stopped asking where Young Heat lived. She told him the address (Charlotte) while crying, trying to plead for her life, but it was futile. He again started to choke her, this time even tighter. Tommy, being a participant in S and M with his girlfriend, started to get turned on by the strangulation. His grip was tight as a python, crushing his prey devilishly on top of Page's lifeless body,

Franky Ziti walked into the room. Tommy was so into his S and M character, he didn't realize she was dead. Ziti yelled at Tommy to stop, but the damage was done. Page was now a memory, and the blood was on Young Heat's hands. Well, as the sick and twisted killer Tommy Two Guns. He got up, trying to hide his erection from Ziti. He was turned on by hurting that young woman. Ziti didn't even comment on what he had just seen. They started to tear the bedroom up looking for any of the jewels. It became clear they weren't in the house. So they left the brownstone. Page's lifeless body lay still on Swave's king-sized bed. Ziti went on the side of the house and clicked the breaker back on. They drove away in the power truck. The only thing they had gained was Young Heat's address. He shouldn't be hard to find in that city. Ziti knew Tommy was a head case, but now he had proof of his weird lifestyle. Tommy drove the truck thinking how he enjoyed killing that pretty fashion model, Candice Gray. He had killed the right one in the wrong person's position. Maybe Page should've listened to her gut instinct. She knew it was a bad idea, but she wanted to please Young Heat. She pleased him with her death. He wouldn't exchange a jewel for her life. She was so young, so naive, and so vulnerable. So long, Page Meeks, you gave your life keeping Young Heat's instructions, staying in character. Ain't that a bitch.

Swave had been busy all day on conference calls to Hong Kong. The Chin brothers were wanting an estimated time when the clothes would arrive. Then he and Pam talked to the Hong Kong city representative, Mr. Lang. He received the photos that would become a billboard in the city. Finally getting a chance to call Candy, she didn't answer. He left a message to call him back. Swave wanted to take her out to dinner then spend the night trying to locate the lost ring, never making an issue about the ring he spent hard-earned money on. He was willing to think positive and help find the spectacular showpiece. He wondered why she wasn't answering her phone. Knowing he'd been spending a lot of time at the office, though he explained it to Candice, still made him feel guilty and compelled to spend some quality time with his fiancée. Pam had taken on most of Kym's load due to severe cases of morning sickness. She wasn't just missing work for no reason. All the conference calls ended. He and Pam went over some projected sales figures. Pam was a wizard with numbers, and Swave was always amazed at her knowledge. He asked Cindy Rae to continue calling Candice until she answered. Cindy also had no luck in reaching the beauty for him. He assumed she had gone out for a while. Probably didn't charge her phone and didn't have the charger. So he decided to end his day at work early, try to beat her home with a surprise of his presence. Then they could go to Philippe Chow to eat some fine Asian cuisine.

Ending the meeting with Pam abruptly, he called Carlos to pick him up in thirty minutes. Pam was enjoying their time together alone. She secretly had a fantasy she wanted to act out ever since she had seen the size of his manhood. Pam wanted to experience his magic between the sheets, trying to hide the attraction she felt for him. Clearly it was obvious to Swave that their relationship was different. Every chance she got, Pam gently touched and brushed against his firm, hard body intentionally. To the naive eye, it seemed harmless and innocent. Honestly it made him incredibly uncomfortable in the workplace. He knew her walking in on him masturbating was the root. A heart-to-heart conversation was definitely needed as soon as they concluded the major details on the international account. He needed her expertise and knew she had connections stretching to Europe, Asia, and beyond. Right in the nick of time, Cindy buzzed him, announcing Carlos had arrived, freeing him from an awkward position. He told Pam they had something to talk about in the morning, hoping to extinguish her fire quietly without causing a uproar. She smiled at him like he was a sliced turkey and Swiss on wheat. He gave farewells to the staff, which was common. Swave the businessman and CEO of the company left the office for the day with a great attitude, thinking about Candy's beautiful, pretty feet. He wanted to buy her a pair of stilettos. Even as a designer, he liked and was inspired by other designers. Before heading home, he told Carlos to drive to Manhattan's Neiman Marcus, always wanting his fiancée to be on the cutting edge of fashion.

He knew she wanted this particular pair of Christian Louboutins. Swave thought the shoes were sexy. More than anything, he loved her to show those beautiful polished toes. Footwear was an absolute work in progress for his company. They started production on Candy Girl sneakers. However, the stilettos and pumps would come later. Swave designed the perfect minidress to compliment the Christian Louboutin stilettos. He and Carlos talked all the way to Neimans. He parked in the parking deck and waited until Swave returned. The whole while, he kept calling Candy— still no answer. He took the elevator to the third floor where the women's footwear was located, imagining the day his brand would be featured in Neiman Marcus. Nevertheless, he was on the fast track to true success. Once his line was popular overseas, every retailer and their mothers would want to carry the line, especially Candy Girl wear. They were intelligently taking a unconventional road for mass appeal.

The store was packed with all sorts of women. Looking around, Swave caused quite a stir with the women, turning a few beauties' heads while browsing for shoes. A blonde saleswoman came to assist him. She was smiling and pleasant. Swave politely asked for the red-bottom stilettos, black, and a size six. She was impressed by his taste. That style of shoe was $600, a nice commission for her helping a hunk. Totally pleased with the limited-edition stilettos, he handed her his company credit card.

Reading the name on the credit card, she turned red in the face. She had actually heard of the brand. In fact, she had recently shopped at his store in New Jersey. Her sister lived in New Jersey, and on a visit, she and her sister ran across to the boutique. The saleswoman was very impressed with the quality of the clothes. Both women raved and planned to support the brand. He was flattered and thanked her for the support, never revealing he was the brains behind the brand. She assumed he was the designer. She asking to take a picture with her for memories. Being a gentleman, he agreed to take a picture with the blonde. Women started to wonder who this dark handsome guy was taking a picture. He shook her hand and walked away into the crowd of customers, thinking of how happy the shoes would make Candice. That was his job, to make his fiancée happy. He called Carlos, telling him he was ready. He picked Swave up in the front of the store efficiently. On the way to Harlem, he called Philippe Chow, making a reservation for dinner. He would take his baby out on the town, maybe even catch a play on Broadway. Whatever she wanted to do was his desire to please Candice.

The radio played Jahiem's song, "You can have anything I've got. / All of me right on the spot."

All the way home, Swave was thinking about the night he had planned. They hadn't spent quality time together since Hong Kong. He longed to hold her and kiss her soft juicy lips. One more stop—he wanted to bring some roses home. So Carlos stopped at the florist. A dozen red roses was the selection, and home was the destination. Carlos played Jahiem's first CD, which always relaxed Swave. Listening to the lyrics and watching the scenery made him feel happy to be living in Harlem among his people and getting inspiration from the Y2K generation. Carlos pulled up outside the brownstone, and Swave paid him. They made plans for an early departure in the morning. A shopping bag from Neimans and a dozen roses filled his arms. At the top of the stairs, he noticed a Fed-Ex delivery note posted on the door addressed to Candice from YH. He took the note, wondering who the hell was YH. Candice obviously hadn't made it back home yet. Opening the door that was unlocked, automatically his defensive guard kicked into alarm. Walking in the house was like walking into a war zone. The house was absolutely wrecked like a tornado had passed through. He dropped the bag and roses, looking for the intruder. The living room had been turned upside down. The kitchen table was broken, and there was blood on the floor. Swave didn't keep a gun in the house; hell, he didn't even own one. Quickly he grabbed a steak knife, continuing to look around the house. In silence, the more he wandered, the more he saw the damage caused.

He pulled his phone out of his pocket to call 911 quickly. He crept up the stairs slowly, trying not to make any noise while walking. The two spare bedrooms were ransacked from top to bottom. He moved closer to his bedroom, expecting to see the same destruction as well. One foot inside the room, and there was his worst nightmare. Candice lay across the bed in a pool of blood. He ran to her, trying to revive her lifeless body. Her forehead was cold, and there was no pulse. "Oh my God" was all he could say. Then he ran to the bathroom with his stomach in a frenzy, vomiting hard from his innermost being into the toilet. He ran back to her side, trying to administer mouth-to-mouth, aware she was gone, but love made him try anyway. Finally he called 911, reporting the crime. Swave couldn't believe this was really happening. This had to be a dream. At least he hoped it was, but unfortunately it wasn't; it was reality. His beautiful love, his fiancée, his soul mate. The woman he would never be able to marry. He was so hurt and couldn't even think straight. This absolutely was the worst day of his life.

The NYPD arrived on the scene and made their way upstairs, weapons drawn, finding Swave sitting next to the dead body, oblivious to the police calling out to him. He was lost in his own train of thoughts, still holding her hand, unable to pry himself away. Finally he noticed the police standing in front of the bed. He was crying and shaking frantically; obviously he was a nervous wreck. The police asked his name and if this was his residence. One officer checked the rest of the room. The other checked to see if the body had a pulse. Negative—she was definitely dead. The officers already assumed that from the faint smell of death. It was hard, but the officers convinced Swave to head downstairs. The bedroom was now considered a crime scene. He pocketed his and Candy's cell phones, walking down the stairs carrying a boatload of grief. One officer followed, while the other called into dispatch. Soon the coroner would be at the scene to gather the body. The officer that accompanied Swave started to ask questions about the crime scene. Until proven otherwise, he was a person of interest concerning the murder, a common protocol for domestic crimes. He called Kym and Pam for support; both made their way to the brownstone in record time. The coroner had arrived, and homicide detectives were also there. Within two hours, the whole property was sealed off with yellow tape. Swave agreed to come to the station to give a formal statement on videotape. Kym and Pam were right by his side like true friends.

His testimony almost ripped the life out of him, reliving how he found his fiancée. He testified that they were in love and planned on getting married. There were no financial problems and no personal problems with anyone. He talked about his business and her being the face of the brand, expounding on his background as well as Candy's background. After a few hours of questions, Swave was tired and wanted to go home. They understood his statement had been a huge help. Kym offered her spare bedroom, but he decided on a hotel. Pam drove him to the brownstone to get some clothes. Then he found himself in a long hot shower in the Hilton in downtown Manhattan. He was happy to have his friends for support but wanted to be alone. He had just lost the woman he loved. Swave told Kym and Pam to handle everything at work. A much-needed break away from everything was evident. The women expected as much, considering the circumstances. In total agreement, the women let him know they were there if needed. Swave took the time to go through Candy's phone to call her parents and Tosha. To his surprise, the phone didn't have her parents' names and numbers. It only contained names and numbers of people he had never heard of until he saw Tosha's and Karen's names. Well, he had to start the process of contacting her parents. He'd never met them; how would he break the news? How would they take it coming from him?

Alone in the hotel room, he was finally able to let down his guard. He had acted so strong in front of Kym and Pam. The truth was he wasn't strong at all. More like the early stages of a nervous breakdown. Looking in Candy's phone, something he never did under normal circumstances, made him wonder, just who his fiancée really was behind closed doors. The pictures in her phone were obviously before their relationship. They featured several with a guy who seemed very close to Candice. She had a few with Tosha and another woman. Then there was one with the unknown guy and Karen. How could that be possible? Now things weren't making any sense at all. How could Candice have taken a picture with Karen before she was obviously pregnant? They had met Karen and Sam in Las Vegas while attending the Toni Braxton concert. He had to calm down; maybe he was missing something. Maybe he forgot something, or maybe his eyes and mind were playing tricks on him. Opening a bottle of Remy Martin, he poured a shot. He needed to lie down and get some rest. This was too much for his brain to compute all at once. Sleep, he needed some sleep. Maybe things would be clear in the morning. It was worth a try, and he had no other choice. The body needed to shut down for a few hours. Swave was totally in the blind about many things. He had picked up Page's phone thinking it was Candy's. The start of a long, twisted deception.

It was wondrous how a few hours of sleep recharged the brain. Swave felt like a completely new man. Having an enormous amount of troubles still pending, now it was time to think about things analytically. All the skeptical thoughts ran through his mind. The fact remained—his fiancée was dead. Nothing in the world would bring her back. Much as it hurt, he had to be strong in order to give his fiancée a special homegoing service. The photos in the phone weren't explainable. At least not without Candice to give a reasonable explanation. For now, he would have to leave the questions for later, although he would do his own investigation soon as the smoke cleared. The main thing right now was to lay his dear love to rest, peacefully and respectfully just as she rightly deserved. If it took every dime he had saved, she would go out in style. The first order of business was to contact Candy's family. He called Tosha's phone, but it went straight to voicemail. He left a message for her to call his phone ASAP. There was some serious information concerning her sister. He left his phone number and ended the call. Tosha didn't answer the phone because Young Heat told her Page was murdered by a unknown force wanting to blackmail them for the jewels. He instilled in her head they probably had Page's phone. Truth was he had mentally already cut his losses and moved on. A true general was able to understand lives would be lost in the pursuit of the American dream, to be abundantly rich beyond measure, enjoying the absolute finer things in life.

The New York press was having a field day with the reports. Breaking news—a young, beautiful model murdered in Harlem. Seems Candice had a sizable following in the industry. She was noticeably romantically linked to the fresh new clothing designer, Eric "Swave" Hawkins." She had been the new face of his clothing line, Palm-Tree, as well as the former spokesperson and model for Neon Vodka. Candy's death was gaining nationwide exposure. Before Swave had the opportunity to contact the Grays, they tracked him down, calling the Palm-Tree office in Manhattan. They reached Pam Orchard, who willingly gave them his number. He answered to hear the terror in Mrs. Gray's voice. Calmly he tried to speak with comfort for the mother who was suffering a tremendous loss. Though he didn't know her, she was just like family. He began to explain to her the horrible chain of events, leaving the photos and suspicions out of the equation, also excluding the terrible condition he found her in—beaten badly and obviously tortured before her death. He gave Mrs. Gray his deepest and heartfelt condolences, expressing sincere, sympathetic sorrow and grief. She felt his heart in those words. They talked for two hours about everything concerning the death of her daughter. Of course she had questions, and he answered them best of his ability. From the conversation Vanessa Gray had with her daughter about how well Swave treated her, like a queen, she knew in her heart he was innocent of any foul play. Mrs. Gray had just talked to her a few days prior. Candice seemed so happy and full of life. Now that was all in the past. A mere vapor in the hot sun quickly evaporated. Swave shared the pre-autopsy report that lead detective Phillip Barnes revealed. His hypothesis on the cause of death was strangulation.

He also gave Mrs. Gray the contact information for Detective Barnes just in case she wanted to ask any further questions or stay close to the investigation. He added that he was paying for the funeral as soon as they released the body. He was flying her home to California for the homegoing services. They promised to stay in touch during the next few days. Mrs. Gray said she would call Tosha to inform her of the family's loss. They ended the call with great emotions for each other, feeling the love through the phone. Truth was, Mrs. Gray admired Swave. She had no ill feelings toward him at all, accepting it as being Candy's time to leave this earth. She was a very spiritual woman and tried to look on the bright side in every awkward and troubling situation. Mr. Gray kept his grief bottled up and went to work to relieve his stress.

Tosha finally called Swave back after receiving a call from Mom, playing along as the hurting younger sister. It was clear Page was killed in place of her twin sister. Mom and Dad and Swave didn't have a clue Page wasn't Candy. The plot had gotten so thick, and Tosha kept quiet, playing along, knowing Candice was really safe and sound. Since Page had played such a convincing role as Candice, Tosha wasn't about to rock the boat. Not before she received some monetary gain. She talked to Swave as if she were weak in spirit—part of the game 'cause she really wanted them to console each other in this time of grief and sorrow. Clinging to thoughts of the first time she saw Swave made her want him even more than ever. The concern in his voice and the loving tone expressed how much he loved Candice. Tosha would claim this opportunity of weakness as her time to thrive. She was aware of the consequences but willing to take a chance, a chance that might land her in the strong arms of her sister's fiancé. She promised him they would speak more about the sudden loss. He wanted to ask her some questions, at least to put his mind at ease. However, he decided to handle his curiosity another time and another way. They ended the call planning to see each other in California, where the family would put Candy's body to rest.

Fourth Quarter

The flight to California was equivalent to a visit with the dentist. Necessary but painful nonetheless. He was greeted at the airport by George and Vanessa Gray. There was an instant love and respect among the three. Vanessa Gray immediately saw what her daughter felt in her heart, the genuine compassion that flowed from his innermost being to his vocal cords and out of his mouth. Not to mention his striking good looks. This man definitely had a presence, Vanessa Gray thought. George reserved his opinion until they had a chance to talk privately, tolerating the nostalgia that came with the visit to California. Everything reminded him of sweet Candice. Vanessa was filled with admiration for him, finding out all the arrangements he had made for both daughters—reserving a plane ticket for Tosha as well as flying Candy's body home to California. It was a shame he wouldn't be her son-in-law. He undoubtedly had the credentials for a great husband, father, and son-in-law. George also had a high level of respect for the man who treated his daughters with such love. Dad was eager to have a one-on-one with him to give his full seal of approval even though it really didn't matter 'cause Candice was gone and never coming back. Now all they could wish for was for Tosha to land a guy half as intelligent and driven as Swave, eventually giving them the ultimate blessing as parents to make them proud grandparents.

Swave gave Detective Phillip Barnes his personal phone number just in case he needed him if any new developments came up in the case. It turned out to be a smart move 'cause the detective called him. New information was revealed by the next-door neighbor. The elderly lady had seen two men dressed in Con-Ed work uniforms, equipped with tool belts and a utility worktruck. They had gone into the brownstone and stayed at least an hour, leaving the residence with clipboards in hand. Two white males were now the suspects in the crime. The detective assured Swave the new developments were top priority. This was a huge break in the case. Detective Barnes was already feeling the heat from the press. They were saying the NYPD wasn't taking the murder seriously. Candice Gray was a vibrant young life who had the entire world as her oyster. The fact that Phillip Barnes had a daughter the exact age as Candice made him passionate about solving the case. He went through the brownstone with a fine-toothed comb taking fingerprints, but no hits came up in the NCIS system. Though Swave vowed to find the killer, he was glad the NYPD was on the case. More directly, he was glad Detective Barnes was serious about the case. Swave shared the new information with Candy's parents. They were both glad some progress was being made. Only a few days, but the first forty-eight hours were the most important.

The two heartless criminals were safely back home in North Carolina. They had accomplished one of the two goals assigned to them after several days of watching Marie. It was obvious Nato was nowhere to be found. At least nowhere around his lover Marie. Before activating the action plan to apprehend Young Heat, Tommy and Franky sat down with their boss, Carmine. This was to inform him of every move that had been made. Carmine knew blood would be shed. He didn't care as long as the task was handled, to retrieve that exquisite, valuable brooch. The wiseguys did have one piece of positive news for the Don. The 50-percent split was not legal and binding. The ownership papers prepared by the lawyer were signed by Sam. A slight twist of the arm by his enforcers now gave Carmine the right to half of Sam's business. He was happy to hear the news and now even more determined to find Nato, the absolute best thief he knew and needed to put the rest of his plan into action. He would stealing a large treasure worth an undisclosed amount from the Arabs that supplied the diamond exchange in the heavily guarded millennium diamond vault located in the heart of Manhattan, New York City. As long as the wiseguys saw a small smile on Carmine's face, they were safe for now. Finding this Young Heat and the brooch would clear the air sufficiently for the two. So after their sitdown at the round table, the Italians were off to putting Operation Brooch, into full effect.

Coming Soon
Tailor-Made Candy II
Revenge!

Au revoir!

Lavish Life 88 Entertainment, INC
P. O. Box 481367
Charlotte, NC 28269
Email: *info@lavishlife88.com*
Website: *www.LavishLife88.com*
Follow us on Twitter, Instagram and Facebook @ Lavish_Life88

Upcoming Releases from Lavish Life 88 Entertainment

Coming in June, 2014
"*The Anatomy of Hip-Hop*"—by Erskine Harden and Anthony Booth.
"*Tailor Made Candy Part 1*"—by Erskine Harden.

Coming in Early Fall of 2014
"*The Final Round*"—by Darnell Jacobs.
"The Upheaval In Rome"—by Donquell Speller

Coming in Late Fall 2014
"*I Dee Claire War*"—by Donquell Speller

Coming in the Spring of 2015
"Tailor Made Candy II"—by Erskine Harden.
"Frost Bitten"—Tony Booth

Coming in the Spring of 2015
"Cognitive Behaviors" by Donquell Speller
"Inside Out the Prison Game" by Tony Booth
"Dalyia the Black Rose"

Available Now In Publication

A short story, "Sabotage to Success" by Erskine Harden now available for $0.99 on all E-Book sites only.

Tailor-Made Candy II

Tosha was amazed as she stood in a trance, watching the muscular frame in a motionless, peaceful sleep. Her mind ran wild with visions of sensual escapades. She wanted desperately to feel his touch, to experience intimacy in a way she had never imagined. She wanted to lie beneath his strong and superior frame while feeling him deep inside her body. The thought of this scenario made euphoric feelings rush her brain which released chemicals in her body causing her to be sexually turned on. The moisture between her legs told the story. She had to seize the moment especially while he was in a vulnerable state.

In her mind, she had the power to persuade him into a promiscuous encounter. She was an opportunist, and this was a chance of a lifetime. Before she made a move the sounds of the squeaky wooden floors alarmed her senses. The old house always alerted its inhabitants of any movements. Snapped back into reality, Tosha knew it was her mother making routine rounds as if she was a security guard working the graveyard shift.

She softly blew a kiss towards her sleeping guest and quickly disappeared into the darkness. Quietly as possible she entered her room, slipping back into the bed just in the nick of time as Mrs. Gray peeped into her room to see her sound asleep. At least she appeared to be, another theatrical performance to her credit. However, the adrenaline pumped through her entire body. She breathed heavily, silently trying to slow her heart rate. Her plan to sleep with Swave and win his heart started to take form. Playing the caring sister of his deceased fiancé was the starting point. Gentle affection leading toward an emotional bond was the strategy. Carefully calculated steps would unite the two. Tosha counted on his vulnerability and her manipulative ways to hook him.

Spending every moment she could with him while he was in California would set the stage. Hopefully, she could maneuver herself into flying back to New York with him. Playing this strategy over and over in her head, thinking about what words to use, clothes to wear, and subliminal signs she would send with her eye contact. She had her work cut out, but Swave would be the ultimate catch. Not to mention she would win over her sister. The hidden contest she participated in against Candice would be over. The whole act was scandalous, but Tosha was fighting for total supremacy. Taking Candice away from life and career, along with using her as a pawn in a crime of deception and fictional death just wasn't enough for her to feel triumph. Tosha had to have Swave for herself like wealth. Having a vindictive core was an understatement, Tosha was a parasite that lived vicariously on others. Candice happens to be her biggest target, and she wouldn't rest until she had totally destroyed every aspect of her big sister's life.

Swave awakens from a dream that seemed so real. He and Candice were enjoying a wonderful vacation on a tropical island. The weather was warm, the water blue, and the sand was white. They rolled around in the sand kissing passionately. The scene was so vivid and clear. Her skimpy Yves Saint Laurent bikini looked amazing. The scent of her green apple shampoo made him smile. While closing his eyes and inhaling the fruity smell that triggered his senses, holding her tight and thinking to himself how lucky he was to have Candice, the grim reality set in, and he was infuriated. He couldn't understand why this was happening to him. Was this a penance for a sin he committed in another life? He was always a good hearted person, never hurting another soul. Hard worker and God-fearing, now he was being punished by the loss of his soul mate. They had become inseparable, enjoying true solid love.

Now he was here in California to bury his one and only true love. Staying in Candice's parent's family home in her room wasn't the plan. He wanted to stay at in a hotel, but Mrs. Gray wouldn't hear of it. The Gray's thought of him as family. Candice had talked so highly of him to her mother. They knew he was a good person. More importantly her parents knew he loved their daughter. In an effort not to offend them, he agreed to stay at their home. It was the least they could do since he flew the body back home and was paying for the funeral.

Assisting her parents with the funeral arrangements and lending them moral support consumed him. He was so preoccupied that his business appointments back in New York had totally slipped his mind. This wasn't normal for his ambitious nature. The only thing that comforted his mind was the trust he had in Kym and Pam. He knew their loyalty and dedication to the company wasn't even questionable.

The one thing that was increasingly troubling to his spirit was Candice's phone and the text picture with her and the mystery man. The last number dialed was to a man named Young. Was he the guy in the text pic? Did he have something to do with her death? Was Candice leading a dangerous and chaotic secret life? What was the Fed-Ex receipt he still had in his wallet for? These were all questions he had to get answers to and soon. However, it wasn't any information he needed to share with the NYPD or the Grays. He deliberately withheld these significant facts.

Patiently waiting until after the funeral, he would start a major investigation. Never breaking the law in the past, he now had the desire to avenge his fiancée's death. It was that fine line that often exists between a law- abiding citizen and a felonious vigilante who takes the law into his own hands. Now wasn't the time though, honoring Candice's life and memory was the immediate task. That meant putting away all the questions and distractions away in order to give his love a beautiful home going funeral. It was the hardest thing he would ever have to do, but it was something he had to do.

The persistent calling and leaving of messages with Swave's secretary finally paid off and Mia received a call from his assistant at the Palm-Tree enterprises. Kym recognized the name from a conversation she had shared with Swave. He told Kym at the request of Candice that Mia would be joining the marketing campaign. Her expertise as a wardrobe stylist, makeup artist, and hairdresser made her a triple threat. She was also the closest person to Candice while they worked on the "Neon" advertising tour.

So as a gesture of professional courtesy Kym returned her phone call. They talked for over half an hour, expressing their sympathy for the loss of Candice. Mia wanted to get the funeral information so she could attend. Also, the entire staff that went on tour with them wanted to show their respect. Carl Mills, the VP of advertising at "Neon," wanted an address to send flowers. Kym sensed the sincerity and gave him Swave's personal cell phone number. Mills would be able to get all the necessary information for her and the "Neon" staff. Normally Kym wouldn't give out his number but in light of the current circumstances and the time factor surrounding the funeral, she decided it would be wise and thoughtful to connect the two.

When the phone call was over, Kym sent Swave a text and telling him that he would be receiving a call from Mia. Kym wished that she could be there to support Swave and to show her respects. However, it was a tremendous work load in New York launching the Candy Girl line as well as the opening of the new store in Hong Kong. Plus, she was very much pregnant and she had to pace herself.

Later that night Mia called Swave after waiting for an appropriate hour because California and New York were in two different time zones. He pleasantly greeted her and she gave her condolences. Swave knew that Candice was fond of her so he didn't have a problem talking with her. He gave Mia the funeral information along with the address of the funeral to give to the other "Neon" staff. He felt it was important that Candice be remembered by as many as possible. The service would be held in Fresno at the family's church, True Vine Fellowship. Family and friends from Fresno could show respect and having additional friends from L.A. would be a great way to honor her memory. So he encouraged Mia to bring anybody that knew Candice and wanted to come.

Before ending the phone call, Swave asked if she was still interested in a job. She obviously had built a rapport with Candice and he wanted to honor his one true love last wish. She accepted his offer and they planned for her to have a formal orientation the following week. As much as it would be hard to do, he knew that the "Candy Girl" campaign had to go on. The best way to give Candice a tribute was to keep the line he created for her alive. He didn't know who would take her place as the face of the clothing line. Whomever it would be, Mia would be in charge of her look head to toe. He had a lot on his plate between dealing with the loss of Candice and trying to expand his fashion line internationally. There was also a burning desire to serve justice on whoever was responsible for her murder.

George and Vanessa Gray handled all the arrangements while Swave silently played his position. The only thing he insisted on was the choice of what she would wear which was a dress he designed for the "Candy Girl" line. The thought never crossed his mind that she would wear it at her funeral.

The whole week was a demanding task as he held back his tears and emotions and tried to appear strong. The reality was the total opposite, he missed her more than words could express. Sensing the front that he was displaying, Tosha took every opportunity to be affectionate with hugs and by holding his hand. Disguised as empathy, she was careful not to reveal her true intentions. Swave thought that she was extremely sweet and compassionate. Although he never looked at her in a sexual or disrespectful light, he still could not help but feel his nature rise when she hugged him. Tosha deliberately rubbed her breast against his chest and he felt her hard nipples which gave him an instant visual in his mind and made him even more embarrassed, by the way, his body was responding to her casual advances.

Tosha, being a master manipulator, noticed the effect she had on him and held him tight as she whispered slowly and seductively in his ear, "I am here for you Swave if you need me." Unsure of himself and in a confused state, he pulled away from her body as he started to feel like he had committed treason. He didn't reply but flashed a friendly smile. Tosha knew she had planted the seed in his brain. Now it was only a matter of time to let it grow and root deep into his subconscious.

The day had finally come to give Candice, the home going service she deserved. The Gray family came together united to give the parent's support. Both sides of the family filled the True Vine Fellowship Church along with friends of the family. There were also people who the Grays didn't know personally. The church was decorated with an assortment of beautiful flowers. It was obvious that Candice had touched the lives of a many people. Along with a packed church, there were also people outside waiting and wanting to pay their final respects. Her parents sat there amazed at the love being shown to their daughter.

As the choir sang old Christian spirituals, tears ran down Swave's face like a stream. Tosha played her role as well -trained actress and held his hand firmly as she wiped his tears away with a tissue. All he could think about was the time he and Candice had spent together. The more he cried, the more the fire of revenge burned within him. He loved Candice more than life itself. Now he had to find the strength to go on and avenge her death. The Pastor, Bishop Harold Nelson Ford gave a touching eulogy. There wasn't a dry eye in the entire church. The highlight of the service was a beautiful song Vanessa Gray sang to honor her daughter. When the coffin was opened for the final viewing of the body, everyone was blown away by her appearance. She looked so peaceful like she was taking a nap. They did a great job with the bruises on her face.

Even in the lifeless state she looked stylish with a wonderful mixed-motif silk gown. In addition to its gorgeous patterns, the dress was covered in geometric beads. Swave had done a phenomenal job with the creation. He noticed Mia, Carl Mills, and the "Neon" staff as they viewed the body. No one would ever imagine that this body wasn't Candice. Page was an identical twin to her sister who no one in the Gray family knew anything about. Nobody except the evil sister sitting and playing along with the game. She didn't care about the pain she was causing her family. The only thing that concerned Tosha was destroying her sister totally. It was amazing how jealousy and envy could consume one's entire being.

As she stood over the coffin beside Swave, she smiled inside thinking how she and Young had outsmarted everyone. Poor Page she thought to herself. Well, better her than me was her mindset. She managed to shed a few meaningless tears for appearance sake of course. She and Swave followed the family out of the church to the awaiting limos. At his side the entire time, Tosha wanted Swave to feel that her affection was genuine.

Chapter 2

News of the young model Candice Gray's murder was shocking and watching the story on MSNBC was very traumatic for Karen as she thought how Candice must have suffered. What was even more frightening was the thought of Youngheat. She knew he had something to do with the murder. Especially after she called Candy's phone and Page answered. They had admitted to the jewelry robbery and now Candice was dead. Her brain started to put things into the proper perspective. Candice and Page were obviously twin sisters and that would explain why Sam thought it was Candice that did the robbery. It had to be Page because it wasn't logical for Candice to commit a felonious act. Youngheat, of course, knew about both identities. He used this knowledge as leverage to commit a crime and blackmail her in the process. The only part of the puzzle she couldn't figure out was her meeting Candice in Vegas. Was this staged or a mere coincidence? How could Youngheat have known where she and Sam were staying? She couldn't answer the questions, but it was clear she underestimated Youngheat. It was like she didn't know him anymore.

Among all the ruthless manipulating things he had done, he now could add murder to his resume, which scared Karen. Youngheat must have killed Candice after he didn't need her anymore. What would he do to her, Sam and the baby she was carrying? It was no doubt she had to cooperate with the plan in order to buy her some time to properly dispose of her problem once and for all. Sam finding out about her involvement would be humiliating but their deaths would be worse.

Thinking about the dilemma she was in from every angle, intensely, taking her time not to make an irrational decision that would cost her family its lives, Karen knew that the bottom line and the common denominator was money. Youngheat did whatever it took to make the all mighty dollar and that was the weapon she would have to use against him. His desire was to accumulate as much money as he could. She would turn his greed into a way to eliminate him once and for all. They had shared some good times in the past. However, things were different these days and she had to think about the future. Her future, which was with Sam and her unborn child. Karen felt the crimes she had committed were a lifetime ago. Her intentions when she met Sam were totally superficial.

Once Karen got to know Sam and experienced the unconditional love he offered, she realized it was no comparison to what she had received from Youngheat. With Youngheat, it was always a hidden agenda. It was always what he could get from her, but Sam wasn't like that at all. He opened her eyes to living a legitimate lifestyle. She was now exposed to a culture and a real family structure that was the total opposite from how she had been living. She now had a real family as a wife and soon to be mother. At first it was only the money and security that hooked her, now it was Sam's true love and caring ways that touched her heart. She had taken her vows seriously and neither hell nor high water would separate her from her husband and child. Youngheat had a fight on his hands.

Youngheat was infuriated that Karen had jumped ship and had not only gotten married but was now pregnant. It was a sign of disrespect and the ultimate slap in the face. It was no way he would allow her to walk away without retribution. Even if she agreed with his plan to talk Sam into buying back the stolen jewels at a discounted price, he would still eventually expose her as a culprit in the scheme. She thought long and hard and came up with an ingenious plan to make Youngheat vanish. First she had to talk to Sam and get him on board with her plan. Only telling him what she wanted him to know, she would handle the intricate details herself; the less he knew, the better in case anything went wrong. One thing she knew for sure was that the lure of money in abundance was tempting. A temptation that he wouldn't be able to resist and a fictional vision was the picture she had to paint.

Jackie and Page wouldn't be a problem to her. Once you cut of the head, the body would die. After she disposed of Youngheat, they would tuck their tails and run for their lives. Even though Page was already dead, Karen didn't know she was killed in her place of her sister Candice. Karen only knew that her former comrades were naïve and she didn't blame them. She knew once her plan came full circle, they would see the light, just as she had. She was now thinking like herself, a strong, intelligent woman.

Being full aware that the detective Alex Lopez was inquisitive about the robberies along with Sam's daughter Kelly's suspicions, his plan had to be full proof and executed with extreme precision. She had to stay steps ahead of them. Sam hadn't opened the jewelry store since the robbery for several different reasons. He was suffering from posttraumatic stress syndrome as well as waiting for the insurance company to pay the claim. He wasn't in any rush simply because the thought of a partnership with Carmine Biasi made him sick. Being forced to sign away half of his empire built from the ground up was devastating. Sam wasn't foolish either; he knew Carmine was a killer. He wanted to be around to raise his child as well as be a grandfather to his offspring. Going to the police wasn't an option; it would only endanger the lives of his wife and children.